And There You Were

MANDA MAZANEC

For Pat, Abi, Sam, and Lily

Chapter One
PAST

Asheville, North Carolina 1994
Chance Johnson

Chance heard the crack of cartilage and watched as the blood spewed across his dad's white shirt. It smeared across Chance's knuckles as he knocked the drunk into the cheap wooden table for a second time, causing it to collapse from the weight of his body.

Wiping the blood with the back of his sleeve before getting back to his feet, the old man lunged at Chance again, swinging a sorry excuse for a right hook toward his jaw. Missing completely, he stumbled forward and fell face-first onto the cold linoleum floor.

"What's going on in there?" Chance's mom screamed, running into their tiny yellow kitchen, her arms reaching for her husband. "You broke his nose!"

"Let me be, damn it." His dad slurred his words together as he pulled his arm away from his wife. "I can take care of myself, Betty!" He placed one hand on the counter and the other on the floor. Pushing up, he got back to his feet but stumbled backward. Standing behind him, his wife broke his fall.

"Damn it!" he swore again. He glared at Chance with wild eyes. Chance knew that look. He'd seen it a thousand times. Barely coherent and shit-faced, he knew his dad wouldn't remember any of this in the morning.

Standing with his feet wide apart, Chance clenched his jaw tightly. At six feet and all muscle, he wasn't about to let a barely functioning alcoholic act like an ass any longer.

"Help him. He needs an ice pack," his mom yelled, frantic.

Chance didn't budge. Instead, he glared back, trying to prove he wasn't the quiet little boy who sat idly by anymore.

"You want to be a man? Then get out! Get the hell out of my house!" his dad yelled, sucking down his own blood.

"Jeremy! Stop! You need to sit down." Chance's mom grabbed his dad by the arm and forced him into a chair. She tilted his head back as she leaned over and pulled a cold compress from the freezer. "Sit still!" Irritation rang in her voice when he tried getting up again.

This time, he listened and remained unmoving, with his eyes closed, as she held the ice pack to his nose.

Then, looking up and catching Chance's eye, she nodded toward the front door, her long brown hair a tangled mess after pulling a double shift at the hospital.

Taking a deep breath, Chance retreated from the kitchen. Quickly grabbing a bag of overnight clothes, he snuck out the door, careful not to draw attention to himself. Careful not to let his dad hear him. It was better this way. Better for his mom. She knew how to calm him down. If Chance stayed, he'd only make things worse.

It was dark outside, but Joe had his lights on out back. Probably heard the entire thing. His house wasn't but twenty feet away.

"I figured you'd be coming," his neighbor said flatly once Chance rounded the bushes. He pushed out a wicker chair using the bottom of his boot, motioning for Chance to sit down.

Placing his bag on the wooden deck, Chance dropped his weight into the seat.

Neither of them said anything for a long moment. Instead, they sat in silence, watching the fireflies dance across the night sky. But when a cold breeze ushered toward them, Joe was the first to speak up.

"You need a sweatshirt?"

Chance nodded, knowing the question meant they'd be sitting outside awhile.

Joe got to his feet, disappearing behind the heavy glass door that now separated them. When he returned, he placed two mugs on the table, steam rising from the hot tea inside. A gray hoodie was draped over his shoulder, and he tossed it to Chance when his hands were free.

"You need to get out of there," Joe said earnestly, motioning toward Chance's house. "No good will come out of staying there. You and I both know that."

Chance wrestled with his words, unsure how to respond.

"You're eighteen now. I don't know what you're waiting for." Still standing, Joe pulled a pamphlet from his back pocket and dropped it in front of Chance.

Before he could respond, Joe continued, "Just think about it. It'll be good for you." He collapsed back into his chair with a heavy sigh. "And your momma will be okay too. She can handle him on her own."

Chance watched as Joe took a sip from his mug. He was right. But knowing it and doing something about it were two vastly different things. He reached for the pamphlet, his fingers slowly lifting it off the table. Silently, he flipped the pages and began reading.

~

Six Months Later
Jacksonville, North Carolina

The heavy wooden door of the barracks creaked open as Tyler Romano burst through without knocking. Shoving his way through the narrow entrance and bumping into Chance on his way, Tyler landed on the bed with a loud thud.

"I still can't believe this is it," he said, grinning ear to ear as he laid his combat boots on top of Chance's black duffel bag.

Chance rolled the last of his green skivvy shirts and tucked them away.

"You'll be headed overseas, while I'm soaking up the sun at Camp Pendleton, meeting all the ladies. We'll be living across the world from one another."

At six foot four, Tyler looked like a giant next to Chance, who rarely felt small in his own six-foot frame. Tyler, who Chance had met in basic training, was the only other marine who hadn't gone home after graduating boot camp. He'd gone straight to Infantry Training School with Chance. It had been six months since either of them had seen their families, but today, that would all change.

Throwing his hands behind his head, Tyler laughed. "I can't wait to see my old man. He's going to give me so much shit though. Look how skinny I am. You're over there packing on the muscle, and I look like I'm withering away."

Chance couldn't help but chuckle. It was true. Tyler was tall and skinny. He'd been skinny the first day of boot camp, but now? Now he was struggling to stay within weight standards.

"You just need a few good home-cooked meals," Chance said, pushing Tyler's boots off his bag.

"Pasta! I bet my little brothers will have a bowl full of pasta ready for me the minute I get home. I can't believe I haven't seen those guys in six months. These next ten days are going to be the best."

Tyler's voice grew excited the more he talked about his family, which made Chance envious. Tyler was close to his family, despite not having a mom. She'd taken off at some point when Tyler was younger, so Tyler had fallen into the caretaker role, looking after his two younger brothers while his dad worked two jobs.

"What are your plans while you're home?" Tyler's breath came slowly as he sat up and planted his feet on the floor.

What were his plans? That was a hard question. Chance didn't want to lie to Tyler. There was no reason to lie. But he also didn't want to talk about it. He already felt guilty enough for not going home sooner, after the Red Cross had reached out to him. Plus, Tyler would feel bad for him and tell him to talk it out. But Chance wasn't like that. Where Tyler was an open book, spewing out details from his childhood, Chance was closed off, letting everything fester and die inside.

"I'll probably hang out with my mom," Chance said, which was the truth. Even if he was omitting details.

They sat in silence for a few moments, which Chance was thankful for. Tyler knew there was more to the story, but the unspoken words were enough for him.

"Here's my phone number," Tyler finally announced, handing him a folded yellow piece of notebook paper.

"The Marine Corps is small. I'm sure we'll see each other sooner rather than later, but just in case."

Chance gave Tyler a half hug as they said their goodbyes.

An hour later, Chance was waiting outside a run-down bus station for his bus ride back home. Wearing civilian attire for the first time in months, a pair of faded blue jeans and a white Duke sweatshirt, he felt more like a college kid than a marine. He knew his mom would appreciate the fact that he was wearing her alma mater sweatshirt, a blue devil, even if only in spirit.

A dark gray bus pulled into the parking lot of the poorly lit bus station, billowing out dirty black smoke. A few cars pulled around back and opened their doors, letting out the passengers who would join him on the bus ride. None of them had waited out in the cold like he had. Chance watched as small snow flurries fell from the sky. He couldn't imagine sitting inside a car on a night like this. Winter had never been his favorite season, but he did enjoy the beauty of the outdoors, and there was something about the way the snow draped itself and clung to nature that made it absolutely breathtaking.

As people exited their cars, he watched as loved ones hugged each other, saying their goodbyes. He wondered if the older couple storing away their suitcases under the bus were on their way to see their grandchildren. And he was curious if the young woman who hugged the clean-shaven man was on her way home to see her family. Maybe the man was being deployed. Maybe she was simply heading to see friends. He gave a half smile. If Tyler were here, he'd probably invent happy stories for each of them.

"That lady over there," Tyler would say, "the one with the oversized coat and brown hat. She's probably on her way to see her five grandchildren, and her suitcase is probably filled to the brim with napkins she saved from the past year. Oh, and presents. Lots of presents. And that woman with the kids? She's taking them on a vacation to a tropical island while her husband is deployed."

Tyler was just a happy person, and people were always drawn to him. Maybe it was his outlook on life. He had, on more than one occasion, told Chance not to live in the past. Tyler had a million reasons to be angry, starting with his mom's desertion of the family, but not once had Chance ever seen him without a smile on his face. Even in boot camp. He could still see the drill instructor's face as he ran across the squad bay to scream at Tyler.

"What are you smiling at recruit?" he'd growled with a raspy voice as he jumped onto Tyler's footlocker. "You think this is funny? Everyone hit the deck."

As every recruit dropped to the floor, Tyler kept smiling. They must have done a few hundred pushups that night, all while Tyler continued to smile.

Just as Chance was getting ready to shove his own bag under the bus, he felt a slight bump from behind.

"Oh, I'm sorry."

The voice was so quiet he might have missed it if he hadn't been paying attention. Wearing a black hoodie and a pair of faded blue jeans that fell past her sneakers, a girl stepped around him. The snow began to fall harder. Bigger flakes now scattered across the sky, making it increasingly difficult to see.

The girl lifted her chin just as the wind picked up, her hood falling from her face. A white fleck landed on her cheek before melting away from the heat of her skin. She wiped the drop it left behind with the back of her hand and then drew back the honey brown hair that stuck to her face, not quite catching behind her ear. Her blue eyes glistened as her gaze met his for a brief moment before breaking contact and looking down at her feet.

Not waiting for his acknowledgment, she walked past him, carrying a small black backpack in her arms. He watched as she climbed the stairs and disappeared onto the bus.

Those eyes.

Those eyes pierced Chance. Not because they were bluer than the ocean. Not because they fit her face so perfectly. No. Because they mirrored his own thoughts. A hidden sadness and a desire to be unseen. He saw it all in that one glimpse.

"All right, let's go!" the bus driver announced impatiently, trying to get Chance's attention so he could close the storage compartment.

He was staring after her, he realized. He blushed. He hoped no one noticed, but it must have been obvious with the way he lingered. Embarrassed, Chance tossed everything except his duffel bag into the compartment and quickly made his way onto the bus.

He quickly scanned the seats and immediately saw *her* toward the back. Instinctively, he walked right to her.

What am I doing?

Catching himself before she looked up, he grabbed a seat across the aisle, within arm's reach of her. His heart raced.

Shit. What am I doing?

Chance froze. This was totally out of character. He stared straight ahead at the seat in front of him. His bag was still on his lap, and all he could think about was the girl sitting so close that, if he reached out his hand, he could touch her.

Is this how it felt? To feel attracted to someone? Chance had never really dated. In high school, he kept to himself. He was too embarrassed to invite his friends to his house, let alone a girl. He'd learned this lesson when a new kid once asked to walk home with him in sixth grade. He lived on the same street, and Chance had promised he'd lend him his copy of *A Wrinkle in Time*. As soon as Chance's hand was on the front door handle, it had whooshed open.

There, his dad stood, half naked, wearing only his long underwear. His brown hair wild, his eyes wilder.

"Tell that damn mom of yours we ran out of beer! Where is she? She's not with you? Damn it, Chance. I told her she better not come back without it. Who is this? You made a new friend? Damn it. Now I need to put on my pants." And, just like that, his dad disappeared back into the house.

Chance stood silent, ashamed and embarrassed.

"I'll just get that book from you tomorrow," the boy whispered before turning and running down the street.

Horrified, that was the last time Chance invited anyone over.

As far as girls went, Chance used his dad as an excuse not to date, saying he was too busy looking after his mom. Everybody knew about his dad. But the truth was, she didn't need him. His dad's drinking had caused Chance to become socially awkward and withdrawn. Low self-esteem plagued him. By the time he graduated high school, he could count on one hand how many dates he'd gone on. The girls were nice enough, but none of them kept his interest, and, in turn, they didn't find him interesting.

But this girl, the one sitting only a few feet away from him? He knew absolutely nothing about her but could see she was nothing like the girls he went to school with. They hadn't made his heart race. They hadn't taken his breath away.

Chance argued with his thoughts as the bus began to pull away from the bus station. It lurched *just a little*, but *just enough* for what came next.

Chapter Two

PAST

Jacksonville, North Carolina 1994
Claire Harding

In the dark stillness of her bedroom, Claire heard the familiar bang as the metal screen door slammed against the frame of the house. Muffled voices outside the window intensified until, on cue, the revving of an engine came to life. She didn't have to look to know it was pulling out of the driveway, indicating she was now alone. Again. It had been this way for the last few weeks. Maybe months.

For the first time since she arrived, Claire let the tears fall, not bothering to wipe them from her face. She wrapped her arms around her legs, letting her body convulse. This was too much. Too hard. She missed her mom. She closed her eyes and willed her mom to hear her. But that was impossible. Her mom was dead. And now? Now she had to live with Alex, her stepbrother, who clearly didn't want her there.

Claire sobbed even harder, her long hair plastered to her wet cheeks. She was unable to understand why she felt so alone. Nothing made sense. She and Alex used to be so close when they were younger, even with their ten-year age differ-ence. But it felt as if, the moment their parents died, they became strangers. And now, at seventeen years old, Claire felt utterly alone.

A few hours later, after she managed to soothe herself and was no longer crying, Claire pulled back the covers and climbed out of bed. Her eyes felt puffy and her nose raw. She stepped into the empty hallway, a sudden wave of dread washing over her. She wanted to go to the bathroom, to splash water on her face, but something about the silence made the hair on her arms stand on end.

It was well past midnight, and Claire wondered when Alex would be home. He never stayed out this late. As a police officer, he ran a pretty tight ship, his predictability always on point. It started with his alarm blaring every morning at six a.m. and ended when he returned home at midnight. Everything in between was regimented in intervals too. She didn't ask questions. He made it clear that his whereabouts were none of her business.

But something felt off tonight. Alex should be home. Something was wrong.

Instead of walking to the bathroom, she turned in the opposite direction. Letting her eyes adjust to the darkness, she tiptoed down the hallway and down the stairs. She continued past the kitchen, drawn to the basement door. Her heartbeat quickened as nerves set in, but Claire, nonetheless, took the railing in her hands. Each step downward groaned and creaked under her weight.

What is that disgusting smell? She held her nose to avoid the putrid odor.

She was too afraid to turn on the light. Too afraid that her brother would return home the second she stepped down the stairs. Instead, Claire once again waited until her eyes adjusted before moving any farther. In the dark, the faint outline of a couch came into view. Next to it, beer cans and old pizza littered a coffee table.

Almost vomiting, Claire cupped her hands over her mouth. She doubted pepperoni would cause such a reaction. Curious still, she crept past the table, scanning the room for whatever the smell was coming from. Images became clearer. A television to her left. A workout bench to her right.

Then, without warning, Claire tripped over something hard. Unable to keep her balance, she threw her hands down to break her fall. She landed in something wet. Her head snapped back to see what it was, but she couldn't tell. On the ground, on all fours, shadows played tricks with her.

It looked like a...no it couldn't be.

But it was. A woman, lifeless, lay on the rug in front of her. Claire's eyes went wide as she screamed.

She pulled herself up to her knees when light suddenly bounced across the room. And in that instance, Claire's eyes dropped to her hands. Thick red blood covered them. Panic shook her as she heard a car door slam. The light disappeared. Her brother was home. She had to get out of here, but her feet felt like they were nailed to the floor. *Shit. Shit, shit, shit!*

Sucking in her breath, Claire pushed to her feet and bolted up the stairs, taking them two at a time. Careful not to touch anything, she ran into the bathroom, locking the door behind her.

As she exhaled, she heard the back door slam shut. Her body shook, and she didn't dare flip the switch. Instead, she stood silent until the footsteps disappeared into the lower level of the house. Then she quickly turned on the faucet and scrubbed her hands until the last bit of blood washed down the drain.

When she finished, she stood with her ear to the door, her heart racing with each second.

What the hell is going on? There's a dead body down there. Alex has to know about it. He's always in the basement. With those guys. But where did she come from? Did Alex kill her? Oh, my god, what do I do?

A loud thump rattled the wall Claire stood behind, shaking her from her thoughts. She heard Alex's voice talking to someone. No. To a few people, she realized as other voices joined in. Maybe three. Maybe four. She couldn't be sure.

Heavy footsteps grew closer. And then another bump against the wall and more cussing.

"Be careful...damn...grab a towel...blood."

Upon hearing the last word, Claire's body went rigid. *Are they moving the body?*

Claire prayed they wouldn't open the bathroom door. Prayed they wouldn't find her standing there, alone in the dark.

Please don't open the door. Please don't open the door.

Fear gripped her heart as she remained still for what felt like an eternity. She knew she had to run. She had to escape. But not now. Not while they were still in the house.

And so, she waited.

Finally, sometime later, after the voices disappeared back down the stairs, Claire worked up enough courage to crack open the door. It was dark. She peeked her head around the corner. Still dark. Even in Alex's bedroom. Exhaling, she tiptoed toward her room.

She didn't make it very far when a shadow caught her attention. She turned her head, a lump forming in her throat. Exiting Alex's bedroom was a tall, slender man, his black hair gelled to the side. His dark eyes glared at her from behind round-rimmed glasses. He didn't speak. He didn't even move. And, for the second time that night, Claire felt tears burning behind her eyes. Seconds ticked by before she forced her feet to inch their way back to her room. When he was out of sight, she closed her door and locked herself inside, releasing the breath she hadn't known she was holding.

The next morning, after tossing and turning all night, Claire awoke to the drone of Alex's alarm. It was so loud she was sure the entire street could hear it. Tossing the covers off, she stretched her legs before planting her feet firmly on the ground. She pulled a black hoodie over her head and stretched a pair of faded blue jeans over her ass.

Images of last night suddenly flooded her memory. She gasped. The woman. The blood. The man in the hallway. She flipped her hands front to back, checking for blood, unsure if what she'd seen last night was real or just a nightmare.

Claire's heart pounded as she eyed the backpack in the corner of her room. She wanted to run. To call the police. But Alex *was* the police. How could this be happening? She had to be smart. She couldn't stay here. If she did, she might be next. Claire had to do this the right way. She had to go downstairs until Alex left for work. She had to pretend everything was normal. That she hadn't seen a dead body. At least for this morning.

You can do this. You have to do this.

At the breakfast table, Claire sank her teeth into a piece of dry toast as Alex read the newspaper, neither of them acknowledging the other. She chewed in silence until he pushed his chair out and stood up.

"I'll be home late. I have some business to take care of once my shift is over," he said, folding the paper, not once looking in her direction. "There's pizza in the freezer if you want to make it after school."

At the mention of pizza, Claire almost gagged on the hard bread between her teeth.

Once Alex was in his car and pulling out of the driveway, Claire leapt from her chair. It was time. She ran upstairs to Alex's room, hoping to find some money. She wouldn't be able to do this if she didn't have cash.

Claire scanned his room. A perfectly made bed, an old oak

dresser, and a small television sitting on an end table were the only pieces of furniture Alex owned.

Clasping the knob to the bifold closet door, nausea bubbled in her stomach as a familiar odor hit her nose. Ignoring the smell, she forced the door open. Her eyes widened, and she almost smiled at the stack of bills sitting neatly on the top shelf. Next to them lay the locket she'd searched endlessly for, the one her mom had given her when she was a little girl. She thought she'd lost it, but there it was, almost gloating that it'd been there just waiting for her to come find it. She clasped it in one hand before thinking twice. With her other hand, she seized the cash. Her throat tightened as the acrid odor became overpowering. She didn't want to look deeper into the closet—she just wanted the money—but her eyes betrayed her as she looked toward the smell. Too afraid to scream, too afraid to move, she swallowed a gasp.

Bare white skin. Crooked arms. Deep brown hair plastered to the same ghostly face she saw last night, lay in a heap by her feet.

They moved her body! Or was this another woman?

She retreated too fast, pulling everything from the shelf to the floor.

Quick. Move quicker. Get out of here.

Claire's hands shook as she reached for the bills, crumbling them into her fists. Her heart pulsed erratically. Her vision blurred. And her face heated. All making it difficult to think or see straight.

Don't look at anything. Get out of here.

But before she could stand up, her hand grazed something small and hard. A rock? Without thinking, she grabbed it, ready to put it back where it came from. But then, there was another one...and another. She arched her brows in confusion as reality set in.

Teeth. There were *teeth* all over the floor.

Sucking in a sharp breath, Claire quickly dropped the teeth. Clutching the money in one hand and the locket in the other, she ran from the room, leaving the woman sprawled out in the corner of the closet.

And she kept running, not once looking back.

Outside, the sun was invisible, hidden by the dark clouds that loomed in the sky. The air was blisteringly cold, and Claire knew it would only grow colder with every hour. Rubbing her hands together to keep them warm, she wished she had grabbed her gloves. But it was too late. She couldn't turn back. Not now. Not ever.

As the wind picked up, Claire increased her pace and made it to the bus station in record time. She stepped inside just as she heard the loud engine of a bus pulling up behind her. She turned to look and watched intently as people began to unload their cars.

"Where's that bus headed?" Claire asked the man behind the counter.

"Chicago. Leaves in five minutes."

"Perfect. I'll buy one ticket." She pulled out a stack of crumpled bills and paid for the ticket before asking if there was another bus heading to St. Petersburg.

"In two hours," he said, already helping the person behind her.

"I'll buy one of those tickets too."

He eyed her suspiciously, but she didn't dare open her mouth. She couldn't tell this man, this stranger, that she was running. That she was hiding from a cop. She needed whatever advantage she could get.

The man handed her the ticket and she dashed to the exit. Peeking outside, it seemed as if everyone had already boarded.

It has to be now.

Claire opened the door, hood drawn down so nobody would see her face. She ran but misjudged her distance, causing her to bump right into someone just as the wind blew the hood from her face.

"Oh, I'm sorry," she whispered, wiping away a fleck of snow that landed on her cheek. Embarrassed, she waited for the man to continue, but when he didn't move, she looked up, only to feel the heat rise in her chest when his gray eyes met her gaze. Cheeks on fire, she dipped her head and walked around him.

On the bus, Claire made her way to the back, choosing an aisle seat. Hoping and not hoping the mysterious stranger would find her. Sit near her. But she couldn't relax, not yet. She wouldn't be able to breathe easy. Not until she was out of Jacksonville and far, far away. She didn't have time to think about that guy.

When Claire glanced up a moment later, she noticed the man she'd bumped into was walking toward her. He was much younger than she had originally mistaken him for, not much older than herself. Probably a college kid, or maybe military with that haircut. His dark brown hair was short and faded around the sides, and while she felt most military guys looked the same, this one stood out with his chiseled jaw contrasting his soft features.

He sat across from her, and the beat of her heart quickened. She turned her head the other way and looked out the snow-rimmed window. What had once felt like a town full of hope was now nothing more than empty promises. The darkness closed in, and Claire let out a deep breath as she fumbled in her pocket for the gold locket she had long outgrown. It was the one thing that brought her comfort.

The interior lights flickered off, and the bus lurched forward, causing her locket to fall to the ground. She bent down to pick it up at the exact same moment as the man sitting across from her did the same.

Her hand brushed the top of his, ever so lightly, but,

rather than moving it away, she looked up, right into his eyes. He was staring at her. Her heartbeat paused. She froze in place. His eyes were remarkably bright in the darkness of the bus. Gray with green bands that drew her breath away.

"I think you dropped this," he whispered.

Her hand shifted slightly, giving him room to move. As he opened his fingers, his eyes never left her gaze. But he didn't give her the necklace, instead he let it sit in the palm of his hand, waiting for her to retrieve it.

She hesitated. She didn't mean to, but once she did, she immediately felt awkward. He was a complete stranger, but she was so incredibly captivated by his eyes.

Shit! I should be hiding. Keeping my head low.

He was a stranger. A complete stranger. He didn't know who she was. He didn't know she was running from the cops. That there was a dead body in her house.

Just grab it!

As the bus turned onto the expressway, exiting onto the ramp, westbound toward Asheville, the first of many stops before her final destination, Claire carefully reached for the chain that held her gold locket. It felt like minutes had passed by the time the locket was in her grasp. As she pulled her hand away, her fingers grazed his fingertips, sending a wave of exhilaration through her body.

She looked away without responding. But she knew he'd felt it too. She could feel his eyes on her, and she'd be lying to herself if she said it bothered her.

"You're welcome." His voice was soft and silvery. If he was being sarcastic, there was no intonation to reflect that. Instead, it was inviting, and Claire couldn't resist turning her head to look at him once more.

When their eyes met again, she blushed and fidgeted with the gold chain.

"Thank you," was all that she could muster, her heart

beginning to pick up speed again. There was something about the way he looked at her. He was serious, yet endearing, and while she had no intention of talking to him, she hoped he would talk to her. It sounded silly as she thought about it, but there was an intensity between them that she couldn't deny.

The bus suddenly came to a stop, sliding ever so slightly in the heavy snow. People started to murmur around them as they wondered what was going on. A few people stood up and looked out the windows. Claire began to panic. Her body grew rigid. They hadn't been on the expressway for more than a few minutes.

There's no way Alex would come looking for me on the expressway. He wouldn't think to check the bus so soon, would he?

"Sorry, folks, looks like there might be a slight delay up ahead. I can see an accident. With all this snow, no one knows how to drive," the bus driver announced on his intercom.

Claire's body relaxed a little as she slumped back into her seat.

"Hopefully no one got hurt," the man across from her whispered.

She looked over at him again. She didn't know how to respond. There was so much on her mind. She gave a wry smirk and looked down. She was comfortable looking away and, right now, this handsome man was making her feel things she'd never felt before, and she liked it. She felt at ease, and the tension seemed to dissipate when he spoke.

"Where're you headed?" he asked.

Chapter Three
PAST

Chance

"Where're you headed?" Chance asked the girl, surprising himself with his own question. Normally, he would have kept to himself and remained quiet in his own company. But there was something about her eyes, the way they looked at him with such intensity and focus. He wanted to know more. It would be a long drive in the snow and traffic, so he let the words slip from his tongue before he could think twice.

"Chicago." Her voice was small but sweet.

She tilted her face, barely looking at him. In the darkness that surrounded them, he could see the paleness of her face behind the dark freckles that speckled her cheeks. Her blue eyes were both striking and soft and, when she met his gaze, he was sure they were smiling at him, even if she was thinking about something entirely different.

Yet, there was something else. A hint of sadness maybe. Wanting to know more but not wanting to pry, Chance took a leap of faith.

"That's pretty far. Is that where you're from?"

She shook her head, hesitating as if she were contemplating a response. Lifting one hand, she pulled back a loose strand of hair and glanced out the window, exhaling as she replied.

"St. Petersburg."

A long pause laid between them until she turned her gaze back to Chance. "What about you?"

Before finding his words, Chance watched as the girl pulled the hood from her head, releasing long strands of creamy brown hair, her once pale face now finding color. And her lips...he couldn't *not* notice her lips. Thick and curvy, the lower lip tucked slightly under as she bit it.

Chance's face grew warm when he realized she was watching him, waiting for a word, any word.

"Asheville. I'm heading to see my folks." Flustered, he bent his head, not wanting to stare. But he couldn't help himself. Her eyes kept drawing him in. "My name's Chance." He held out his hand, intending to be polite, but when she glanced down at it, he closed his eyes, another wave of embarrassment washing over him.

He began to withdraw his hand, his eyes flickering open when he felt the softness of her fingertips as she laid them in his palm.

"Claire," she reciprocated in a hushed whisper.

After a few seconds, they withdrew their hands, both letting go at the same time. The sensation sent a wave of pleasure through his body.

Still gazing at each other, Chance felt an urge to keep talking. He didn't just *want* to know her anymore, he *needed* to know her. "That chain, be careful with it. The clasp in the back is broken." He nodded in the direction of her other hand.

"How'd you know?" A puzzled look crossed her face.

"I noticed the clasp was pushed forward. Which means it was broken and stuck like that or was about to break. I don't want you to lose the locket. It looks like an antique," Chance said, finally feeling confident enough to string a few sentences together.

He watched as she glanced down at the necklace, running her finger across the gold locket, as if recalling a memory that held a story she didn't want to forget.

"It is. My mom gave it to me when I was little. It's been broken for a few years now," she said, lifting her head as she finished the sentence. She closed her hand tightly and looked at him. "Thanks again. And I'm sorry for outside when I bumped into you."

The corners of his mouth curved up. "That's okay, I wasn't in a rush. You're just lucky it was me you bumped into, and not a poor old lady," he said playfully.

"I suppose you're right. That might have been a bit more awkward, seeing as I ran off without much of an apology."

The way she spoke gave him goosebumps. She was making fun of herself. And that smile. It was infectious.

The bus inched forward as it maneuvered around the accident. Claire turned her attention out the window, as did most of the passengers. But Chance kept his focus on Claire. Her demeanor changed, almost as if she were holding her breath, afraid of something. He wondered what she was thinking about, what was on her mind.

Realizing this would be a long drive, he figured Claire would want to be left alone. Heck, on a typical day, he wanted to be left alone too. He was about to say something when Claire interrupted his thoughts.

"Chance?" she whispered.

"Yes?" The sound of his name coming out of her mouth exhilarated him.

"Since it's such a long ride, do you want to maybe sit here, next to me? Maybe keep me company for a while?"

Chance could see how hard it must have been for her to

ask. Both because he was a stranger and because he could still see fear in her eyes, as if she had something else on her mind.

"I'd love to," he said without hesitation.

He grabbed his duffel bag and slowly got to his feet. Claire, too, got up and nestled herself in the seat next to the window. Chance sank into his new seat, feeling the heat rise between them.

Over the next few hours, Chance and Claire sat side by side, stealing glances at one another as the bus drove through the night. Curled up next to him, Claire listened as Chance shared the details of why he was heading home.

"I should have been home already. The Red Cross reached out last week, but I didn't know what to make of it. At first, I thought it was my dad."

At that statement, he felt Claire's questioning eyes prodding him for more information.

"For as long as I can remember, my dad's been a borderline functioning alcoholic. That line is so thin, though, he's tripped over it more times than I could count. Anyway, I thought the Red Cross was calling to tell me he was sick. I mean, with the way he drinks, I wouldn't be surprised if he had liver failure. And I didn't want to go home. Not for him." A pang of guilt ripped through him as he continued. "I know that sounds awful. But it's the truth."

Claire nodded, still listening.

"Yesterday, they called my command. They pulled me out of my last day of training to tell me it was my mom. That she's in the hospital. That she's in critical condition." Chance paused, suddenly aware of how open and vulnerable he was. He thought of Tyler. "Talking is good for the soul," he'd said on more than one occasion.

Claire adjusted her weight, sitting straighter, and grasped his arm. She watched him intently, her eyes locked on his. He looked at her in return, her face only a few inches away from his own. He could see that his story washed away some of her worries, whatever they were, at least in this moment. But how could he continue with his own? The pain was too much, and if he spoke the words, he might not be able to stop himself from crying.

As if reading his mind, Claire spoke up. "You don't have to answer this, but do you know what happened? Have you been able to talk to your mom at all?"

And there it was, the question he knew was coming. Pain stabbed at his heart, recalling the conversations he'd had over the last twenty-four hours.

"I can't talk to her."

Claire gripped his arm a little tighter, releasing the tightness in his chest. Exhaling, he continued. "After calling my house all day yesterday, I finally gave up and called my neighbor, Joe. He told me everything."

A tear formed in his eye, but he didn't bother to wipe it away. He was going to finish this story whether he wanted to or not.

"My mom's been battling breast cancer for the last year. She didn't want me to know about it. She's been dying... slowly. And I never even knew about it. Joe told me it progressed quickly over the last few weeks. And now...now she's not responsive."

Claire clapped her hand over her mouth and tears fell from her face.

Chapter Four
PAST

Claire

Claire wiped her eyes, unable to stop the tears from falling. Instinctively, she tightened her grip on Chance's arm, floundering for something to say. But there was nothing. Words couldn't do anything, couldn't change anything. She, of all people, knew that. And, somehow, she still felt compelled to comfort him.

With another slight squeeze, she drew his focus toward her.

"I'm sorry," he said, his eyes still wet.

"Don't be sorry. You have nothing to be sorry for." She wanted to wipe the tears from his face, to feel his skin. The intimacy of the idea made her heart skip a beat.

"I didn't expect to share all that with you. I haven't told anyone yet."

"I wish I could tell you it'll get easier, but it won't," she said, surprising herself with her own words.

When his eyebrows furrowed, quizzically, Claire took in a deep breath and continued. "I haven't really talked about this either, but..." Her voice trailed off, trying to find the right words. She closed her eyes. Memories floated through her thoughts as she tried again. "My mom and stepdad died a few months ago. The pain is still there. It doesn't go away."

"Is that why you're going to Chicago?" Chance asked. He wiped his eyes with his free hand before clasping hers again.

He peered into her eyes as if looking into her soul. At that moment, she wanted to tell him everything. She wanted to start with why she was on the bus and work her way backward. She wanted to be comforted and told that everything would be okay, that no one would come looking for her. It had been so long since she'd been held, hugged, or felt safe.

And Chance was right here, so close to her. Holding her hand. But he was also a stranger. If she shared the details of the past few days with him, he'd think she was crazy.

She looked away and pulled her hand back. Her heart ached with flashes from her memory. Her bloody hands. The teeth. The money. The woman and her tangled body. And then, of course, Alex. Did Alex know Claire was missing yet? That she'd found the woman in his closet? Someone would come looking for her. That much she knew. She'd stolen a lot of money from Alex, and she was fairly sure it was connected to the dead woman and all the men who had been at the house with Alex the night before. *All those men.* They would *all* come looking for her, wouldn't they?

"Tell me about your mom," Chance asked, breaking the silence. "I mean, you don't have to if you don't want to. But you can."

Her attention snapped back at the sound of his voice.

"You went somewhere. You weren't with me," he said, sounding worried.

Her eyes glistened with more tears.

"I don't know where to begin."

Chance's hand rose to her face, where he brushed her

cheek with his thumb. She hesitated at his touch, but the gentleness was comforting, so she leaned into it and closed her eyes. More tears escaped, falling off her freckles.

"Tell me anything. You don't have to start anywhere in particular."

How was this man so capable of calming her? She stared at him for a moment, noticing for the first time his large build compared to her tiny frame. He was nothing short of attractive, but there was something more. Something deeper.

"My mom was so beautiful," Claire started, her voice cracking upon her first few words. "She was a dancer. She performed all over the country. When she had me, people told her that her life would be different, and she'd have to settle down, but I think that gave her drive, drove her ambition. She took me with her and, for the first seven years of my life, it was just us. We lived in Florida, but we traveled all the time, all over the country. At least until she met my stepdad, but, even then, it didn't completely stop, it just slowed down."

Claire recalled the details as if they were happening in real time. She saw her mom standing in front of her as a toddler, slipping her pink ballet shoes on for her first mommy and me ballet class. She could still feel her mom's long brown hair dangling in front of her face, brushing against her cheeks as she tied the string that helped secure them to her chubby little feet. She remembered feeling proud and exhilarated as her mom introduced her to her instructor, introducing her to the dance world for the very first time.

"Why is that?" Chance asked.

"Hmm?" Claire asked, lost in thought.

"Why is it that it slowed down once she met your stepdad?"

"Oh, you know. Dating and marriage. She started taking jobs closer to home so she could be home more often with us.

She started taking jobs at different dance companies, teaching choreography. I think she also wanted me to have a more stable life. Traveling became harder when I was in school. But my mom taught me everything. She taught me how to read, how to ride my bike, how to apply eyeliner, and even how to change a tire."

"What about your dad? Or your stepdad?" Chance asked, avoiding the obvious question about how her mom died.

Brushing her hair away from her face, she told Chance she'd never met her real father. He had left long before she was born, probably with no clue that she even existed. Her mom had always been honest with her, and, because of that, she had no interest in looking for him.

Knowing the inevitable was near, she finally laid it all on the table for Chance. He was the first person she'd ever told, and she didn't know what feelings it would bring her. Neighbors had tried to convince her to see a therapist to cope with her loss, but there hadn't been time. Their deaths had been so sudden, and, since she'd had to move in with Alex, she'd packed up and moved quickly.

"My stepdad was great. I mean, he came into my life when I was eight, so it was hard at first. He sold commercial real estate and was always pretty busy schmoozing clients. But he was available for me and showed support whenever he got the chance. He never missed my dance recitals and treated me like his own daughter."

Claire looked at Chance, realizing she was acknowledging her stepfather in a positive light, something she rarely did anymore. In truth, she hadn't thought about those dance recitals in a long time, but it brought back a fondness she'd missed. Wanting to stand out and show off his money, her stepdad always brought her the prettiest, and largest, bouquet of flowers. And while it embarrassed her in front of her friends, she now recognized his desire to connect with her.

"My stepdad, Mark...he died too," Claire continued. "They were out in the gulf, just beyond St. Petersburg. They decided to take their sailboat out at the last minute to celebrate one of Mark's sales. They asked me to go with them, but I told them I had plans to go to a friend's house. When I got home, they weren't back yet, and it was dark. They never took the boat out by themselves that late. I started to call the neighbors, everyone I could think of. And then the doorbell rang."

Claire paused for a moment as she inhaled. "An officer stood on our doorstep and asked if my parents lived there. He told me that someone called in an abandoned sailboat. The coast guard searched it. They weren't there. Nothing seemed to be missing, and their lifejackets were still on board. It took them five days to locate their bodies. My mom was found first and then, shortly after, Mark's body was recovered. They drowned."

Claire was crying again, remembering the moment the officer asked Alex to identify her mom and Mark. Claire demanded to see her mom, to see if there was some mistake. Her mom was a good swimmer, and she knew better. She would never go into the water without a life jacket, especially in the Gulf of Mexico. And Mark, he was an even better swimmer. But when they took her down to the cold morgue and pulled the sheets from their faces, the only thing she could do was cry and bury her face into Alex's shirt.

She looked out the window and watched as the snow blew across the two-lane highway. It enveloped the bus, making the landscape in the distance come alive in the dark. Chance reached for Claire's hand, interlocking his fingers into hers. She felt surprised, but allowed it, relaxing just enough to finish her story.

"My mom had no other family. I was her family. Since I'm only seventeen, I was told I had to live with my stepbrother. That's what she wanted. She wrote it in her will. So, for the last few months, I've been staying with him in Jacksonville."

"Is he a marine?"

"No, but he's a cop," she replied, shaking her head.

Chance released a deep sigh and scrunched his face, but he tightened his grip on Claire's hand. She liked the feel of it, and she liked the comfort in his demeanor. She would have been happy to sit this way the rest of the ride, but curiosity dug at her heart.

"Are *you* a marine?"

"Yeah. I had to get out of my house. I couldn't stay. Not with my dad's drinking problem. But, now, maybe I should have."

"It's easy to second-guess yourself. I do it all the time. I mean, I'm doing it right now," Claire said.

"What do you mean?"

Before Claire could continue, the bus swerved, its wheels sliding underneath them. She clutched Chance's hand even tighter, Chance squeezing it right back. One of the kids at the front of the bus cried, and she heard someone behind them gasp.

"That was scary," Chance said matter-of-factly.

Claire opened her eyes, not even aware they'd been closed. "You weren't scared, though, were you?"

"No."

She thought she saw a smirk cross his lips and instantly felt butterflies. His eyes sparkled, and she couldn't help but smile back.

What am I doing? Claire wondered. *How did I get here? How am I holding a stranger's hand? Why is he telling me about his mom, and why did I tell him about mine?* She knew the answers didn't matter. Not at this moment. She liked this. She wanted to stay like this forever and not let go.

"So, you never really answered my question. What's in Chicago?" Chance asked again, drawing her back into reality.

"Freedom," Claire responded, not wanting to tell him the truth. That there was absolutely nothing for her in Chicago. She didn't want to tell him that she bought the ticket because it was the fastest way out of Jacksonville. Or that the thought of Chicago actually frightened her.

"Freedom sounds good," Chance replied, drawing her hair back away from her face.

A smile crossed Claire's lips as she let her eyelids fall, feeling his hand linger on her cheek. Her heart pounded, a desire that ran from her heart to her chest.

When her eyes flickered open, she met his gaze.

Chance inched forward slowly, his hand lowering to her lips, grazing the bottom with his thumb. Heat rose through her body, the intensity between them rising.

"Can I..." he started to say before clearing his throat. "Can I kiss you?" he asked, his hand already drawing her near.

With the slightest nod of her head, her lips parted before he took her in. The warmth of his mouth discovering hers. His touch was both soft and electric. When Chance began to pull away, Claire closed her lips around his, forcing their lips to remain locked for a few more seconds. Her body melted into his and, through their clothes, she felt their hearts beating in a rhythmic session.

But, like everything else good in life, their kiss came to an end. Their lips finally parted, making way for breath. The attraction was strong; there was no denying it. In any other world, she would have taken the initiative to kiss him again, showing her interest. But this wasn't real. They were on a bus. He would be getting off shortly, to go live out the rest of his life, while she...while she wasn't sure where life would take her.

"Come with me," Chance said, breaking the silence.

"Come with you?"

"Yeah. I don't know what you mean by freedom, but you should come with me to Asheville. I have a little over a week left before I fly to Japan. You should come with me."

"Come with you?" Claire asked again, this time understanding him, but not quite knowing how to react.

Chapter Five
PAST

Chance

The next day, as morning light glimmered across the fresh snow, sneaking through the sheer curtains, Chance found himself standing at the entrance of his parents' bedroom. Alone. Feeling somber, he glanced around, unable to get his mind off Claire while also paling at the thought of his mom.

Selfishly, he wished Claire had come with him. The request had surprised them both the moment the words left his mouth, but he didn't want to lose Claire, as silly as it sounded. Their encounter had been short, but, in those few hours, they'd formed a connection unlike any other he'd previously experienced. It was as if they'd been placed on that bus, together, on purpose. As if fate had brought them there.

Disheartened, he still understood when Claire told him she couldn't get off the bus in Asheville. She insisted her brother would come looking for her and she needed to get as far away from Jacksonville as possible. Which meant she had to leave North Carolina.

But he didn't let her refuse without putting up a fight. Even after she'd finally confessed what caused her to leave her stepbrother's house, he tried to convince Claire there must have been some mistake. Some sort of mix-up. How could someone kill a woman...and leave her there? In the movies, people got rid of bodies, they didn't keep them locked inside closets.

Claire had grown quiet at his questions, unable to say more than "I'm sorry," which made him feel ashamed he had even spoken in the first place.

As the bus neared his stop, the lights flickered on.

"Kiss me again," Claire had pleaded, her eyes filling with tears. Leaning in, Chance nestled his nose against Claire's, the heat from their breath warming him as he placed his lips on hers. He felt her body shudder beside him.

"I'd kiss you every day if you'd let me," Chance whispered back as their lips parted. Stroking his cheek, she exhaled. Each of them knew this was goodbye.

Claire's hand slowly retreated when he stood. He didn't want to leave. He wanted to stay. In a perfect world, he would get to know her, date her, and bring her home to meet his mom. But that was unrealistic, and pain stabbed at his heart.

Reaching down for his bag, he picked it up and slung it over his shoulder, never taking his eyes off Claire. With a small curve to his lips, he nodded his head and walked off the bus.

Outside, the cold wind was harsh, biting at his cheeks. Chance tried to find Claire through the snow-covered windows but couldn't make out more than a few blurry figures. He stood there, painfully, staring, hoping Claire at least knew their connection had been real. He waited until the bus pulled away before turning his attention away.

Putting his thoughts of the night before aside, Chance walked toward the closet. Solemnly, he reached up to grab the box of pictures that lay hidden beneath a pile of old sweatshirts.

"Do you remember when we went to Lookout Mountain in Chattanooga?" he could still hear his mom asking.

"Yeah, I was six, right?" he'd asked, confirming what he already knew.

"That was my favorite vacation. I wish we could go back again one day." She'd nodded with a faraway stare and a smile that lit up the room.

Chance hadn't known why she asked that question last year, but it was stirring in his head now as he sorted through all the old family photos.

Flipping through them, one by one, Chance recalled various memories until he came across a picture of his parents on either side of him. His dad in jeans and a Beatles T-shirt, his mom wearing jean shorts and a black tank top. Behind them lay the seven states that were claimed to be visible from their viewpoint.

"Look how gorgeous your mom was there," his Aunt Debbie commented, sauntering into the room, admiring the picture in his hand. "I'll never forget how happy she was when you guys went on that vacation."

She smiled, which made Chance smile.

"Yeah, it was her favorite trip," Chance said, remembering as if it happened yesterday. Ironically, it was his favorite trip too. It was the last time he recalled his dad being happy and sober. His mom had begged his dad to take them, something about it holding a significant place in her heart.

Still staring at the image in his hand, Chance closed his eyes and, for a moment, he was brought back to the eighties.

The wind whipped through his hair as he stuck his hand out the window, allowing the breeze to infiltrate the car as they drove down the highway. His mom insisted they drive straight to the Incline Railway—ignoring his dad's plea to check into the hotel first—promising the view would be worth it. After being in the car for almost four hours, Chance's dad was reluctant, but agreed to do what she wanted. Once they found a place to park, she hurried them out of the two-toned beige Ford Grenada and rushed them to the railcar, where they all squeezed on.

"Hold on tight, Chance," she exclaimed as if he were still a toddler. Her hair swirled across her face as they ventured uphill.

When they made it to the top of the mountain, he watched as his dad stood speechless, mesmerized by the vast terrain spread out in front of them. Grabbing his wife in a tight embrace, he bent her forward and kissed her forehead.

"It's gorgeous, Betty. We should have come sooner."

They stayed in Chattanooga for three days, exploring and learning about the historical events it was known for. They ate at small diners. One, he recalled, was so tiny, it only had three booths. His dad laughed so hard he grabbed his mom out of the booth and twirled her around in the tiny aisle, dancing with her as the other families clapped. It was pure magic.

He also recalled a cemetery but couldn't remember why. And then, he remembered his dad's mood shift. Not right away. Not instantaneously. But he suddenly remembered the beer, one by one, until his dad was no longer able to drive home.

"He'll be all right, sweetie. He's just really sad." It was the first of many excuses his mom gave for his dad's loss of willpower.

"Your mom would want this picture," Chance's aunt said, drawing him back to the present. "I'm going to run to the store and make a few copies." She wiped her tear-streaked eyes.

"She'd like that," he agreed, handing her the picture.

"Chance, please don't beat yourself up about this. You had no way of knowing she wouldn't make it through the night." Leaning over, she kissed the top of his head.

After she left, he sat in his own thoughts, tears streaming

down his face. Mad at himself for waiting so long to come home. Angry that his mom had been taken from this world too soon. He wished he could go back in time, come home sooner. Tell her he was sorry. He wanted one more day with her. One more hug. But he'd been robbed of that. He thought it was his dad who was sick that entire time. It was his dad's fault.

When his thoughts shifted to his dad, anger squeezed his throat. He stood up and walked back to the closet, ready to place the box back on the shelf where it belonged, but, as he glanced down, another picture stole his attention. It was of his dad, a younger version, while he was still in the army.

There were four other guys in the picture. Sitting side by side, next to a large tank, they looked tired and dirty. They wore battle fatigues and olive green cotton jackets and pants, each one holding their M16 service rifle proudly. Chance remembered seeing this picture as a kid. It hung on their refrigerator throughout his childhood, but he couldn't place when it had been removed. He never asked questions. And his dad never talked about it. Black and white, and kind of blurry, it was still easy to spot his dad. Not smiling, but not angry. The men looked to be taking some time to relax or maybe to regroup themselves. Based on how young they all looked and their expressions, he guessed it was taken at the beginning of the Vietnam War.

Flipping it over, he noticed the last names of each of the men written across the back. He ran his finger over the words, noting dates next to everyone except his dad. Three of the guys, Butler, Stanley, and Jones, all had 1968 scribbled next to their names. Howard had 1975 next to his name. He suspected these were the dates the men had died, but he wasn't quite sure, as his dad had never mentioned them.

As he flipped the picture back over, he heard the front door creak open and then bang shut. Chance tossed the picture back into the box and quickly placed it back on the closet shelf. He could hear his dad in the kitchen, the familiar sound of the refrigerator opening and the crack of the beer that came next.

"Oh, it's you," his dad mumbled, collapsing into the wooden chair when Chance joined him in the kitchen. He propped his feet on the edge of the table, his boots still on.

Chance didn't respond, irritation washing over him. He'd seen his dad at the hospital in the middle of the night after he'd gotten back. Joe had left him a letter on the door stating to come right away. But right away hadn't been fast enough. He arrived just minutes too late.

He did, however, make it in time to witness his dad falling apart. From the doorway, he could see his dad sobbing uncontrollably, his body almost completely on top of hers. The nurses had to help pry him off her.

Chance had waited in the hallway until his dad was escorted out. Joe followed right behind them, wearing his officer's uniform. Noticing Chance, he drew him in for a tight bear hug, his own eyes swollen.

"I'm so sorry, Chance. I'm so sorry," he repeated as they neared his mom's bedside.

In the last six months, his mother's body had transformed. Her eyes, once small, had sunken into her skull, exposing dark circles around the perimeter of their lids. Her skin, previously so vibrant and full of life, had become as pale as the moon. Even her arms were skinnier and bruised.

In shock, Chance sat next to his mom and clasped her hand into his. He hadn't expected to see her this way. He thought he'd have more time. He wanted more time. He couldn't understand why this was happening. Why couldn't it be his dad? His mom had always been there for him. She was a good person. His dad was nothing but a drunk. Chance didn't even feel guilty wishing his dad could take his mom's place.

Leaning over, Chance whispered in his mom's ear, hoping her soul could still hear him, letting the hot tears fall to her face.

"I love you, Mom."

His dad coughed and cleared his throat as he took a swig from his beer can before turning the television on. Clenching his fists, Chance began to walk away, not wanting to be in the same room with his dad.

As he turned toward the door, a thunderous voice boomed across the TV. "Breaking news in Jacksonville, North Carolina," News Anchor Mike Lipman announced to his audience at home.

Chance and his dad both winced at the loud voice. Lowering the volume, his dad sat back and pulled out a newspaper that had been on the table next to him, not paying particular attention to the screen.

Chance stopped in his tracks. The city mentioned, Jacksonville, caught his attention.

"Can you turn it back up?" he asked, not looking away from the screen. When his request went unanswered, he walked over to the TV and turned it up himself.

"In the news tonight, the bodies of four women have been found in Wilson Bay, near Wilson Island. None of them have been identified yet, but it has been confirmed that they were all young, probably in their early twenties. The investigation is in the early stages. We will have more information as this story unfolds. If you have any information that can help the Jacksonville area police department, please..."

Before the news segment finished, Chance was out the door, leaving his dad alone in the kitchen.

A few minutes later, Chance sat on a familiar wooden chair in his neighbor's kitchen. Light radiated throughout the room as Joe handed him a mug with a rooster on it, with hot tea inside. As Joe set down the cream and sugar, he offered Chance a spoon.

"No, thanks, I drink it black now."

"Never did think I'd see the day you turned down cream and sugar." Joe laughed as he placed the spoon next to him.

"How you feeling today? Did you at least get some sleep?"

Chance shook his head.

"Listen, I know you're upset and angry. Hell, I would be too. But you have to understand something. Your mom was a proud woman. She loved you, and she knew it would destroy you if you knew she was sick. She knew you'd put your life on hold, and she didn't want that."

"She put you up to it. Didn't she?" Chance asked, referring to the Marine Corps.

"Bless your mom, she was a wonderful woman. I did as she asked. And it was the best thing for you."

Joe would do anything his mom asked. Chance knew that. His mom spent years helping him through a rough patch, and Joe, in turn, returned the favor.

Though he had graying hair, Joe was only in his early forties. He'd been married once, but Chance had never met his wife. Joe never talked about her at great length. But, from the bits and pieces of conversations they'd had over the years, Chance knew she'd been the love of his life. They were young and in love. She had gotten pregnant. They got married. And then they bought the house he was currently sitting in. Then, one day, Joe received a call while on duty. It was from the hospital. His wife had been in a terrible head-on collision with a semi-truck. At six months pregnant, they tried to save both her and the baby. But, in the end, there were too many complications, and they both died during surgery, before Joe arrived at the hospital.

Chance's mom said he was never the same after that,

which is why she checked on him so often, bringing him food every time she cooked a meal.

Chance was too young to remember those days, but he did recall the years that followed. Joe threw himself into his law enforcement career and their community and started coaching when he heard Chance was trying out for Little League. That's how they grew so close. Joe was like a big brother in a way.

"That's not why I'm here," Chance said, setting his mug to the side.

He propped his elbow on the table and leaned his jaw against his hand. "What do you know about the women found in Jacksonville?"

"You mean the women who were found dead?" Joe asked, looking confused. After Chance nodded, Joe continued. "Well, I mean, I probably know just as much as you do. They just announced it on television. Why are you asking?"

Chance didn't know how to respond, but he never kept anything from Joe. He was the one person Chance felt he could trust. But Joe was a cop, and if he didn't choose his words correctly, he could be endangering Claire's life.

He sat quietly for a few seconds, thinking about what to say. "Do you know where the women were found?"

"I haven't heard anything beyond what you heard on the news. What's this all about?"

Letting out a deep sigh, Chance decided to tell Joe everything. Well, everything except for the magnetic connection he and Claire shared.

He started with how he met Claire in Jacksonville. How she seemed nervous and worried. He told Joe that, by the time they were halfway to Asheville, she had begun opening up about who she was and why she was leaving Jacksonville, detailing how she'd lost both her parents and had moved in with her stepbrother, and how Alex was probably a murderer.

"I'm scared," she'd told him. "I think Alex and those guys killed her. I think there might be more too. And I can't call the police. Alex *is* the police. No one would believe me. I don't even know if I believe myself." Her voice shook with each admission.

Chance focused on Joe. "She told me she thought she saw a dead woman in her brother's closet *and* the basement, but she wasn't sure if it was the same woman or not."

Joe's eyes grew wide. "Okay, hold on here a second. She said she 'thought' she saw a dead woman in her brother's room, and then she ran?" Scratching his head, Joe got up from his seat. "Chance, you realize what you are telling me is that a woman fled the scene of a crime, right?"

"What was she supposed to do? If he's a cop and she told anyone, they might not believe her. And then what?"

Slumping into his chair, Joe placed his head in his hands. "And you want me to help look into this, I'm guessing? How well do you know this girl...Claire? Do you know her last name, where she went? Anything?"

"No." Chance kept such a straight face, he was sure Joe saw right through him.

"Okay, so you clearly have the hots for this girl. I'll look into this a little and see what I can come up with, but with such little information, I honestly doubt I'll be of much use. It's going to be tricky if this guy is a cop. I don't want to draw any suspicion. Some precincts get territorial, and if I start snooping, they might wonder why."

As Chance began to stand up, Joe cleared his throat and stood up with him. "If I look into this, you need to promise me something. You need to focus on your grief."

"I'm fine," Chance shrugged.

"No. You aren't fine. You're angry. And I'm afraid if you don't face it while you are home, you might get into some trouble down the line."

Turning his back, Joe reached above his kitchen refrigerator. Pulling down a white envelope, he handed it to Chance.

"Your mom wrote it for you just a few weeks ago. She asked me to give it to you when she was at the hospital. You might want to sit down when you read this."

Chapter Six
PAST

Chance

Later that evening, lifting the tab on the envelope, Chance finally withdrew the letter Joe had given him earlier that day. Now, as his dad slept, snoring on the couch, Chance walked out onto the back porch. In the dim light, contrasting the night sky, he began to read.

My sweet baby boy,

I know you have questions, lots of questions. And I doubt this letter will answer them all. But if you listen with your heart, maybe you'll begin to understand.

I want to start at the beginning, before you were born. It was 1972, and I had just volunteered to be a nurse with the Army Nurse Corps. This was all at the tail end of the Vietnam War. I know this may sound strange to you, considering I've never mentioned it in the past. But you also have to remember, the Vietnam War was not talked about or discussed upon returning home, for both soldiers and nurses alike. For the men, it was harder. Women had it easy in comparison, or at least I did.

As a volunteer, I arrived in South Vietnam with the

Army Nurse Corps and worked at a field hospital that closely resembled an oversized tent. I wasn't there long, but long enough to meet a man. It's sort of cliche to say this, but he was tall, dark, and handsome. He was a soldier, and the years of war had been etched into his face, the lines deep and his skin tanned.

He came to see me one day, his hand requiring a few stitches, and while our visit was brief, I couldn't help but get lost in his eyes. He came back to see me the next day and the day after that. And though I told him we'd both get in trouble if he continued, I secretly wished he'd keep showing up.

As the weeks wore on, thousands of soldiers and nurses began pulling out of Vietnam. The day I told him I was returning to the United States, he pulled me aside and told me he loved me and that he'd marry me one day. And you know what? I believed him. We wrote to each other almost every day, and I longed to see him again, to get lost in his eyes.

Finally, in March of 1975, a letter arrived asking me to meet him in Hawaii for his R&R. And on April 18th, we married, just the two of us, underneath the Hawaiian sun.

Unfortunately, the man I loved so dearly had to return to Vietnam.

"I have unfinished business to take care of," he said as he kissed me goodbye. The news was already reporting that more soldiers were being pulled from Vietnam. That they would be returning stateside in a matter of time. But my new husband said he wanted to see things through to the end. He'd invested so much time in Vietnam that he needed to be there to see his men get home safely. He promised me this would be the end though. He promised he'd come back home, and we'd be able to start a family. But fate had other plans.

Eleven days later, my husband, Simon Howard, was killed in the Fall of Saigon. I'll never know all the details, only what has been told to me, and even those details are only fractured stories. Bits and pieces that cause nightmares. One thing I know, he died a hero. He died trying to help evacuate American troops.

Simon's body was flown to Chattanooga to be buried near the rest of his family. It was that morning, before the drive over, that I found out I was pregnant. On the worst day of my life, on a day of unimaginable grieving, I found out I was blessed with you. Through the pain and tears, I couldn't help but smile, knowing that your dad kept his promise. A family. Maybe not with him. But he created a family. You and me.

At his funeral, I met all of your dad's friends, and they shared stories of a man I loved. But over time, as they all left and returned to their own families, one man stayed back. He helped me tackle everyday living. He wasn't even from Asheville, but he told me that Simon was his very best friend, that Simon had saved his life countless times, and that he would do anything for me as Simon's wife.

As I grieved the death of a husband I barely knew, I also panicked over raising a child without a father. Simon's friend, now my friend, also grieved. Not just for the loss of Simon, but for so many of his friends lost to war. We grieved together, and over time, we, too, fell in love. I considered myself lucky because it was a deeper love than anyone could possibly imagine. This friend became your new father and my husband, demanding that I marry him the day you were born, although I made him wait. But he was the first to hold you and the first to say he loved you, which made my heart melt. How could I have been so blessed with not just one love, but two loves?

I'm sorry for never sharing this story with you. I always imagined telling you as you got older, but it became more and more difficult. Your father has his demons. He has seen things you cannot begin to imagine. And as you saw those demons begin to arise, you began to pull away. I was terrified that, if I told you the whole truth, you would disown him as your father, and I knew that would tear him up even more. But I see now that it didn't matter. The drinking was never tolerable in your eyes, and I should have put my foot down. But, you see, your father is a great man. He's always loved us, and I vowed to always love him. I know he has nightmares from the war. But you can't possibly understand what it was like for him to come home to people sneering at him and muttering disgusting words. He lost so much and yet dedicated his life to us.

Now, as for my cancer. I decided a long time ago that I wouldn't tell you because you'd put your life on hold for me. I didn't want you to see me fall apart or become someone other than your mom.

Your father has taken great care of me, but, for the last year, it's taken a toll on him. He has struggled, as you can see. He needs you now more than ever. You both need each other.

I love you, Chance. You are my beautiful baby boy. Promise me that you'll look out for your father. Don't give up on him.

Love Always,
Mom

Chapter Seven
PAST

Claire

Tears poured down Claire's face as she sat in her own misery. She watched Chance as he searched for her through the darkened windows before he turned around and disappeared into the night. If she'd only said, yes. Yes, a million times. More than anything, she wanted to stay with him, to feel his warm embrace. But it was too late. And now, he was gone.

And who was she kidding? Her feelings for Chance were unrealistic. She barely knew him. Staying with him in North Carolina would be dumb. Way too risky. Claire needed to get as far away as possible. Once she got to Chicago, she'd create a plan. But the idea was still out there, like a cloud floating in the sky, and she sulked in her seat, remembering Chance's soft lips and penetrating eyes.

As the bus rumbled across the gravel road and slid back onto the expressway, she shoved aside the conflicting thoughts. She wiped her cheeks as she watched the snow somersault from the sky, lighter and softer than before. Feeling heavy, Claire adjusted her weight in the seat and let her eyelids fall, letting sleep find her.

Hours later, a sudden jolt awoke Claire, waking her from the same nightmare she'd been having for weeks. On a wooden dock, her mom and stepdad stood, their backs to Claire, ignoring her insistent screaming until she couldn't take it any longer. She tried running to them, trying to warn them not to get into the water. But the distance never grew shorter. Finally, turning in her direction, her mom placed her bony hand in the air, warning Claire not to come any closer. And while she was still too far away to see clearly, she still noticed the wrinkled and swollen skin that sagged from her arm and the hollowed-out eyes that were missing.

And then, her parents stepped off the dock, plummeting into the black water.

Claire heard herself screaming in her sleep, begging her mom to come back. But the jolt woke her up like it always did, leaving her with sweat dripping down her neck and her pulse racing.

"Last stop!" a voice rang out.

How long have I been sleeping? Claire wondered as she opened her eyes, thankful to have been pulled from the nightmare.

The sky was still dark, but she could almost see the changing of colors beginning to take place across the horizon. The sun would be up shortly if the clouds stayed away.

Out of the corner of her eye, Claire caught sight of something near her foot. Reaching down, she grabbed hold of a torn piece of yellow notebook paper, a phone number inscribed on the inside. *Did Chance drop this?* Holding it firmly in her hand, she brought it up to her heart. It couldn't be, could it? Maybe she'd call him when she was safe. Maybe, just maybe, this wasn't the end.

"Is this Chicago?" Claire asked the bus driver as he pulled into an empty lot.

"Sure is. Union Station is a few blocks that way," he said, pointing down the dark road.

Climbing down the stairs, Claire's sneakers landed in a pile of black slush, leaving her feet cold and dirty. Even before sunrise, Chicago seemed to be bustling with business. With no gloves, scarf, or hat, Claire knew she would stick out like a sore thumb. All around her, people pushed past, zipping by with their arms tucked tightly in their pockets, trying to stay warm. The streets were filled with the same dirty slush she landed in moments ago, the sidewalks no better. And while she only had a few blocks to walk, her socks and feet had already begun to feel like icicles.

In the distance, a siren blared, throwing Claire into a frenzy. Fear took her by the shoulders and shook her. *What if Alex is here right now, looking for me? He might have friends here.* Cops were connected everywhere. She knew she had to be careful. She began to tremble as doubt built within her chest.

What am I doing? She didn't know anybody—not a soul—in Chicago. She wanted to cry. Her mom would know what to do. She would hug her and make her feel safe. How she longed to feel safe. The idea of hiding in Chicago scared her. Sure, it was almost a thousand miles away from Jacksonville, but if Alex had committed murder, he'd go to the ends of the Earth to find her, to shut her up. Claire was certain of that.

Logically, her brain told her to go to the cops. Here, in Chicago, they might not have ties to Alex. They could help her. They could look into it and then...

No. She couldn't. They'd look into it, and Alex would find a way to hide it, to cover it up. He'd lie. The body was probably already gone. He knew how to cover things up. And then they would make her go back and live with him because she was only seventeen. She was still a kid. No. She definitely couldn't tell the police. Not anything.

But, in the back of her head, as she made the decision not to report anything, she also knew this was exactly how bad things happened. It was like watching a bad movie play out. She knew she would be the one yelling at the actors to just call the police because now they were making it worse.

A few moments later, after crossing the last street, Claire found herself entering Union Station, too cold to appreciate or marvel at its size or beauty. Finding a seat in the center of the station, away from the frigid air near the doors, Claire sat down on a small wooden bench. Feeling small and insignificant, she instinctively traced her finger over her locket, trying to calm her nerves.

The sun had finally risen, peeking through the overhead windows, casting shadows across the people who walked by. Her eyes darted from person to person, noting the rush of bodies that seemed to flow effortlessly and with purpose. She felt oddly out of place, the only person not moving, not running to catch a bus or a train or even a taxi. And the noises. The echoing of voices, the loud engines. It was all too much, and she buried her head into her sweater, pleading for it all to stop.

Be brave. Make a plan.

But what kind of plan? How does one make a plan when they have no plans? Her mom always told her to have a plan in place, but it sounded contradictory, which made Claire angry. How could her mom manage to make her angry when she was dead? Frustrated with herself, she lifted her head and was suddenly drawn to the wall opposite her, catching sight of a poster draped across the brick wall showing a man dressed in a midnight blue coat, outlined with red seams, that seemed to gleam in the morning light. Wearing a white hat and matching white gloves, the man stood, proudly carrying a rifle.

Her eyes shifted to his brass-plated belt and back up to his chiseled face.

He's a marine.

As Claire stared at the recruiting poster, she couldn't help but think of Chance. Her hand reached inside her pocket, feeling the crisp edges of the paper that lay inside next to her locket.

She paused for a second...and then it hit her. Chance. She had to call Chance. This was what her mom would have wanted. No, not to rush back into Chance's arms, but to seek his help. Being brave also meant being vulnerable.

Claire waited for the shop to open inside Union Station and paid for a prepaid calling card with some of the money she had stolen from Alex.

Then, finding a pay phone near an outside wall, yellow paper in hand, she picked up the receiver. She was about to dial the numbers when she second-guessed herself and placed it back in its cradle. Everything inside her wanted to hear his voice, but she was so nervous. What would she say? She knew she couldn't go back to North Carolina, even if Asheville *was* hours away from Jacksonville. She couldn't risk being in the same state. Alex would find her. Even if Chance couldn't help her, which she knew would be unreasonable anyway, she wanted to hear his voice. She could almost imagine it now. Soft, masculine, and empathetic.

She picked up the receiver once more. This time, she listened as the dial tone echoed in her ear. She flipped over her calling card and punched in the numbers and then proceeded to punch in the numbers from the yellow paper. The phone began to ring. Once, twice, three times...

"Hello?"

Three hours later, Claire was on another bus. This time, heading to New York—Staten Island to be exact. Not exactly what she imagined when she'd tried to call Chance. Instead, she was on her way to meet another man, a complete stranger.

His name was Tyler Romano. He'd answered the phone

and, after a long pause, Claire finally mustered up enough courage to ask for Chance.

"Chance? You have the wrong number," he said. "Wait. You said Chance? Chance Johnson?"

"Yes. I think that's his last name. But I'm not really sure." Her voice wavered as she clutched the phone tightly.

"Chance doesn't live here. I mean, Chance lives in North Carolina. I'm his buddy, but I honestly don't even know his phone number."

Claire felt defeated as her heart sank. Her shoulders felt heavy, and just as she was about to hang up, the man on the other end continued. "My name is Tyler. Can I help you with something?"

"I don't know. I'm not really sure why I was calling in the first place. I just..." Her voice trailed off as her throat tightened.

"Hey, listen, if you need anything, please just say it. Chance and I met in the Marine Corps. Both of us are on leave right now. I'll see if I can track him down somehow. Can I ask you something though?"

"Sure," Claire replied, still feeling utterly hopeless.

"How did you get my phone number?"

Claire hesitated before sharing the details of how she found the phone number, thinking it belonged to Chance. Tyler listened and asked questions and, before long, Claire was beginning to open up more and more, tiptoeing around the most intimate of details, leaving out her feelings for Chance and that she was on the run. She sensed Tyler was a nice guy, genuinely trying to gather what information he could so he could better locate Chance for her. But what did it matter if he *did* find Chance? It's not like Claire had a phone number where she could be reached.

Tyler must have sensed a change in her tone, because the next thing she knew, he was asking if she was in a safe place.

She hesitated. What had she said to him to make him think she wasn't safe? If she told him yes, it wouldn't be a lie. Or would it? She knew that, while this building provided her shelter from the cold, he wasn't referring to that.

And then, without hesitation, she began to sob. She wasn't strong like her mom. She wasn't brave.

Scared, she poured her soul out to this complete stranger, telling him everything, from the dead woman in Alex's bedroom to her running to Chicago with no place to turn.

"Let me get this straight. Your parents are gone. Your stepbrother is a cop but is involved in some murder. And you ran away?" His voice was tender and soft as he spoke. If he was judging her, he didn't let on.

"Claire? Do you have enough money to buy another bus ticket?" he asked, forcing her to redirect her attention.

"I think so."

"Have you ever been to New York?"

And just like that, Claire followed Tyler's insistent pleas to purchase a bus ticket to New York.

"You have nowhere else to go, and I wouldn't be able to live with myself if something happened to you," he said, declaring he'd do whatever it took to get in touch with Chance.

When asked why he was doing this for her, his response was simple.

"That's what friends are for. Now get on that bus, and I'll meet you at the station when you arrive."

Chapter Eight
PAST

Chance

After reading the letter his mom had written to him, Chance remained glued to the wooden chair in complete shock. Hands shaking, he reread it another time, not believing his eyes. *My dad isn't my biological father? My mom was married before?*

He had already been angry, but he was downright *furious* now. He'd been lied to his whole life.

With clenched jaws, Chance rolled his shoulders back as thoughts of tearing up the letter spiraled in his head, but Chance stopped his hands from proceeding.

Chance rose to his feet and shoved the chair into the table, then yanked the glass door open to step inside, away from the forbidding cold. Turning his attention to the grating sounds coming from the living room, his eyes landed on his dad...or whomever the man was.

What do I call him now? How am I supposed to react to any of this?

Asleep in the oversized recliner, a brown blanket half sprawled across at his legs, he was snoring like a freight train.

The television was still on, and there were more than a half dozen beer cans scattered about.

Furrowing his brows, Chance pressed his lips together. Anger bubbled inside his stomach and his chest tightened. Chance knew he had to get out. He couldn't stay here. Not tonight. Not with this man who couldn't stay sober for a day. The man who wasn't even his father.

Turning his attention away, he caught sight of the car keys on the coffee table, and, without a second thought, Chance grabbed them and tore off into the night.

The next morning, Chance awoke to the sound of sirens blaring and heavy metal blasting. Barely able to open his eyes, he was fully aware he wasn't at home, lying in his own bed. His head pounded and ached, and he wished someone would turn down the music.

Finally, prying his eyes open, lights flooded his vision. He instantly regretted it and shut them again. Maybe this was a dream. No, a nightmare. It had to be.

Sliding his hands down, he felt nothing but skin, his bare ass exposed. He tried to grab a blanket, a pillow, anything. But he wasn't on a bed. He was on the floor, and there was nothing close enough to reach.

"Good morning, sunshine!" a sharp voice announced extra loudly, trying to compete with the music coming from another room.

Glancing up, Chance squinted his eyes tightly, trying to focus on the woman who stood before him. Silhouetted by the sun, he noticed she was tall, with long blond hair that hung well past her shoulders. Fully dressed in a pair of black slacks and a white shirt that hung low across her chest, she turned to open the last of the blinds, making Chance's eyes water.

"Do you know where my pants are?" Chance asked hoarsely. His throat was so dry it felt like he'd swallowed a thousand cotton balls.

"You don't remember taking them off, now do you?" She laughed, tossing him his jeans.

Completely embarrassed and totally out of his element, he rolled over and worked his jeans on over his hips.

"What exactly happened last night?"

"Last night?" She laughed again as she grabbed a broomstick from a closet. Before continuing, she reached the broom up to the ceiling and began banging it repeatedly until the music grew quieter.

"You mean last night *and* this morning?" she asked. She propped the broom up against the wall and then turned around to face him.

Chance closed his eyes. He couldn't have. His cheeks grew hot, and his stomach tightened, suddenly feeling nauseated, feeling every sip of the alcohol he'd ingested last night. She was a beautiful girl, but she was older, probably by at least ten years. And blondes weren't his type. How would this have happened?

Feeling lightheaded, he zipped his pants and sat down on the cream couch behind him. He remembered driving to a pub in downtown Asheville, which had a reputation for serving underage kids. He'd had a few drinks as he lounged on the barstool, feeling every bit of his self-pity. But he couldn't recall much else.

"Oh, honey, don't you worry. Nothing happened. I mean, it *could* have happened, but whoever this Claire girl is, she ain't me. You're not so much my type either...kind of young. Especially to be pining over some girl who isn't even here." She smiled, and for the first time, she actually looked sympathetic.

As she neared him, he stood, unsure what to do, still not quite sure how he ended up here, naked on her floor.

"Your shirt," she said, handing him the gray T-shirt he'd been wearing last night.

As she turned away, he noticed her sad eyes barely looked

at him. But they flashed an amused smile when he pulled the shirt over his head, wincing in pain. Every muscle in his body felt like it was on fire.

"Hurts, huh?" she asked with a noticeable southern accent.

"Yeah, I don't get it." He clenched his teeth and grimaced.

"You really don't remember, do you?"

He shook his head, hunched over, holding his ribcage.

"Sit and I'll tell ya. I know it hurts." She nodded toward his stomach.

"Last night you walked right up to me and said you were taking me home. Well, that didn't go well with my date." She giggled. "It was actually really amusing. I mean, you actually saved me from a terrible date. The guy was awful, and once he hit you, well, I told him I'd rather go home with you than him."

Chance tried to remember it but couldn't. Everything was a blur. He vaguely remembered a guy twice his size getting angry and sucker punching him in the ribs.

"How'd I end up here?" he asked, not knowing if he really wanted all the details or not.

"After he hit you, you fell backward pretty hard. I sort of took pity on you," she said with a wink.

Embarrassment washed over him as she simultaneously recalled the events and tidied her living room, picking up the pillows he'd probably tossed to the floor. He hung his head, ashamed of his actions when she continued.

"I hadn't realized just how drunk you were though. Tom, the bartender, came around and helped you off the ground. Told me you'd been there for a few hours, drinking alone. Once we got you onto a chair, you started calling me Claire. I knew, right then and there, that your heart must have been broken. Breakups are tough, and it was actually refreshing to see a man so broken up about it," she said earnestly.

Chance watched her as she spoke. She was a storyteller for sure, animated when she needed to be, but casual in tone. And there was something mysterious about her. Why would she bring him here, a complete stranger?

"Tom fed you some pain medication and ensured you had plenty of water. I just kept you company; it was the least I could do, since you saved me from that arrogant prick. But within an hour, I noticed you weren't sobering up, and I was ready to head home. Tom said he'd call you a cab, but you didn't have any money left on you to pay the cab driver. Tom's a sweet man, but he would have called the police because he doesn't like charity cases. Me, on the other hand? I love them when they save me from my own self-destruction."

Chance narrowed his eyes, confused. When their eyes met, she put down the garbage bag and sat next to him with a deep sigh.

"Oh, I don't mean, like, I'm going to self-destruct, but look at me. I'm thirty-one years old and I live alone, next to a bar. It was fun for the first few years. But the only men I meet nowadays are arrogant pricks, liars, cheaters, or taken. You, you're in the 'taken' category. Your heart belongs somewhere else. Listening to you talk about Claire was so refreshing. It made me have faith in humanity again. I guess taking you home was sort of selfish on my part though," she said as she slumped deeper into the cushion.

"If we didn't...how did I..." Chance started to say, unsure of how to ask.

"If you mean, why were you butt naked on my floor, it's because you walked right into my apartment and undressed yourself. You were on the couch when I went to bed, so how you ended up on the floor is questionable. You fell right to sleep, so I left you there. You were a true gentleman." She laughed as she finished, but he sensed a hint of sadness in her voice.

"And this morning, you slept right through all those sirens. There was an accident down the other way, and I'm fairly sure there were at least a dozen cops and ambulances driving by." She stood back up, smiling again.

"By the way, my name's Valerie. I don't want to kick you out, but I sort of have to head into work. I have some coffee over there if you'd like some before you leave."

"Coffee? Crap. What time is it?" he asked, realizing what today was.

Chapter Nine
PAST

Chance

A few hours later, Chance was making small talk with neighbors he barely knew and family that came in from out of town, his head pounding. His aunt had made all the arrangements, opting out of a funeral home and having a celebration of life at his parents' house. While not very large, the setting was suitable for people to come and go. Tucked back, away from the street, their house sat on an acre of land. In the summer, the trees provided a fortress of shade. But, today, the bare branches only amplified his emptiness.

The forecast showed the likelihood of more snow, which was unusual for this time of year, but Chance's aunt set out folding chairs and tables on the back patio anyway. She also placed pictures around the house, portraying his mom as a vibrant little girl, loving wife, and doting mom.

"She was so gorgeous." Thelma sniffed as she tiptoed up behind Chance, wiping her nose with a tissue. They looked at a black-and-white picture of his mom with her white nurse's hat and uniform, probably from when she graduated nursing school. Thelma lived across the street and was a few years older than his parents. She lived alone, her children all grown up and moved out, living in various parts of the country. Thelma had become friends with his mom when they first moved in, and now he wondered if she'd known about his mother's cancer, curious who his mom let into her life. He wanted to ask, but he didn't feel it was appropriate, especially here in their house, during a period of mourning. It wouldn't do him any good anyway. The answer would likely only hurt more.

"Yeah, she was always beautiful," Chance replied, careful not to make eye contact or to add any unnecessary detail. He knew if he did, it would only draw out a longer conversation, and he just wanted to get through the night, though he knew full well he'd have to indulge in more conversations than he'd like.

From the corner of his eye, he saw Joe approaching and turned around to greet him.

"Hi, Thelma. Hi, Chance," Joe said first, giving Thelma a hug. "Do you mind if I steal him for a minute? I wanted to chat with him for a bit, if you don't mind," Joe asked as he pulled himself from her embrace. He patted Chance on the back.

"Oh, no, of course not. You two go talk. I'll go find your Aunt Debbie."

When Thelma stepped away, Joe pulled out a notepad covered with writing.

"First of all, how are you feeling? Any better after that shower?" He chuckled. Joe had picked him up from Valerie's apartment. He had been amused that Chance had claimed Valerie as his own and found it even funnier that he got decked for it. But he was also impressed that Valerie was kind enough to take him in, and, if Chance wasn't mistaken, he could have sworn he'd seen the two of them exchange glances as he got into Joe's squad car.

"I've been better. What do you have there?"

"So, I finally have some information for you about those

women from yesterday. Looks like they identified one woman so far. Her name was Robin Harris. She was only twenty years old. She had been reported missing for about two weeks and was a student at the University of North Carolina. One of her roommates mentioned she responded to an odd inquiry in the newspaper and hadn't been seen since. The other three are all young women too. The theory right now is that these women were all abducted, probably from college campuses. They got lucky identifying Robin because she had a few tattoos. If it wasn't for that, it might have taken a lot longer. All of the women had their teeth removed, making dental matches impossible."

"Did you say they were missing their teeth?" Chance asked. He replayed his conversation with Joe the day before, but he didn't recall mentioning the teeth. Claire had though. He could still see Claire's face in his mind as she told him about the woman in the closet and the teeth on the floor. Her worried expression, her touch, as her grasp tightened in his hand.

"Yeah, each one of them had their teeth pulled out. Some of this information has already been leaked to the press, so I'm pretty sure what I am sharing with you now will be in the news shortly."

"Joe," Chance said, "I'm certain that Claire's brother is a part of this now. She told me about the teeth. She mentioned them falling from a shelf in his closet.

"I believe you, but you don't understand. It's not like I can accuse the Jacksonville Police Department of having a dirty cop, especially when I don't even have a name. I could lose my own job for that kind of accusation." Joe sighed as he shoved the notepad into his back pocket.

"We can't do nothing though. Claire is out there. Afraid he might find her. What happens if he does? What happens if he finds another woman and does this again?"

Joe stood silently next to him, hands on his hips. He probably knew Chance was right, but he didn't have much to go off.

"I have an idea," Chance finally announced. But, just as the words left his mouth, a loud bang erupted from the kitchen. Both Joe and Chance turned to look. His dad lay sprawled on the floor, a beer can safely in the clutches of his hand.

"Got it!" He laughed as a few plates belatedly clattered to the floor.

Chance headed for the open kitchen door.

"Chance," Joe said, reaching to stop him, but he shrugged him off.

"What's going on?" Chance demanded, eyes narrowing on his dad. Two men backed off after lifting his dad to his feet. When his dad couldn't meet his eyes, Chance felt the anger rising.

"You're drunk! Of all days, you're drunk! I shouldn't have expected anything less. You are a complete disaster. I don't understand how Mom put up with you for so long."

By this time, a crowd had gathered.

"Chance," Joe called out to him again.

"Who do you think you are, talking to me like that?" his dad finally said, slurring his words, barely audible. He reached to place his beer on the table but missed. It hit the linoleum floor hard, and foam sprayed in all directions, hitting onlookers.

"You're a sorry excuse for a human, you know that? Mom wouldn't just be disappointed, she'd be disgusted." And with that, Chance turned and walked out the door.

Chapter Ten
Present

27 years later
St. Petersburg, Florida 2021

Claire

Walking along the sugary white sand, Claire watched two pelicans float across the tranquil sky, scanning the crystal-clear waters below. One dove and nabbed a fish before soaring effortlessly back into the sky. A smile crossed her face as she breathed in the salty air and the sand creased between her toes.

Checking the time on her phone, Claire let out a silent exhale. She knew she needed to start work, but a few more minutes wouldn't hurt. This was her favorite time of day, and it was only recently that she was even able to enjoy watching the ocean again. Even so, Claire scooped up her shoes and made her way back to the little café that sat isolated across the street from where she stood along the shoreline.

Knowing it'd be a long morning, Claire set her laptop on a small table in the corner of the patio and looked at her screen in dismay. How would she finish her novel when her heart wasn't in it? With a deadline quickly approaching, Claire

"

knew she'd have to call her editor and request more time, but she also didn't want to hear her friend complain on the other end. She'd already received two extensions, and even those hadn't been easy feats.

Stretching out her arms, she decided to grab a cup of coffee before diving into the remaining chapters of her latest romance novel. The bell to the café dinged as she strolled to the counter with her coffee-stained ceramic mug.

"Hey!" Sasha said with eyes that sparkled and a killer smile that Claire wished she had. As Beach Brew's only morning barista, Claire had grown close to Sasha in the past few years. With almost two decades between them, Sasha was closer to her daughter Molly's age, but she considered her a friend, nonetheless. She radiated confidence in the way she walked, talked, and smiled. And her striking red hair and bright freckles made it easy for her to become the perfect muse for Claire's latest novel.

"Morning. Can you fill this up with whatever dark roast you have brewing?" Claire asked, setting the mug on the counter, offering it to Sasha.

"Of course."

"Do you have plans this weekend?" Claire asked, making small talk, but also genuinely curious.

Sasha had just begun telling Claire about a man she'd matched with on a dating website when the bell to the door rang again, indicating another customer had walked in. Claire didn't turn, as she was used to people coming and going. Instead, she listened to Sasha ramble on about the possibility of a date. That was, if the man worked up enough courage to ask her out.

"It's a beautiful morning...no rain in the forecast," a gentle voice hummed behind her.

"It is," Claire agreed as Sasha handed her the freshly filled mug. Slipping her hand between the handle and the neck of the mug, Claire turned around and lifted her gaze.

She immediately locked in on *his eyes* at the same moment his gaze dropped to hers. Not having a firm grasp, the mug slipped from her hand and shattered across the floor. Claire stood there, silent, wide-eyed, as hot coffee spread around her feet.

Sasha shrieked, the surprise catching her off guard. But Claire couldn't speak. Frozen in place, a flood of memories filled her head all at once. He, too, stood motionless, seemingly also in shock.

"Chance?" she gasped after catching her breath. She was sure her dismay was written all over her face. Was she imagining this? Had she manifested him here? For years, she'd hoped to see him again, and here he was, right in front of her. Was he real? She hadn't fallen, hadn't hit her head. No. This was really him.

"Claire," he replied, narrowing his eyes with the same skepticism she had. One word. One syllable. That's all he had to say, and her heart fluttered.

"Are you two all right? No one got burned, did they? I'm so sorry." Sasha's face crinkled as she came running around from behind the counter with a dish towel. With her bright red hair in a high bun, she began picking up the shattered pieces of white porcelain that had once been Claire's favorite mug, the one Molly had given her when she published her first novel.

"Claire, I'm so sorry about that mug," Sasha said, knowing how much it meant to her. "Are you okay, sir?" she continued, directing her attention to Chance as she frantically wiped the hot coffee near his feet.

Still frozen within his gaze, flashes of the last time Claire had seen Chance came rushing back. It was shortly after 9/11. After the Twin Towers had fallen, after Tyler had died.

She recalled the look on Chance's face when they locked eyes then, the first time in almost seven years. She hadn't expected to see him that day. She'd never found Chance, and she had long given up. Tyler, too, had stopped searching. But, on that cold September day, inside the confines of the cemetery, Claire looked up as the wind brushed her cheek. Through the gray, luminous mist, surprise caught Claire off guard. Her heart skipped a beat, and she sucked in a sharp breath as her eyes met Chance's gaze from across the plot where Tyler's body would be laid to rest.

Wearing his dress blues, Claire figured Chance had come to offer his condolences and might even be a pallbearer, helping to conduct the ceremony honors that Tyler's dad had requested. But what were the odds of Chance showing up? After all those years?

She continued to watch him as the priest offered a prayer. Her lips parted, and she held her breath. And then, suddenly, the tears poured down her surely mascara-streaked face. Claire brought one gloved hand up and wiped the moisture away. And, in that brief moment, she thought she saw confusion cross Chance's face. She wanted to say something to him. To run to him, to be comforted by him. To tell him she had looked for him for years.

But all that hope was lost the moment her daughter started crying. At three years old, Molly couldn't comprehend the gravity of what was happening. And so, instead of calling out to Chance, she bent over and scooped Molly into her arms.

When she turned back around, Chance was gone.

She expected to see Chance later, after the funeral. She wasn't sure where or when, but she assumed he would be there. But, after the casket was lowered, and after people said their goodbyes, Chance was nowhere to be found. And then she cried again. For not only had she lost her best friend, but she'd also lost the love of her life...again.

"Do you live here, in St. Petersburg?" Chance asked now, breaking the silence.

"Yes. I mean, no, not here," Claire said, breathing quickly, with butterflies in her stomach. "I live on the bay side," she continued.

Nervously, she bent down to help Sasha pick up the pieces of her mug. He, too, bent down and slowly gathered what he could as Sasha went back to grab a mop.

Standing back up, Chance placed the small fragments into his cupped hand.

"I'm just here working, I guess you can say," she said, gesturing outside to the table under the palm trees, afraid to take her eyes off him. "What about you?"

"I'm here for the next few days. I'm speaking at the National Psychology Conference at the Tradewinds this weekend," he said in the same gentle voice she remembered from so long ago.

Sasha came back out with the mop and continued to apologize profusely. Even though Claire told her that it wasn't her fault, Sasha still insisted that Claire would get her coffee free of charge for as long as she wanted. She then insisted Chance order whatever he wanted on the house. But, as a true gentleman, Chance declined. He ordered his coffee and tipped her heavily.

When they both had their coffees in hand, they stood awkwardly silent, neither making the first attempt to walk away. Years had divided them. And, while they were strangers, their brief past still drew her to him, as it had on the bus all those years ago. Her feet felt rooted into the ground, wanting, waiting for him to say more.

But when his gaze shifted away from her, her heart began to beat faster. She was nervous. She had to do something. She couldn't let him slip by again without saying what she'd wanted to two decades ago.

"Will you be free tonight?" she asked, her breath catching on the last word, unable to tear her eyes away from him.

Silence filled the space around them as he gazed at her. She didn't want him to stop looking, but she wanted him to speak. To say something. Anything. Her heart pulsed and her lips went dry. Licking them, she felt her entire chest rise in anticipation.

"I can be," he finally responded, his whisper almost lost in the breeze.

"Would you like to get some dinner? There're a few places right along the beach near the Tradewinds that have some great seafood. I can meet you over there."

"I'd love to," he said smiling.

Chapter Eleven
Present

Chance

"With more research today than ever before, we know that veterans have a high risk of developing post-traumatic stress disorder, especially those who have seen combat. But we also know that combat itself is not the only deciding factor. Sexual trauma and violence also lead the pack. Anything that negatively affects one's life in a traumatic way and causes depression, sleep problems, and drug or alcohol use are common telltale signs that someone is experiencing PTSD. Often, we use these symptoms to determine treatment of our patients. You have an alcohol problem, let's treat that. You have depression, let's treat that. What we need to be doing is finding the root problem of these symptoms."

Chance cleared his throat and continued. "Now don't get me wrong. I know there are some of you in this room who are saying, 'That's not me. I always find the root cause first. I know what I'm doing. I've been doing this for years.' If you can honestly say that, then this part doesn't apply to you. What should apply to you is how we plan to reach our patients before they stop showing up and give up. The statistics keep rising. More veterans are taking their lives than ever before. If we, as their therapists, psychologists, and social workers, know that our patients are at risk when they walk into our office, then we should be doing a better job of taking care of them. Keep them coming back. It's hard enough for most patients to admit they have a problem, often blaming themselves when things go wrong."

Chance spoke to the crowd from the stage. He'd been asked to speak about PTSD by his mentor, Valerie. She was unable to attend the conference and felt that, with the combination of his research and his real-life experience, he would be able to impress upon his colleagues the importance of reaching out to their patients, setting a higher bar for a better mental healthcare system.

"So, I want to ask you all, before I leave here today, what will you do the next time your patient cancels their appointment or fails to show up? Rather than charging them a cancellation fee, how can you be a better provider?"

Chance had already discussed the fact that most male veterans wouldn't even acknowledge depression in the first place, being taught from an early age that showing sadness is a sign of weakness. And that it's only amplified during boot camp. Women, on the other hand, will show more vulnerability, unless it's tied to sexual trauma. In that case, they are at a higher risk of not sharing all the details, afraid they caused the violence in the first place.

Instead, both genders have a high risk of turning to violence, drugs, and alcohol. He thought about his dad when he spoke about drinking and how combat could turn even the healthiest brain into mush under the wrong circumstances. Most of his colleagues pretended to understand, having studied for years, even specializing in this area. He saw them nodding their heads in agreement, but he knew that, for the vast majority, they still would never quite get it.

He left the stage feeling content, knowing Valerie would have approved. But he also felt incredibly disappointed because he knew most of the providers here wouldn't change a thing when they went back to their practices. Sure, they smiled and congratulated him on a great presentation, but the likelihood of anyone actually putting forth the effort to improve was slim to none.

Back in his room, Chance thought about Claire as he got ready for the evening. He had known there was a small chance of running into her when he agreed to the conference at Valerie's urging. A patient had left one of Claire's novels in his office last year. At the time, Chance had no idea she was a writer. Actually, he hadn't known much about her at all. He tried not to think of her. Her name ushered in a mix of emotions that often led to anxiety. But when he saw the novel sitting on the sofa, his eyes grew wide and his mouth dropped open when he recognized Claire's name emblazoned across the front cover.

Claire Harding.

It couldn't be, he thought at the time. Maybe it was just a coincidence. Somebody else with the same name.

Opening the jacket cover and flipping to the last page, Chance lost his breath. There she was. Claire. Her long honey brown hair pulled to the side. And she'd taken her name back. No longer Claire Romano, she was Claire Harding again. What was he supposed to do with that information? Shock ran through his veins as he tried, day after day, to get Claire out of his thoughts. But the more he tried not to think of her, the more he ended up dreaming about her.

It was only natural that his curiosity took over, and he began to research her whereabouts. While he had no social media accounts of his own, it wasn't hard to find a website dedicated to Claire as an author. She had three books out, her latest, a national bestseller. On her Instagram account, while not being specific, she noted living back in St. Petersburg, Florida.

But, if he actually believed they'd meet by coincidence, he would have bet against it. The odds were stacked against him. In a city of a couple hundred thousand, there was just no way for them to run into each other.

But then fate took control. And there she was, more beautiful than ever. Age treated her well. Her skin, no longer pale, was vibrant and full of life. More freckles dotted her cheekbones, the bridge of her nose, and her forehead. Her eyes were still radiant and soul-searching, as if one couldn't keep a secret from her if they tried. Fine lines had formed exactly where they should, from living both a life of hardship and of happiness.

And now, here he was, about to meet her for dinner. How on Earth did this happen? Their short conversation from earlier replayed endlessly in his mind.

Turning on the shower, Chance jumped into the hot, steaming water, and lathered his body with soap. He continued to think about Claire, wondering if she was thinking of him as he ran shampoo through his wet hair.

After he got out and toweled off, he told himself this was just a casual dinner. No big deal. But as he pulled on his beige khaki shorts and white polo, he couldn't shake the butterflies in his stomach, feeling like he was a teenager all over again.

Just before seven o'clock, Chance arrived at Crabby Bills, the seafood restaurant Claire recommended. Worried there might be a wait on a Friday night, he arrived early and asked the hostess if he could get a table for two out on the back tiki deck.

"It might be a while," she said, not looking up from the seating chart.

"That's fine," he replied after checking the time on his phone.

Noticing a couple emerge from their seats at the bar, Chance made his way over and grabbed the empty chairs, which were in direct line of sight from the main entrance.

"Can I get you a drink?" a tall brunette with colorful tattoos asked as he sank into the chair.

"Just water, thanks."

The woman looked at him and shrugged before dropping ice into a tall glass.

In the past, those looks often bothered him, sometimes even caused him to grow angry. He could sit at a bar and not drink alcohol. There was no crime in that. But now, it didn't matter. He was used to it.

Reaching for the water, Chance took a sip to wet his lips and calm his nerves. Over the rim of the glass, he noticed the entrance door open. Claire stepped inside and, instinctively, his chest tightened, and his breath went shallow.

Wearing a baby blue sundress that hugged her at the waist, Claire was even more beautiful than he remembered from earlier.

Catching his eye, she advanced toward him, her long golden hair swaying with each step. A small smile curved at the corners of her mouth.

Pushing out his stool, Chance stood when Claire approached. "I figured we could sit here until our table is ready. I asked for a seat outside. I hope that's okay with you," he said as he pulled the stool out for Claire, conscious of how close their bodies were.

"Of course. I would have recommended the same. It's a beautiful night, and I bet we'll have a great view of the sunset since there're no clouds in the sky." Her voice was wistful as she slipped into her seat.

Chance couldn't take his eyes off her as she spoke. Watching as her fingers gently tugged at the strap to her dress, he noticed she wasn't wearing a ring. Either she'd never remarried after Tyler, or she didn't wear rings. He hoped for the first and then instantly felt embarrassed. *What does it matter if Claire is married or not?* She must have noticed his expression because she quickly folded her hands in her lap.

Feeling the warmth rise in his body, he cleared his throat. "Would you like something to drink?" he asked, still fixated on her eyes. When she glanced at his water, he continued. "I don't drink. But you can order anything. It won't bother me."

She eyed him curiously but didn't respond.

"It's a long story."

Before Claire opened her mouth, the server called out Chance's name, letting him know their table was ready. Chance stood up and allowed Claire to lead the way, following the server to the back deck. Claire had been right. There were no clouds in the sky, and the view was amazing. Blue skies stretched as far as his eyes could see. The sun, already low, was burning yellow and orange, ready to be engulfed by the horizon. The atmosphere was nice, too, calmer, and more peaceful than inside by the bar, where it was too loud to hold a conversation. Out here, as they took their seats, they had a chance to actually speak and be heard, allowing his nerves to finally break free.

"You look nice," Chance began as they took their seats at a small table set apart from the rest, allowing the two of them to be alone.

The same small curve he'd seen before formed at her lips, but her body tensed at his compliment.

"Thanks. I don't dress up much. Actually, I don't go out much. I wasn't sure what to wear."

It was his turn to smile.

"You're staring," Claire said, biting her lower lip, clearly uncomfortable.

"I'm sorry. It's just...I still can't believe it's you." He

shifted his gaze away for a brief second before bringing it back up again to see her, to take her all in.

"It is," she said, smirking. The lines around her lips curved, and her blue eyes sparkled as she spoke.

"Do you know what you're going to order?" Claire asked, opening the menu, redirecting the attention away from her. "The blackened salmon is pretty great, but so are the crab cakes."

"I'll take your word for it and order the salmon."

Just as Claire folded her menu, a slight breeze caught her hair, tousling it over her face. As she reached for her hair, the menu slipped to the floor at her sudden movement. Both she and Chance bent down at the same time, trying to catch it. Chance reached it first, but Claire's hand grazed the top of his hand as she leaned in for it too. The touch was electrifying and brought back images from two decades earlier when their hands met as he picked up her locket from the floor of the bus.

Looking up, he opened his mouth to speak, wanting to say something, but not finding the words. He saw it in her eyes as well. She felt it. He knew she did. Electric shocks ran through his veins, even as Claire withdrew her hand. It was like nothing he'd ever felt before. It was the thing he'd been missing in all his past relationships. But this sudden feeling that washed over him didn't bring back that comfort he'd longed for. While his heartbeat quickened, his body also tensed. Something didn't feel right. Seeing Claire also brought back memories of Tyler.

Thankful for the server, Chance looked away, afraid Claire might see his confusion, his conflicting thoughts. They ordered their food, Claire requesting a sweet tea to go with her meal. In the distance, Chance heard the ebbing of the waves as they hummed across the sand. A few blue herons drifted overhead as they made their way to a new landing perch away from the crowded beach.

Claire tilted her head and finally spoke when the server walked away. "You just went somewhere."

Shaking his head, he apologized. "Sorry, sometimes, I just..."

"It's okay. Do you want to talk about it?"

"There's so much I want to talk about. But maybe, let's just start with today?" He felt the sincerity in every word she spoke. He wanted to be up front with Claire. He wanted her to know he was here on business. That tonight was just one night, just like it had been so long ago. But that only made his jaw tighten. He hated that he was here and could only give half of himself. She knew this though. Tonight came with no expectations. But damn she was so gorgeous. And her voice. It was so sweet and calming.

Chapter Twelve
Present

Claire

Claire couldn't believe her eyes. If she wasn't sitting right here, she would have thought she was lost in a dream. Her mind had played tricks on her for years, and she often cursed the world around her for toying with her emotional heartstrings. But it was real. Chance was sitting right there in front of her. She felt his eyes on her and, while his look confused her, she wanted him to keep staring. It made her feel desirable again. Sure, she'd had men look at her in the past, but their eyes only looked at her exterior. Chance, however, used his eyes to stare through to her soul. There was a difference in how that made her feel, but she had somehow forgotten that long ago.

"So, how was your conference today?" Claire asked, deciding on small talk first, trying hard not to dissolve into his eyes.

"It went well. Better than expected, actually. It was the first time I presented."

She watched as he swirled his water to the right and then back to the left, not placing it back on the table. She felt the heaviness in his voice and waited for him to continue, but when he didn't, she asked him what the presentation was about.

His gaze shifted to the water beyond the deck. The sharp rise and fall of the waves.

"It was about post-traumatic stress disorder. I was specifically talking about veterans. My mentor and I have been trying to push the mental healthcare system in a more proactive direction. There are too many veterans who slip through the cracks, and if the providers are more proactive than reactive, I believe we can make a bigger difference, save more lives."

He spoke with such passion and conviction that she had no doubt he could change the world with just his heart alone.

"I take it you're a psychologist then? After you left this morning, I googled the conference, but I didn't see your name as a speaker."

"Well, I don't have my doctorate degree yet. They typically only have doctors speak at these, but my mentor asked me to cover for her since she couldn't make it."

Their food arrived, and the server lit the candle on their small table. The sun, now vibrant orange and red, was just beginning to fall behind the water's edge, leaving darkness in its place. Fairy lights flickered on above, making the night sky look magical.

"I don't think I've ever seen such a beautiful sunset," Chance admitted between bites.

"That's one of the reasons I love it here. Even on a cloudy night, I love the way the sun sets across the gulf," Claire said, taking a bite of her food. "What made you want to be a psychologist?"

Avoiding the question, Chance looked back at Claire. "What made you want to become a writer?"

"How'd you know I was a writer?"

"One of my patients."

"One of your patients?" Her eyebrows arched.

"Maybe a year ago, a patient of mine left your book on the couch when she left. By the time I noticed it, she was gone. It took me a hot minute to realize your name was staring right back at me. I mean, I wasn't exactly sure it was you at first. The name kind of confused me. I thought you were going by Romano all these years." His voice held bite, she noticed, and was more accusatory than confused.

"Chance," Claire started, but didn't know how to continue. Overwhelmed with emotions, she closed her mouth and let her shoulders slump. On the one hand, Claire wanted to give in to her desires. She hadn't let a man into her life for as long as she could remember, and if she were being honest with herself, she didn't think she'd ever felt so overpowered by infatuation. Not since the first time she'd seen him. Every man she'd ever met was compared to that single night. The tension between them, the heat, and that moment he let his lips fall onto hers.

On the other hand, she couldn't help but feel like a fool. He'd known about her and where she lived, taking time away from his day to google her. But he'd never tried to reconnect with her. And that brought back images of New York. Tyler's funeral. He'd disappeared without so much as a word.

In that instant, Claire began to question everything. She didn't know Chance. She hadn't spent more than a few hours with him, and that was when she was seventeen. Maybe she'd romanticized him all these years. She had to, to keep moving forward.

"Yeah?" he replied, responding to his name.

"How come you never came back for me at Tyler's funeral? How come you knew I was a writer and never thought to look for me?" Claire spoke with desperation. She felt a knot forming inside her stomach. She knew she wouldn't like his answer, but she felt like she needed the truth, no matter how much she might dislike it.

When Chance didn't answer, Claire stood up, rubbing her damp palms on the fabric of her dress.

"This was a mistake." Claire pushed her plate back and set her napkin on the table. "I don't know what I was expecting." Opening her purse, she pulled out some bills and placed them on the table. "I wish I could have thanked you back then. You saved my life, you know that? And for that, I'll always be grateful." Sucking in a sharp breath, she excused herself without explaining. She pushed in her seat and turned her back to Chance, quickly making her way to the beach. She didn't look back.

Chapter Thirteen
Present

Chance

After paying the rest of the bill, Chance found himself walking along the shore toward his hotel. Pissed that he allowed Claire to leave so abruptly, he cursed under his breath. Then, taking off his shoes, Chance dug his toes into the cool sand, waiting for the water to lap around his ankles.

A part of him wanted to catch up with Claire. To apologize. To explain himself. The moment their hands met, a surge of adrenaline sent shock waves to his core, like firecrackers flying in all directions through the night. He felt it happening, causing his heart rate to intensify. In one millisecond, he wanted to bring Claire close. To touch her face. To press his lips against hers. But just as those thoughts crashed through his mind, his hands clenched at the thought of her and Tyler, even after all these years.

It was probably for the best that Claire left. His thoughts were still too fuzzy, and he didn't want to say something he might regret. Hell, he was more than qualified to remain calm, but she did something to him that he couldn't quite control.

Still, it didn't take away the heaviness he felt deep in his gut.

Missing the sunset, the only light visible was what radiated from the moon. It reflected in the water, illuminating just enough of the sand for Chance to continue walking. Water dripped from his feet as he made his way back up the beach. In the distance, he heard a hushed laugh. Lifting his head, he noticed a young couple sitting on a towel in the distance, holding hands as they got lost in one another.

Feeling disappointed in the evening, Chance dialed Valerie's number.

She picked up on the second ring, like she always did. "Hey sweetie, how's it going?"

"Good."

"Just good?"

"Yeah. How's my dad?"

"You're deflecting."

"I'm good. How is he?"

Chance heard Valerie's exhale. She wouldn't ask again. She knew him well enough to leave him be, knowing he would talk to her when he was ready, but he could also hear the question in her voice.

"He's good. Took him to a meeting tonight. He complained the entire time. Said, and I quote, 'I'm too damn old to be going to these damn meetings.'"

She laughed, which made him smile. He could picture his dad saying those exact words, probably with brows furrowed and a deep frown as he walked to the car begrudgingly. At seventy-nine years old, his dad had a love-hate relationship with AA. Said he needed to go in order to stay sober but despised hearing sad stories. In September, he'd have seventeen years of being clean and sober. Chance was proud of his dad. It had taken him a while to get to this point, and he was happy with the progress with not only that, but with their relationship that grew from it as well.

"Did you do anything else today? After the conference?" Valerie asked, still fishing for details.

"Not really. Got a bite to eat. Heading back to the room now." Chance knew he'd eventually talk to Valerie. But not now. He hadn't spoken about Claire in years, and he still had to sort out his thoughts before opening his old wounds to her.

By the time Chance hung up with Valerie, he was already back in his room. He got undressed, brushed his teeth, and washed his face. He looked at himself in the mirror and thought about the question Claire had asked him at dinner. Why hadn't he gone back for her after Tyler's death? He could create any excuse he wanted to, but the fact was, it was only himself looking at his reflection in the mirror right now. Lies would do him no good.

"Because I loved her. And she loved somebody else," he said aloud.

Just remembering the funeral burned the back of his eyes. How could he have been in love with a woman he had only known for a few hours? How was it that he had felt it with such magnitude and such force, and she didn't? She had moved on and gotten married. And not to just anyone, but to his friend from basic training. On the flip side, how could he be mad? Tyler was a great guy. He was nice and caring. The type of guy who would take the only shirt he had off his back for anyone. But it didn't take away the hurt, the pain, the jealousy.

Chance brushed off his feelings for Claire as infatuation, and, for years, he dismissed any feelings he had toward any woman he dated afterward. He held them at an arm's length, never letting them see the real Chance. Never letting them get close to him. Always comparing them to Claire.

Most women realized this, and their relationships fizzled

out rather quickly. But there were two women who did manage to last long term. Well, if you consider one and two years long term, that is. For a forty-five-year-old man, some would consider that to be pitiful. And he would agree.

On his one-year anniversary with Pamela, Chance spent the night at the hospital. She had thrown a vase at his head after screaming that he was incapable of using the words "I love you." It had cost him four stitches to his skull.

With Becca, he tried harder and found the words he had longed to say to a woman, but he hadn't felt the electric feeling he had felt with Claire. So, every time he said it, he felt like a fraud. Unlike Pamela, Becca was calmer and patient. They were both forty by this time, and Becca sat him down one day before their two-year anniversary. She had been married before and was far more experienced in relationships than he was.

"You say you love me, and, while I believe you do on some level, I don't want to feel like I'm second best."

Chance hadn't told Becca about Claire, nor had he told any of his previous relationships. But Becca was wise and picked up on the subtle cues he hadn't even seen himself.

"We're comfortable with one another. But I don't want just 'comfortable.' I want, when someone looks at me, to have them really look at me. Like they can see into my soul with searing desire. Like they want to rip off my clothes."

Then Becca kissed him goodbye.

Still looking at his reflection in the bathroom mirror, Chance saw the wrinkles that bored into his forehead. The scar in his left temple he'd gotten in the Marines while on deployment, right below his hairline. He saw the tired eyes of a man who could no longer lie to himself. He was in love with Claire, still, after all these years. It was she who held his heart.

Chapter Fourteen
Present

Claire

Claire woke the next morning tangled in her sheets, still upset by the night before. Rubbing her eyes, she stretched. Not wanting to wake. Not wanting to face the day. How had she misjudged the signs, the shared glances? She was no expert at love, that much was obvious. But from the minute Chance looked at her in the café, she recognized the attraction she had felt so many years ago, which had left an imprint on her heart.

In the past, friends had said she romanticized her encounter with him on the bus. They told her she'd been young and naive, that, if anything, it was purely lust that attracted her to him. Some had even told her he was probably a creep, looking for a sexual encounter of some sort. But Claire never viewed it the same way. She had felt lust on many occasions in her life. She had wanted men in her younger days, men she had no intention of keeping around. Only wanting their bodies and what they could do to her, the frustration leading to a world of passion. That was lust. And, while lust was fun, she'd wanted more.

She doubted her friends, never believing Chance had been

after her for her body. And while she had, on many occasions, thought about what *Chance's* own body would look and feel like, that wasn't the only thing on her mind. Back then, on that cold winter night, they had forged a bond that was so deep, so vulnerable, she felt it impossible to replicate.

But now, she didn't know what to feel, what to believe. She felt foolish for holding on to a memory for so long. It wasn't like she ever truly believed he was her soulmate. Okay, so maybe she *did* believe that. But now? Damn. She didn't know how to feel.

Pulling her hair into a loose bun, Claire's stomach ached. Today was going to be difficult. Finally dragging herself from her bed, she walked into the kitchen, where Shadow was already scratching at the door.

"I'm coming, I'm coming," she said to her four-legged friend. Unlocking the latch, Claire slid the door open. Shadow, a rather large black lab, dashed outside, chasing the squirrels that mocked him from the patio just moments earlier.

After Shadow grew tired from barking, he ran back inside to eat. Meanwhile, Claire worked on applying some light makeup, evening out her skin tone and bringing life back to her cheeks. Still tired from the restless night, she fetched her black-rimmed sunglasses from the kitchen table before giving Shadow a quick belly rub. Then, leaning over the dog, she grabbed her bag and keys and headed out the front door.

Inside her Jeep, she turned up the radio and pulled out of the driveway, noticing the empty black truck across the street, again...for the third time that week.

It was odd, seeing that truck where it was parked. Claire was pretty friendly with all of her neighbors, and she was fully aware that the person living across the street was on vacation. She'd have to text the woman later to make sure everything was okay, that she knew someone was parking in front of her home. It wasn't like the city, where people parked wherever they could find a spot. Claire lived in a small suburban town. A truck like that might go unnoticed once, but not three times.

About twenty minutes later, Claire walked into Beach Brew. She so loved that it was small and quaint and walking distance to the water. Claire loved everything about it and what it offered. It was the first place she'd come when she arrived in St. Pete a few years ago. It was close enough to the water that Claire could look at it and enjoy a cup of coffee, but far enough away that she didn't have to step foot in it.

Over time, she'd built up the courage to stand in the sand. And then she found the courage to tiptoe into the water. And, after she'd lived there a year, she was finally able to push past her parents' deaths and swam in the clear waters of the gulf, something she hadn't done since she was a teenager.

Inside the café, Sasha was working behind the counter as usual. Today, her bright red hair was pulled into a braid that ran down the length of her back.

"Morning, Claire. You're here later than normal. I almost didn't think you'd be coming. I was just about to text you," she said, nodding toward her phone. "Bold roast?"

"Yeah. Just getting a late start. I still need to finish this last chapter." Claire exhaled, not wanting to think of anything but the coffee.

Sasha was one of the few people Claire shared her writing with before she sent it to her editor. She seemed to have a great insight into character development, and it was fun to sit and pick her brain. More often than not, she'd bounce ideas off Sasha and see where they landed. Although Sasha had dropped out of college before Claire met her, Sasha was beyond creative and doing very well for herself, running the café and teaching both yoga and meditation.

This latest novel, however, just wasn't wrapping up the

way Claire had envisioned it. And while she knew she could talk to Sasha about it, she also felt like scrapping the entire thing.

"So? Are you going to tell me?" Sasha's eyebrows arched, a grin covering her face.

"Tell you?" Claire responded flatly. She knew where the question was leading but wasn't in the least bit ready to discuss it.

"Oh, come on, Claire. That perfect specimen of a man yesterday. Who was he?"

"Oh, nobody."

"Nobody? I don't believe that for a second. You barely noticed me when I was cleaning up the coffee around your feet. You can't tell me he was nobody."

"He was just somebody I knew a lifetime ago."

"Well, he's awfully dreamy. And wow! The way he looked at you. I'd die for a man to look at me the same way. Did you guys ever date?" Sasha asked as she made her magic happen behind the counter.

"No, it's a long story."

"Well, I'd love to hear that story sometime," she said, setting a new gray ceramic mug on the counter.

When Claire looked at it curiously, Sasha explained.

"He came in this morning, real early. Looking extra dreamy. He was looking for you. Bought this mug and asked me to give it to you the next time you came in."

By lunchtime, Claire couldn't concentrate any longer. Staring at her computer, barely able to focus, her eyes felt like they were bleeding. She must have read and reread the same sentence a hundred times, unable to move forward with any sort of ending. Chance was the only thing she could think about. Not knowing why he'd agreed to meet her for dinner. Not knowing why he never came to look for her. Not having closure. It was all too much. Imagining how dreamy he might have looked this morning, she saw him in every character she wrote about.

When she couldn't take it any longer, Claire shut her laptop and climbed into her car. Speeding through the streets, she made her way to the Tradewinds in record time. She had to find Chance. She had questions, and he was the key to those answers.

"I'm here for the conference on PTSD," Claire said to the receptionist at the front desk.

"Umm, I think you're referring to the National Psychology Conference." the short lady kicked back at her like she'd said something stupid.

"Yeah, that's it. I'm looking for one of the presenters. His name is Chance Johnson." Claire continued, ignoring the woman's annoyed expression.

"We don't have names. And you have to have a paid ticket to get into one of those rooms." Clicking her pen, she waited to see if Claire had anything else to add. When she didn't, the woman turned around and went back to what she was doing.

Claire's chin dropped slightly as her lips pressed together. Upset and unsure what to do next, her feet backed up. Looking up, her eyes went wide, and her mouth pursed. There he was again. Standing right behind her. As if fate purposely planted him there.

"I couldn't help but overhear that you wanted to join one of the presentations."

Claire caught her breath in surprise.

"Did you get the mug?" he continued, his voice steady, his eyes intense.

"Chance. We need to talk."

Grabbing her hand, he pulled her behind him, leading the way to one of the back exits. His grasp was firm but gentle, and, all at once, she became dizzy with desire. Her heart quickened with each step. Once they reached the sand, he released her hand but took her by the hips to draw her close. Her chest constricted with anticipation as she felt his heart beating against hers. He inhaled deeply, as if taking her all in. When he exhaled, she followed suit. Their breathing in unison. She looked up at him, his eyes penetrating hers.

"Chance..." she began, but before she could continue, his hands were cradling her face.

"I love you. I've always loved you. The moment I saw you on that bus. I can't lose you. Not again."

His voice was soft, and her heart melted as he held her tighter. He brushed the hair that had fallen from her bun away from her face. His touch was gentle as he let his fingers linger on her cheek.

"I don't care that you and Tyler got married. I don't care about any of that anymore. I—"

"Wait, what?" Claire pulled back, stopping Chance midsentence. "Married Tyler? Is that what you think?"

They stood a moment in silence under the afternoon sun before Claire continued. "I never married Tyler. Is that what this is all about? Is that why you left the funeral? Because you thought I was married to him?"

Looking down at his feet, Chance shook his head. "You weren't?" he asked, as if seeing her for the first time since he came to St. Petersburg.

"No."

"I saw you up there. And afterward, someone mentioned your name. They called you Claire Romano. I don't understand."

It was Claire's turn to reach for his hand. She clasped his hand tightly in her own.

"Let's go for a walk."

Chapter Fifteen
Present

Claire

Taking her sandals off, Claire placed them under a bright yellow umbrella. Chance followed suit and took his off as well. After rolling his pants cuffs, they walked toward the water, the soft sand warm as it touched their toes.

Claire, this time, led the way. They moved slowly, their feet leaving footprints behind as the waves receded, only to be washed away when they returned. Their fingers laced together as if they had been created to fit this way all along.

"I loved Tyler." Claire spoke calmly and without reservations. "He was my best friend. He had a heart of gold. And I miss him terribly."

Chance listened, knowing exactly what she meant. He envisioned Tyler as she spoke, recalling boot camp and infantry training battalion. His jokes, his smile, his willingness to help everyone out.

"Do you know how I met Tyler?"

"No," he said, shaking his head slowly. "I assumed it had to do with the Marine Corps. I hadn't known you joined until the day of the funeral."

"I did join. But I didn't meet him that way. I met him because of you." Her breath came out easy, more relaxed. "I joined the Marines because of you too." She squinted her eyes in the sun, watching as he leaned forward, taking one step at a time along the sand.

When Chance furrowed his brows and scrunched his nose, not understanding what she meant, she continued. "When you got off that bus, all those years ago, do you remember what you asked me?"

A brief pause sat between them before Chance responded. "I asked you to come with me." His voice softened.

She stopped walking and stood facing him, looking up to meet his eyes. "Yeah. And I wanted to, I really did. But I was only seventeen. And your mom was sick. And you were leaving for Japan. I mean, everything happened so fast. One minute I'm running for my life and the next I'm falling head over heels for a man I just met. I didn't think it was real. I kept believing I'd wake up one day. That all of it was something between a dream and a nightmare."

He squeezed her hand just as the wind lightly blew at her blouse. A shiver went up her back, and the sensation made her aware of how close their bodies were, her bare shoulder to his cotton shirt.

Tugging at his hand, she changed direction, finding the perfect place to sit, close enough to feel the breeze floating off the water, but not close enough to get wet. He sat next to her, his hand still in hers. But, in that moment, she wanted him to touch her somewhere else...her arm, her face, even her thigh. But she didn't dare inch closer. Not yet. Instead, she continued.

"I was so angry with myself for not going with you. By the time I reached Chicago, I was scared, worried, terrified. I had no idea what I was doing, where I would go, or how I would get my next meal." She lowered her head, feeling Chance's skin as he adjusted his fingers.

"When you got off the bus, you dropped a piece of paper. It had a phone number on it, a phone number I believed was yours. When I finally mustered up enough courage to call it, I had this whole thing planned out in my head. What I would say, how I would say it. I wanted to change my mind, to come with you. But then Tyler answered, and my entire world took a detour. And then you, you somehow saved my life, and I couldn't even thank you."

Lifting her head, she watched as he brought his eyes to hers, questions dancing in them.

Over the next hour, as they sat in the warm sand, Claire told Chance about the events that played out when she got to New York, being careful not to leave anything out.

"Tyler had this old soul about him. He was protective and sweet. And his dad, wow! They were like twins somehow, only separated by years. Tyler didn't hesitate to explain my situation with him. He said if anyone could help, it was him. At first, Tyler was insistent on finding you, but do you know how many Johnsons live in Asheville and the surrounding area? And it's not like we had cell phones or the internet back then," she said, cracking a smile. "He tried the operator a handful of times, but, when that led us nowhere, we went back to the drawing board."

The sun was hot, but she doubted Chance noticed, except when he leaned over to wipe the perspiration off her shoulders. Closing her eyes, Claire held her breath, feeling his soft fingers as they touched her bare skin.

"On the second night I was there, we watched the news. Nothing new had been reported about the dead women, just the same as the night before. I woke up screaming from nightmares. I'm not even sure Tyler slept that night. When I woke up in the morning, I heard Tyler and his dad talking about what they should do. Tyler's dad was insistent that the police would help, that New York cops had no ties to those in Jacksonville. But Tyler reminded him that, without my last name, they had no idea who the dirty cop was, and he was afraid that would only make things worse."

Chance brought his hand back to hers, sliding them together, exploring it with the tips of his fingers, sending tingles down her spine. Claire went quiet, letting her shoulders rise and fall from the tenderness of his touch. How he managed to do that surprised her, and she wondered if she had the same effect on him. Taking a deep breath, Claire instinctively loosened her fingers for him.

"I wanted to leave. I felt like I was intruding on strangers. Nice strangers. And I felt like an inconvenience. Just when I was about to pack up and leave, the news came on. Both Tyler and his dad started yelling for me to come quick. When I entered the living room, I saw Alex's face on the television screen. The reporter called him a person of interest. Tyler got excited, asking if that was him. I nodded but remained quiet. I knew there were more men involved. When Alex's face disappeared from the screen, mine replaced his. A reporter said I was missing and, that if anyone had information on my whereabouts, they should call their local police. They claimed I could be in danger."

"I still don't understand how I play a role in any of this," Chance said, his voice low. "I literally left. I wanted to help you, but I literally left the country early, before my ten days were up. I was probably on a plane to Japan at that time." His fingers stopped moving along her hand.

Claire paused to look at him and gave a gentle smile. She shifted in the sand and angled toward him, away from the water. Wanting to touch him, she found the strength to lay her hand on his bent knee. His hand followed, and he placed his on top of hers.

And there it was, the butterflies were at full speed, charging against her chest wall, begging to be released.

"I finally allowed Tyler's dad to call the Staten Island police. When they answered, they claimed they were receiving tons of messages from witnesses across the country. Witnesses that claimed to have seen me as far as Iowa, California, Kentucky. They asked if there was any specific information that could link me to Alex as proof, something no one else would know. When I got on the phone and gave a description of the dead woman in his bedroom, the woman on the other end went quiet. She said she would have a detective come out immediately."

Claire stopped again and looked out at the clear water that lay in front of them.

"You can stop. You don't have to keep going," Chance said. "It won't change my mind. Whatever happened, I—"

Clearing her throat, Claire interrupted him. "No, I want you to know. So there's no confusion. It's just...well, I haven't really told anybody this story. Only Tyler and his family knew." They stared deep into each other's eyes as Claire picked up where she left off.

"After the phone call, a detective was at Tyler's house within an hour. He was pretty matter-of-fact and to the point. He explained he was working with another detective, who lived in Asheville, who was helping the case. Said, since it was an inside job, they were using the support from nearby cities. Detective Joe Daniels from the Asheville Police Department spoke to me on the phone."

Chance sat up a little straighter. She could see he was beginning to understand.

"Detective Daniels told me that you helped solve the case. He said you told him to look for the couple who drowned in

St. Pete in order to find the last name of the police officer in Jacksonville. That my parents were the key to his name. He also added that I should change my last name in the meantime. Said he knew there were other men involved, but Alex was keeping quiet, so changing my name was in the best interest of my safety. He told me that was also your idea."

Chapter Sixteen
Present

Chance

Even as he was hearing it, Chance couldn't quite believe it. After all these years, Joe never told him any of this. Claire was right though; he did tell Joe about looking in St. Petersburg to find the name of the couple who drowned. He figured it was easiest to find them because they'd most likely have the same name as her stepbrother, which would, in turn, help him identify the dirty cop in Jacksonville. He also suggested the name change. He figured, with such a high-profile case, Claire would be in danger until all the men were behind bars.

He hadn't waited, though, to find out any of the details of the case. He had been so angry over the revelation of his dad not being his real dad, and then witnessing his dad make a mockery of himself the day of his mom's celebration of life, that he split. Calling his commanding officer, Chance made arrangements to leave for Okinawa, Japan, ahead of schedule.

"I never married Tyler. I only took his last name," Claire said quietly, looking into his eyes.

Chance gazed back. "I guess I assumed. I heard someone call you Claire Romano. And you had a kid. That girl. I mean,

I understand now. And if you were married to him..." His voice trailed off.

"Molly," Claire smiled. "And Tyler *did* ask me to marry him. Many times. Molly is our daughter." Claire looked away suddenly, as if the mention of these details triggered another memory.

At the turn of her face, the wind picked up, ruffling the loose strands of her hair near the front of her face. He instinctively brushed the ones closest to him behind her ear, touching her face as he did. Biting her lip, she leaned into his touch, causing his pulse to quicken. He wanted more than anything to pull her close, to touch her lips. To taste them on his. He wanted to take away all her sadness, but he knew she was just beginning to scratch the surface.

"Changing my name didn't make things any less scary. Having Alex locked up didn't stop me from thinking about those other men. Detective Daniels kept in touch with me over the next few days, walking me through what I should expect, at least from a legal standpoint. When he told me you were already out of the country and didn't know how to get a hold of you, I began to rethink everything. I cried and cried and cried. Tyler stayed with me and tried to do everything he could to help. But, in hindsight, I was finally grieving. I was grieving for the loss of my parents. I was grieving for the loss of those women. And I was grieving for the loss of what could have been between us."

He felt the heaviness in Claire's heart with each of her words.

"With Tyler having to leave for Camp Pendleton, I figured I'd have to leave too. I'd have to figure out what my next step would be. But Tyler's dad insisted I stay. Told me I had to stay and that he wouldn't take no for an answer. He was so sweet and so full of life. That's where Tyler got his spark from. They were the spitting image of each other. So, for the next few months, I stayed there. I helped take care of Tyler's younger brothers and finished my GED. But once I turned eighteen, I knew I couldn't stay. I mean, Tyler's dad would have allowed me to stay forever, but I couldn't. I had to grow up."

Claire paused before continuing. She took in a deep breath, then exhaled. "Do you remember asking me what was in Chicago and what my response to you was?"

Chance nodded his head. "You told me freedom."

"Yeah, freedom. But I never really achieved any kind of freedom. Definitely not in Chicago. And not in New York either. They were both Band-Aids, temporary fixes that were just buying me time. I was still hiding. Alex had been charged with first-degree murder by then, but the other men still hadn't been identified. The only way to freedom was through myself. I had to find out who I was, and the only way I was able to do that was by joining the Marine Corps. I thought about you and your dad and how you joined to get away from home. I thought about Tyler and how he joined to find a better version of himself. I decided to join for both reasons. I needed to be independent. I had to be strong. And I knew the Marine Corps would provide me with both. When I enlisted, I felt my mom's presence the entire time. I knew she would have been proud of me."

They sat silent for a while, watching the waves rush on shore. They saw people pointing at a few pelicans in the distance, flying overhead, diving for fish with their large bills on the ready. And in those moments, Chance imagined what Claire had gone through, the trauma she endured, the pain she must have felt. The loneliness. He knew that loneliness all too well and how bitter it tasted.

And then Claire continued, breaking the silence. "I got incredibly lucky and got stationed at Camp Pendleton, near Tyler. We grew close to one another, but nothing serious. He wanted more, but I couldn't give him anything more than what I'd already given him, which was friendship."

Chance thought about that for a moment, but then images of that little girl drifted into his mind.

"I know what you're thinking. If that were true, how did we end up with Molly, right?"

Feeling ashamed for wanting to know when it really wasn't any of his business, he nodded.

Claire turned away. It took her a few seconds to speak, but when she did, her voice came out in slow painful breaths. "I was barely twenty. I had no family, no mom. And I couldn't even tell people my real name. I wanted to die. Like, really die. I don't think Tyler really knew how bad it was. One night, we just got drunk. Really drunk. And he was there. And I wanted to be loved. And he loved me. If he hadn't been there that night to drink with me, I honestly don't think I'd be here today. And, well, nine months later, Molly was born."

Chance took her hand and squeezed it and then released a breath he hadn't known he was holding. He lifted his other hand to her chin and turned her face toward his. Her eyes were full of tears.

"I did love him. But not in a romantic way," she cried.

"Tyler was a great guy, and I am so incredibly grateful you had him." Chance felt his stomach tighten. Hearing her words pained him. Not about Tyler. Not about Molly. But the fact that she had been so sad she wanted to end her life.

"He was. And he continued to beg me to marry him. And I probably would have if..." Her voice trailed off as she looked away again, this time only for a brief second before looking back at Chance. "If he hadn't gone off to be a hero. The stupid ass," she laughed, wiping the tears from her eyes.

"Tyler and I moved back to New York after the Marines. I found an apartment down the street from his dad, and he found one a few blocks away. He was on his way to pick Molly up from my place when the Twin Towers were hit. He'd just left the fire station when the news began broadcasting everything. But you know Tyler. When something happens, when people need help, he'd run to them.

"Molly was three years old when he died. She never got to see her dad again. It's been a long time, but I still remember it like it happened yesterday."

Chance watched Claire as she continued to wipe the tears from her eyes. He, too, could remember the details of that day. He'd been assigned to recruiting duty in Woodbridge, Virginia, the previous year. On the day of the attacks, he was at Quantico Marine Corps Recruiting Command when another marine yelled out that a plane had hit the Twin Towers. Chance hadn't believed him, but when they turned on the television overhead, they watched as not one, but both towers were struck by planes. The room became silent as they watched the horror unfold. Not a word was spoken as they watched the news coverage of what still haunts millions of people around the world.

And then, within an hour, they received word that the Pentagon was also hit, this time by a third plane. Since the Pentagon was so close to Quantico, the base had been put on lockdown. All phone service went down. People couldn't make outgoing calls, and those who had loved ones at the Pentagon grew increasingly worried as time ticked by, the only source of communication coming from the television.

Chance considered himself extremely lucky. He hadn't lost anyone he directly knew at the Pentagon. His friends had made it out alive, some even helped as they awaited first responders. But that wasn't the case for the other one hundred and eighty-nine military personnel, civilians, and passengers aboard American Airlines Flight 77 who lost their lives.

It wasn't until two days later, when he was watching the near constant and continuous news coverage of the attacks, that he saw Tyler's face appear on TV. He was listed as a first responder who lost his life that ill-fated day.

As Chance opened up about these details, he explained to Claire that he asked to help take care of Tyler's funeral. As a veteran, Tyler earned and deserved to have a full honors ceremony. But he hadn't expected, nor could he believe it, when he caught sight of her.

"I don't blame you for being with Tyler. I get it. I guess, at that moment, I was just shocked. I couldn't understand it, and I didn't want to. It left me in a bad place. I had always wondered if what we shared was something we *both* felt, or if it was just in my head," Chance admitted.

Through her tears, Claire gave him a smile that could light up a thousand rooms. But just as she began to speak, Chance's cell phone rang. Shifting in the sand to pull it out of his pocket, his heart sank when he looked at the phone number.

"I have to take this. I'm sorry. It'll only be a minute."

Claire nodded her head in agreement.

"Hello?"

The voice on the other end was rushed and hurried.

"Sure. I can be there in about ten minutes. I'll look for you when I get there. Thank you."

"You have to go," Claire stated.

"Unfortunately. They want me back at the conference to answer some questions. There are a few doctors and therapists who want to meet with me. I'd tell them to wait, but this is kind of a big deal, and I don't want to lose their support."

Claire stood and took both of his hands into hers, helping him out of the sand.

"Walk with me?" he asked, raising his eyes.

"Of course."

She was absolutely gorgeous, and he wanted nothing more than to scoop her into his arms and kiss her. He'd been wanting to do that the entire time. But he didn't. Instead, they turned back toward the hotel.

They didn't talk much on their way back. Instead, they held hands like teenagers in high school. Chance thought back to the night before when he saw the other couples and imagined what it might be like to walk hand in hand with Claire when they got older.

When they arrived at the Tradewinds, Chance took a risk and asked if Claire would like to meet for a late-night dinner, promising to make it up to her for the night prior, as well as for their past. He was in town until tomorrow afternoon, and he really wanted to see her again.

"I'd love to, but I actually have another date," she said with a half smile.

He should have known. How could he assume that Claire would be single after all these years?

"I understand," Chance said softly.

"You could join us," Claire offered with the grin he couldn't get enough of. It was the way her smile curved in one corner of her mouth, while the other side created a crease in her cheek. And her perfectly round eyes glistened in the sun, causing her expression to invite him in.

Chapter Seventeen
Present

Claire

"Join you?" Chance asked.

Chance looked confused, and Claire felt kind of guilty for portraying the question out of context, but his expression was also cute and endearing. She wondered if he was imagining her with another man. At the thought of it, she felt silly.

"Yes. Join me and my *daughter*. She's performing at the Straz Center in Tampa. She has the leading role, Cinderella."

"She takes after your mom?"

Claire smiled, appreciative that he remembered what she had told him about her mom.

"I wouldn't miss it for the world."

"I'll pick you up a little after six then?"

She wasn't expecting anything more, but her desire for it was another story entirely. Their talk on the beach was what she needed. Coming here today, she hadn't the slightest clue as to how it would unfold. But recalling his words, "I love you," made her feel something she hadn't ever experienced. She had loved Tyler, but in a compassionate way one loves someone they've grown used to. In a way that shows they care for one another in a genuine way. She loved her daughter that way, too, but more out of maternal instinct. Stronger than the love she had for Tyler, this love would have given her life in sacrifice. And, like with Tyler, her love for Molly had grown into a beautiful, unbreakable friendship. Over time, she considered Molly to be the single greatest love of her life. Until today. She wasn't downgrading Molly's relationship with her. But when Chance spoke those three words, she felt her life shattering into a million pieces, only to be fused together again, instantaneously. A romantic love she'd longed for but had given up on years ago.

And now, without expecting it, but deeply desiring it, she responded as Chance bent down and pulled her body close against his own, closing the distance between them, their fingers still intertwined. As his fingers released from her grasp, he brushed them slowly against her arm as he reached for her face. With open palms, he held her and locked his lips onto hers, pressing them gently against her own. And, although it was soft, it was also firm. The magnitude it held was like shifting tectonic plates. As if this kiss, this sole kiss, could spark a volcanic eruption.

They pulled away, only to catch their breath, their lips parting slowly.

"Mr. Johnson?" a sharp voice interrupted them, causing Claire to peel herself away from Chance's warm embrace.

Turning in the direction of the voice, Claire noticed a petite young woman pushing her glasses up the ridge of her nose and tossing her blond hair over one shoulder, waiting to be recognized.

With little patience and a look of annoyance, she asked again, "Are you Mr. Johnson?"

"That's me," Chance replied, out of breath.

"They're waiting for you down here. Follow me." With a turn of her heel, she marched away without hesitation.

"I'll see you at six," Chance said, his gray eyes glowing. And then he was gone.

It was still early when Claire arrived back at the café. She knew she needed to work, to finish her novel, but her mind was elsewhere. Her editor called while she was driving, and rather than answering like she always did, she pressed the end button, sending her to voice mail. She knew why she was calling, and, in the past, she would have explained what was going on and why she needed more time, requesting another extension. Tessa might yell, she might even scream, but ultimately, she knew her friend would understand. And if Claire as much as mentioned Chance, she might even score some brownie points. But now, Claire felt renewed. She didn't want to discuss her book with her friend, not until it was finished.

An alert caused Claire's phone to vibrate. Looking down, she read the message she was trying to avoid.

Don't ignore me. I need an update.

Instead of responding, Claire chose avoidance. And then she shut her ringer off completely.

Setting her laptop on the same small circular table in the corner of the café's porch, Claire recalled Chance again and his unexpected appearance yesterday. She replayed the events in her head, realizing she had long expected that chapter of her life to remain closed. With that door wide open now, she smiled to herself and began clicking away at the keyboard. She knew exactly how she was going to end this novel.

Just after four o'clock, Claire stopped typing. She wasn't ready to read over her work quite yet, but she was satisfied with her new ending. Glancing at her phone, she noticed the time. If she moved quickly, she'd have enough time to drive home and get ready. Maybe even have enough time to shower.

Packing up her things, she looked out at the gulf. She smiled at it, thinking how proud her mom would be of her today. She'd come a long way. After a few long moments, she grabbed her bag, slung it over her shoulder, and climbed into her Jeep Wrangler and hit the road.

Chapter Eighteen
Present

Chance

After turning away from Claire in the lobby, Chance walked with a skip in his step, even though his knees felt like Jell-O. And he found it nearly impossible to catch his breath as his heart pulsated against his rib cage. The smile, however, was the one thing he left alone. He knew he was glowing, riding a high he hadn't felt in years. And that intensity transferred over when the short blonde introduced him to a room full of his peers.

"You told us to rethink what we will do the next time a patient cancels an appointment. Or when they just don't show up. What do you suggest?" an older gentleman with gray hair and round glasses asked, starting off the Q&A.

Grabbing a bottle of water from the podium, Chance took a sip to coat his dry throat before speaking.

"Reach out to them. More often than not, a simple phone call can make a world of difference. But, let me be clear, I don't mean a call to tell them to reschedule or that they missed an appointment. I mean, ask them how they're feeling."

Standing straighter, Chance moved from behind the podium and stepped off the stage, inching closer to the man, but making eye contact with everyone in the room.

"Don't ask them why they missed the appointment. That

will only create more anxiety. If they don't answer, which most of them won't, leave them a voice mail, letting them know you care about them and their health. Ask a question that requires a response."

Chance ran his hand through his hair as he let out a deep breath. "I know that takes more time, and, for most of you, your assistants or office managers have been the ones to make your phone calls. I recommend you flip the script. *You* make those phone calls. Build a better relationship with each and every one of them."

A man across the room stood up, this time younger than Chance. "I have a lot of veterans who come in with trauma and PTSD. Most of the time, they only come to my office because a family member begged or coerced them to. And then, of course, they don't come back." The man pointed at Chance as he continued. "I've done what you're saying. I've called to check up on my patients. But the most I get is that they've already heard everything, and they don't need my help."

Chance made his way over to the young man, maneuvering around other doctors to reach him.

"Thank you for trying." Holding out his hand, Chance gave him a hearty handshake.

"But, you saying that shows that you know what you are doing still isn't good enough. Let me be very clear. Most veterans have the same mentality. It's been ingrained into their brains that going to the doctor makes them weak. You, my man, are the enemy."

Chance turned to look at everyone as he continued. "My father is a Vietnam War veteran. Do you know how many therapists he didn't call back? How many appointments he canceled? How many people gave up on him? Until, finally, my mentor, the woman who sent me here today, recommended a new approach? She called him. She texted him. Every damn day."

Chance's cheeks flushed as he recalled what he'd been told over the years. About his dad cussing Valerie out, telling her to mind her own business. But Valerie kept right at it, knowing that what he needed was a shoulder to lean on, even if that meant being his punching bag.

"Even when my old man wouldn't respond, she kept at it. She began to forge a bond between them, even though he wasn't actively seeking treatment from her. And then, one day, he walked into her office. People are looking for human connection. They need to know they aren't alone." Chance raised his voice. "Telling them in a one-hour session is very different from showing them."

Chance walked out of the conference room an hour later with his chin high and a lightness in his chest. Sharing stories about his dad, and other veterans, usually weighed him down, but, today, their stories, their outcomes, had been the center-piece of transformation. After his kiss with Claire, Chance hadn't thought his day could get any better. He was wrong.

Feeling the adrenaline coursing through his body, Chance ran up the stairs to his room. Breathing heavy but barely breaking a sweat, he pulled his phone out from his back pocket. He still had plenty of time. Opening the curtain to the shower, Chance turned on the water as hot as it would go. As the steam began to rise, Chance tore off his clothes, eager for the night ahead. Looking through the clothes he'd brought with him, he suddenly realized he wasn't sure what was appropriate attire for the theater. Thankfully, he'd exchanged phone numbers with Claire right before she left, so he decided to text her.

Chance: *Never been to the theater. What's the protocol on dress attire?*

He waited, not sure if she would respond or not. But he

didn't have to wait too long. The little blue dots, indicating that she was typing, appeared on his screen within seconds.

Claire: *Depends on what you brought. If you have khakis, go with them.*

She ended the text with a smiley face, which made him smile to himself.

Chance: *See you soon.*

At six o'clock, Chance was waiting inside the entrance of the hotel with flowers in hand. After his shower, he'd still had enough time to run down the street and purchase them at a small florist shop. However, once he paid for them, he began second-guessing himself, hoping he hadn't gone overboard.

Just as Chance was about to step outside, his phone vibrated. The green light alerted him that he had a new message from Claire.

Claire: *Pulling up now.* Again, it ended with a smiley face.

Chance pushed his way outside to see a black, two-door Jeep Wrangler pulling into the parking lot.

"Nice ride," he said, noticing that both the top and doors had been removed. He climbed in, and instantly his breath was taken away. Claire was drop-dead gorgeous. Even sitting in the driver's seat, without a clear view, he could see that her navy blue, very strappy dress hugged her across the chest and hips. It was elegant but casual at the same time. Her warm brown hair, with golden undertones, was gathered together, low, near the base of her neck, held by a gold clasp. And her eyes. When she looked across at him, her eyes seemed to reflect his own thoughts, and he could see himself getting lost within their magnetic pull.

"Ready?" she asked with a slight smile.

"Yeah, but first, I wanted to give you these." He handed her one of the bouquets. An assortment of pink, purple, and white peonies, carnations, roses, and lilies.

"The other one is for your daughter. I hope you don't mind."

"You didn't have to do that. But it's thoughtful, and I'm sure she'll love it like I do."

"One more thing."

Claire looked at him with a puzzled look.

"You look gorgeous."

Claire tilted her head to the side with an uneasy smile. And it instantly took him back to them sitting next to each other on the bus when they first met. It was the same modest smile that told him she wasn't comfortable with compliments. At that moment, he wanted to tell her she was the most beautiful person he had ever laid eyes on. He wanted her to feel beautiful and believe it.

"Thank you. You look good yourself. I see you took my advice on the khakis," she responded, diverting the attention away from herself.

After clicking the seat belt together, he reached for her hand. Feeling the ease of her skin, another rush of adrenaline caused his heart to speed up. Claire responded and opened her fingers, allowing him to lace his fingers between hers. He hadn't held another woman's hand like this in a long time, he suddenly realized. If he had, it didn't have the same feeling or meaning. This was entirely different. The touch was both exhilarating and intimate.

They didn't talk much on the drive, but they didn't need to. Occasionally, Claire would point things out and tell him about her favorite places as they passed by. She explained how she moved back to St. Petersburg just a few years ago, after Molly graduated from college. She said she would have moved sooner, but she didn't want to be an overbearing parent.

"Plus, I had Tyler's dad to think about. I couldn't just leave him alone."

"How was he when you left?"

"He didn't need me. I think that's what made it harder." She laughed, but her voice dropped at the mention of it.

"He turned seventy-five last year, and do you know what he did?" When he shook his head, she continued. "He up and got married. Can you believe it?"

Chance laughed but found the idea endearing. To find love so late in life was magical.

"I visit him at least two times a year. Molly and I usually fly up there around September, and we visit Tyler's grave. And then we go back in the summer, whenever it works for Molly's schedule."

"Tell me something else. Something I don't know about you," Chance requested, wanting to know more about her life.

"That's a hard one. Anything? Let me see. Okay, I have something. I once ate a live fish."

"What?" he laughed, taken aback by her admission. He watched as she bit her lower lip, ready to bare it all.

"Well, I was kind of a quiet kid. I didn't have many friends growing up. One day, at my neighbor's birthday party, a bunch of kids were daring each other to do ridiculous things. When one of the girls dared someone to swallow the goldfish, I volunteered. Figured if I did, everyone would think I was the coolest."

"Did it work?"

"Not in the slightest. I got sick the second it went down my throat. And no one wants to be friends with the puker."

"Quiet and brave," Chance said under his breath as he squeezed her fingers.

Chance took her all in as she continued to laugh at herself. It felt so natural to sit back and listen to her, to watch her smile. He felt like this was what life was supposed to be like. This was how his life should look.

Chapter Nineteen
Present

Claire pulled into the parking garage at the Straz Center for the Performing Arts with an hour to spare. While Chance suggested they go find their seats, Claire, instead, insisted they take advantage of the cool evening air by taking a stroll along the Riverwalk.

"I've been to plenty of these. I know where our seats are." Her chest rose and fell with an excited breath, and she slid her hand into his. "Follow me."

Outside, on ground level, Claire led Chance to a cement bench near the Straz Fountains, only a few hundred feet away. Together, they sat and watched the water rise and leap into the air, replicating multiple miniature geysers, only to tumble back down, spilling over the brown bricks and into the blue pool.

"You're staring again," Claire said coyly, noting the way Chance hadn't taken his eyes off her.

"I can't help it. I mean, you're more gorgeous now than I remember." He took his free hand and brushed the wisps of hair away from her face, his fingers tracing behind her ear.

Her cheeks warmed at his touch. Feeling desired, wanted, craved, Claire couldn't remember the last time she felt this way. But she loved every second of it, wanting more of it.

"Tell me something. I don't want to step on your toes

again like last night. But I'm deeply interested. What made you want to write?" Chance asked, easing the tension he initiated.

Claire sighed as she watched people pass by in all directions. Some stopped to take pictures by the fountains, while others took pictures in front of the river. She knew this question would come back up again. Writing was a big part of her life. But her writing was complicated. How could she explain so haphazardly?

"It was a collection of events," she began, forging ahead with her memories. "I mean, I always wanted to write. My mom encouraged me when I was younger. She told me to dream big and then write it all on paper so it could come true. Something about seeing it. Touching it. It made it more tangible in her eyes. The older I got, though, my insecurities crept in, self-doubt, not believing in myself. Those sorts of things."

She thought about some of the big events in her life and then continued. "After we met, after the ordeal with my stepbrother, I hid from a lot of my pain. I was still young and processing my grief. When I was in the Marine Corps, I finally found a counselor I liked, and they recommended writing to get out my frustrations and stress. Although, at the time, it was mostly just journaling. And then I had Molly, and my journals began to collect dust."

She turned her body inward, her knees touching Chance's legs. Chance shifted, too, closing the distance between them. The closeness brought a tingling surge up her spine. Easy. Like it was meant to be. But recalling the events she was about to share with Chance still brought pain. Letting out a slow breath, Claire closed her eyes for a brief second.

"You don't have to continue," Chance said, squeezing her hand tightly.

Lifting her eyelids, Claire went on. "No. It's fine. I'm fine.

It's just, well…I haven't shared some of these details with anybody since court. And it's been so long."

A sudden gust of wind caught Claire by surprise, causing her dress to ruffle in the air. Chance hurriedly placed his hand over the material, holding it in place on her knee. The warm sensation from his hand was exactly what she needed to continue. She wanted to continue.

"When Molly was about seven months old, my commanding officer called me into his office one day. Said that a civilian detective needed to speak to me about Alex's trial."

Chance looked up at her, meeting her serious expression. "Joe? Joe Daniels?"

"Yeah," she nodded, her eyes lifting.

"Did you meet him?"

"He flew out and met me at Camp Pendleton. Said it was better to talk in person than over the phone. I didn't mention any of this the other day because I feel like I live in these chapters of my life, and I try not to let them bleed over into other chapters. I know that sounds silly. But it helps me stay sane." She sucked in her full lips until they were almost paper thin.

Chance nodded, watching, staring at her with every word.

"Anyway, Detective Daniels told me Alex had taken a plea bargain earlier in the year, but only to second-degree murder for one of the women, not all of them. Claimed he had nothing to do with the others, and since I only saw one woman…" She paused, finding the strength to continue. "With the plea deal, he agreed to name some of his accomplices. In turn, he'd receive a reduced sentence of fifteen years. With those names, they were finally able to arrest two of the three other men."

"Wait, he only received fifteen years?"

She watched his reaction mirror hers from twenty years ago. "Fifteen years wasn't enough, I know. Especially since three of those years were considered time served. But Detective

Daniels said since it was such a high-profile case, with Alex being a cop, that if they went to trial, there was also a likelihood Alex would go completely free."

Chance narrowed his eyes and shook his head, a look of disbelief etched all over his face.

"But there's more."

"More? What do you mean?"

Claire spent the next few minutes telling Chance what Detective Daniels told her, recalling the events of her parents' deaths all over again.

"Your parents' death case was never closed. Were you aware of that?" Detective Daniels had asked Claire. "Their bodies were found without life jackets, and when you told the police they were good swimmers, the police began looking into their personal lives to see if there was any foul play. Once you moved in with Alex, they found a stack of evidence pointing fingers right at him. But, before they could act on anything, he was already being arrested for the murders of those women. While he was in custody, they continued to build a case around him. Did you know Alex asked your parents for two hundred thousand dollars before he went down to visit them?"

"Two hundred thousand dollars?" Claire gasped, not sure she'd heard him right.

Shaking his head, he continued. "He was in debt. A lot of it, according to some letters we found in your stepdad's office. But he refused to pay Alex or loan him the money. The letters turned ugly, and there was a lot of fighting between him and your stepdad. But, right before he came down to visit, there was a change in the message's tone from Alex. He claimed he had some vacation time he needed to burn before he lost it. Said he wanted to come spend time with them."

Claire thought about it for a moment, not sure she understood. Her parents hadn't mentioned any of this. But why would they? She was just a teenager when all that happened. But it was still shocking to hear the words.

"There was also a voice mail on the answering machine from your stepdad to your mom the day Alex came down to visit. It said for her to be careful and not to trust him." Adjusting in his seat, Detective Daniels wet his lips before continuing. "Anyhow, with some digging, a St. Petersburg detective finally found video footage of Alex's car down at a marina, a few miles away from the pier your parents used for their sailboat. Alex rented a speedboat under the name Robin Harris, and even used her credit card. That was the woman we were able to identify at the beginning of all of this. The video was a little blurry, but it showed him returning within an hour after leaving the dock."

"What are you trying to say? That Alex had something to do with my parents' deaths too?" She sobbed, tears streaming down her cheeks.

"Detective Daniels said he wanted to personally tell me before they charged him with my parents' murders," Claire told Chance. "Said he'd been close to the case for a long time and felt he owed it to me on a personal level." Taking each breath slowly, her chest rose and fell as she stared into Chance's eyes. "Then he told me Alex wanted to see me."

Chance's eyes widened and his lips parted. "Did you see him?"

"I didn't go. Not right away, at least. After Tyler, after his death, I finally went. And that's when I really started writing. Everything he told me. Every disgusting detail. I wrote it all."

"But you've never published any of that, have you? I've only seen your novels," Chance asked, confused.

"There's a book out there. It's under a pen name. I didn't want to be associated with it. But I also felt like the story had to be told. Alex was very filtered. He was forthcoming when he wanted to be, but he also kept a lot of details hidden. I always felt like there was more. So, rather than focusing on him, I focused on the women. I told their stories. By the time I finished, I needed a change. I wanted something light to write about, something that people could smile about. And, by then, I felt like I was ready to be Claire Harding again."

"What happened with Alex then? What was the end result?"

"He was convicted. They gave him two life sentences, no chance of parole. I didn't go to his sentencing, but I heard he was very apologetic and claimed that our parents' deaths were an accident."

"And what do you think?"

"I think Alex got caught up in something bigger than himself, but I also think he's a compulsive liar." Glancing over Chance's shoulder, Claire noticed a man in a black jacket watching them. The man flinched upon being caught. Claire's stomach tightened and her throat restricted as she held her breath.

Chance turned around, noting her sudden change in demeanor.

"You okay?" Chance faced Claire again, pulling the palm of her hand close to his heart.

Blinking hard, she looked at Chance and then back to where the man had been sitting. But he was gone. Twisting on the bench, Claire looked around wildly, scanning every face, but found nothing.

"Talk to me. You just went somewhere," Chance said softly, bringing her palm to his lips.

"Did you just see that guy? The one with the black jacket?" Her words came out fast and fierce as she released her hold from Chance, standing to look for the man in the black jacket. Her heart pounded with each breath.

"Claire?"

Turning her attention back to Chance, her brows

furrowed, not realizing what just happened. But the sound of her name drew her back to him. Standing inches from her, Chance extended his arm, repeating her name again.

"Claire."

"I swear there was someone watching us. He was just sitting there. And then he wasn't."

Ignoring Chance's invitation to take his hand, she pointed to the spot where she'd seen the man. Watching. Waiting. But maybe she imagined the whole thing.

"I'm going to take your hand," Chance whispered, reaching slowly to clasp her fingers between his. Taking a step closer, he pulled her hand to his chest.

"Do you feel this? Slow down your heart rate. Breathe with me." Chance placed his warm hands on top of hers as she began to feel the steady rhythm of his heart. Her eyes locked on his until she suddenly felt silly and shook her head.

"I...I swear there was someone there."

"Claire, you've lived a life filled with trauma. Revisiting your past will do that to you," Chance said, inching his way closer. Releasing Claire's hand, he pulled her into a tight embrace, wrapping his arms around her back.

A few minutes later, the two of them stood up and made their way back to the theater. Claire felt a sense of comfort as she walked with Chance by her side. She hadn't told anyone about Alex's conviction except for Tyler and her therapist. Not even Molly. The only thing Molly was aware of was that her grandparents had died in a boating accident. Maybe Chance was right. Maybe the spoken words put her on edge, causing her to see things that weren't there.

"That was amazing. I mean, I'm completely speechless," Chance said after both the intermission and at the end of the show. "I've never seen anything like it before. And your daughter, she looks just like you."

"She was in costume and makeup, and she was so far away

you couldn't possibly tell that she looked any more like me than she did to the woman sitting next to us." Claire laughed, taking Chance's hand and leading him into the lobby.

"She looks just like you, Claire." The way he said her name gave her goosebumps. And for the first time that night, she thought about it being his last night there. He told her he would be leaving tomorrow, sometime in the afternoon, and she suddenly felt an emptiness in the pit of her stomach.

"So? Do I get to meet her? Can we give her these flowers? I don't know how any of this works. Maybe you don't want me to meet her."

It was cute the way he babbled on, and she wanted to kiss him right there. Instead, she smiled and directed his attention to the side door where the cast was beginning to come out.

"Mom! Over here!" Molly shouted above the crowd. In a white ball gown with rhinestone sleeves, Molly was absolutely breathtaking. Claire knew Chance wouldn't know, but Molly looked more like Claire's mother than Claire.

"That was great! You were wonderful. Everyone was wonderful!" Claire yelled above the noise, giving Molly a quick hug.

"Thanks. I had a bit of a slip during rehearsals. But I..." Her voice trailed off as she noticed Chance. Her mouth fell open.

"This is my friend Chance. Chance, this is Molly."

Chance leaned forward, away from the crowd walking past, and handed Molly the bouquet of flowers he had brought. "These are for you. Your mom has told me a lot about you. The show tonight...it was beautiful."

Molly was still in shock, Claire could tell, but she finally pulled herself together enough to take the flowers. "It's nice to meet you."

Molly then looked back at Claire. "I'm sorry, Mom. I know I said we'd do dinner, but I promised the gang we'd do dinner too. Can we take a raincheck? Maybe do dinner next weekend?" She looked at Claire with raised eyebrows, and Claire knew what she was thinking.

"Sure, sweetie. I'll call you tomorrow. Great job again."

As they turned to leave, she knew Molly was still watching them, which made her smile.

Chapter Twenty
Present

Chance

There was something incredibly intoxicating about the way Claire walked, talked, and looked at him. He was drawn to her in a way he had never imagined possible. And he was positive Claire felt it too. The way her face glowed when she looked at him, her smile gentle. The way she rested her hand in his palm.

Chance helped Claire pull a black windbreaker over her head before they hopped on the expressway, the temperature dropping a few degrees. They drove back toward St. Petersburg with the wind blowing in their hair. The moon hung high, guiding them across the I-275 bridge over Old Tampa Bay, until stratus clouds began to scatter across the sky, swelling, threatening to burst at their seams at any moment.

"Look out over there. It looks like it's about to pour," Chance yelled, competing with the sound of the other cars on the road as he pointed at the sky.

"I'll pull over once we're across the bridge. We can put the top back on." But, as if the heavens had heard and decided to play a trick on them, water began to pour from above.

Claire looked at the open sky, laughing and smiling. "I hope you don't mind getting wet."

Chance watched as her eyes danced, water dripping from her face. He held a hand out, trying helplessly to block what he could from obscuring her view. But it was useless. Even the windshield wipers couldn't keep up with the steady flow of rain that penetrated the windshield. It was coming from above and through the sides, leaving them with zero chance of staying dry.

But, as Chance watched Claire drive, he noticed that she didn't seem to care, which made him laugh too. She turned her head and pointed, keeping her eyes on the road, yelling something inaudible against the noise of the rain. Following the direction of her extended finger, relief washed over him as he saw the end of the bridge coming close.

Slowing down, Claire pulled to the edge of the road and stopped along the shoulder. Chance was out of the Jeep first, but Claire was close behind, pulling the top up and over their heads.

"Clip that in under the visor," she yelled to him.

He did as she instructed and then met her around the back to help clip and secure each side window. Stretching above her helped, but Claire probably wouldn't have needed his help, even if he weren't there. She was more than able to take care of herself, which made her that much more attractive.

As the last window snapped into place, Chance stood watching Claire, her hair in a tangled mess that stuck to her face and neck. His heartbeat quickened, and his body tensed, hyperaware of hers. Her dress, once flowing in the breeze, was now drenched, clinging to her every curve.

She turned, her eyelids dripping with water. Mascara running down her face. Chance couldn't help himself anymore. He reached for her at the waist. After taking a slow, deep breath, Chance pulled Claire close to his chest, her body wet against his. The cold rain dripped down their faces, sending goosebumps down their bodies. He wiped what water he could from her cheeks, and, when he felt her heart quicken, too, he guided her head toward his. Leaning forward, he pressed his lips to her neck, tasting the rain and the salty air on her skin. He felt her exhale, and, as she took another breath, he inched his mouth down to where her neck and freckled shoulder met and kissed her skin again, deepening his touch.

Chance ran his hands up her back, under the windbreaker, feeling her bare back between the straps of her dress. At his touch, Claire arched her back and then, as if on impulse, she stood on her tiptoes to meet his lips. Caught in the moment, Chance withdrew his hands, bringing them to her face, engulfing her as the rain continued sliding down every inch of their bodies.

Cars began to honk as they whizzed by, passing them on the road, but neither of them noticed. Not until a semi roared by, blaring what sounded like a foghorn.

Slowly, Chance pulled away, his lips leaving hers. Her eyes were still closed, but, as she began to open them, he grinned at her, feeling every ounce of love he hadn't known he had, never knowing what true love felt like.

"We should get out of this." She exhaled, squinting.

"Yeah," he agreed, taking a moment to catch his breath before releasing her.

He ran to the driver's side and opened Claire's door so she could climb in, and then pulled her wet dress up beside her. Then he ran to his side, careful not to slip in the mud that was forming from all the rain.

Once inside, he stared at Claire, lost in the moment, unable to utter a single word.

"We're soaking." Claire laughed, fine lines curving around her mouth.

"We are. I've never driven in rain like this. With no roof."

"It's a first for me too. I live closer than your hotel. Let's head back over there first. I have to get out of this dress."

At the mention of getting out of her dress, Chance clutched her free hand.

Chapter Twenty-One
Present

Claire

They pulled up the brick road to her small house in Historic Roser Park. The rain hadn't let up, pelting the vinyl top of the Jeep in rhythmic succession. They ran inside, saturated from what had turned into a storm. Thunder rattled above the treetops as streaks of light lit up the sky.

Claire flipped the switch to the hall light once they made it indoors, but the lights didn't turn on. She threw her keys on the small table next to the door and made her way to the kitchen and flipped that switch next, but that didn't work either.

"The power's out," she called down the hall.

Just then, Shadow sprinted out from the living room and ran between Claire's legs, rubbing his side against them.

"You definitely don't want to go out in that rain. Maybe later," she told him, patting his head.

Chance laughed at her words, causing Shadow to lose it. Making a mad dash down the hall, all four paws scraping the hardwood planks below him, Shadow jumped at Chance, trying to lick his face.

"Shadow. Down," Claire commanded.

Chance, still standing on the carpet in front of the door, eagerly bent at the waist to pet Shadow, who instantly dropped to the floor at Claire's voice.

Making her way back to the two of them, Claire eyed Chance's wet shirt, stretched across his muscles, suddenly thinking about their kiss outside in the rain. It made her body ache with desire. She knew she should slow down. Knew she should offer him a towel. But, instead, when he ran a hand through his wet hair, she couldn't take it any longer. Slipping her hand into his, Claire invited him into her bedroom, closing the door to Shadow.

Standing in front of him at the foot of her bed, in total darkness, it took a few moments for her eyes to adjust. Claire reached her hand up, touching her palm to his chest, feeling his heartbeat and the warmth of his breath. Wanting, waiting, yearning for Chance to touch her back.

Taking a step closer, Chance reached for the bottom of her windbreaker and slowly pulled it off, over her head, as if reading her mind. And when he reached for the straps to her dress, she held her breath and closed her eyes. His touch was warm and soft and sent a flutter through her stomach.

Slowly slipping the straps from her shoulders, Chance bent down and scooped up the bottom of her wet dress, pulling it off the same way he had the windbreaker, this time breathing her in as he dropped it to the floor. Her eyelids flickered open as he traced her bare skin with one finger, dragging it down her arm, and over her hand.

"Claire," he whispered, his mouth to her ear. The sound of her name made her body burn with desire.

"I'm going to kiss you." His voice deepened, full of hunger and passion and love.

With her hand still in his, Chance brought it to his face,

resting it there as she parted her lips, waiting in anticipation, her heart beating wildly. His lips met hers a second later, wet and warm and longing for more. She ran her hand across his face, feeling the stubble on his cheek, until their lips parted, allowing them time to breathe.

Chests heaving, Claire lifted Chance's shirt over his head, feeling the heat rise from their closeness. She unbuttoned his pants and dropped them next to her dress.

Chance ran his fingers across her back and lifted her, deepening her desire for him, then laid her down on her bed, touching her lips the way he had that first night she met him. The memory made her dizzy. She ran her fingers through his wet hair as she anticipated what was coming next.

But the moment came to a sudden halt when an alert sounded from Chance's phone. She wanted him to ignore it, to keep touching her, to kiss her. Her adrenaline was running high. And he did, at first, but then paused and waited for the ringing to stop.

But when it rang again, he sat upright.

"I'm sorry, I have to get that," he whispered.

She felt his body move, and she let out a sigh of disappointment as she watched him reach for his phone.

"Hello?" His voice was raspy, out of breath. "Wait. Slow down…Okay…Where are they taking him?"

Claire felt the intensity in his words and sat up, still wearing her bra and panties that had been soaked through, exposing her bare skin underneath.

"It's storming here and it's late. I doubt if I'll be able to get a flight out tonight. I'll see what I can do about changing my flight to the first one out in the morning. Keep me updated, please."

Before he ended his conversation, Claire was already up, grabbing towels to dry them off.

"Do you want to talk about it?" she asked, handing him a towel.

"It's my dad. They think he had a stroke. He's on his way to the hospital right now. I'm sorry," he continued, his gaze shifting back to her.

"No. Don't be sorry. Is he okay? Can I do something?"

He stood tall, almost completely naked. Only a solid pair of black boxer briefs covered his lower half. He wrapped the towel she'd given him around his torso. Then he extended his arm out to her and draped her towel around her body. He pressed himself against her, rubbing his hands up and down her back to warm her.

Lightning lit up the room, and thunder crashed in the distance. And then, as if nature was aware of what was happening, her lights flickered on.

"I need to check flights. I really am sorry. You don't know how bad I—"

Claire pressed her finger up to his lips. "It's okay. I understand. I'd do the same thing. Go check flights. You can use my laptop over there if you want. I'll throw your clothes in the dryer now that the power's back on." She smiled wearily.

Chance didn't let her go right away. Instead, he held her tightly, and she sank into his arms. But, as he released her only seconds later, she felt disheartened. She was concerned for his dad and felt bad that Chance had to hurry home. But it didn't take away the pain she was beginning to feel. What did she expect? That's what she told him that first night when they met for dinner. What had she expected tonight? To sleep with him? Even if they hadn't been interrupted, he would still be leaving tomorrow. What was she doing? This wasn't like her. She didn't open her heart for it to break.

She opened the bedroom door to Shadow lying on the floor where they had left him. He jumped up and ran past her, into the bedroom with Chance, ignoring her for the new guest. *Traitor,* she thought, amused that Shadow was more interested in Chance than her.

Inside the laundry room, she slipped into a dry shirt and a pair of faded jeans that she had sitting in a basket. She tossed Chance's wet clothes into the dryer and turned it on. Back in the kitchen, she poured water into a kettle and placed it on the stove, warming it to make hot tea.

Looking out her kitchen window, Claire watched as the storm downsized to a drizzle. Chance came up behind her and nuzzled into her neck, wrapping his arms around her. She closed her eyes, imagining her life like this. To be able to laugh and kiss in the rain, to take long walks on the beach, to be touched by a man who loved her, and to love back. She hadn't told Chance how she felt. Though she was sure he knew, she still wanted to say it.

As quickly as the images came, she wondered if this was just destiny keeping them apart. The two of them, bumping into each other, years apart, only to be left alone in the end. Maybe it was better that she hadn't said those words. If she openly admitted to them, she would only be left hurt, more than she already was in that moment.

Chance took a strand of her still-damp hair and brushed it to the side, exposing a bare spot along her neck. Still holding her hair from behind, he bent his head down to kiss it.

"I found a flight that leaves at six a.m.," he said softly, lifting his head.

She could see their reflection in the window. His face was solemn and serious. She didn't know how to respond. Instead, they stood there until the whistle blew from the tea kettle. She turned around and cradled his face with one hand and kissed him gently on the lips before letting go. She walked to the stove, shut off the burner, and poured the water into two ceramic mugs, careful not to knock over the tea bags.

"Your clothes will be dry soon," were the only words she

could string together. There was a pain in her stomach, a dull ache she couldn't get rid of. She felt selfish for feeling so disappointed. His dad was in the hospital. What was he supposed to do? It would be wrong for him not to go. But it left them in this weird spot, and she didn't like that feeling. Not one bit.

Chapter Twenty-Two
Present

Chance

At four in the morning, after showering and packing, Chance waited for the Lyft driver outside the entrance of the Tradewinds. It had stopped raining before Claire drove him back to the hotel. She had offered to wait, to take him to the airport, but he already felt bad enough and knew she wouldn't get any sleep. They'd finished their tea together, as his clothes finished drying, before driving off in silence. It was painful. Chance wished he'd said something, anything, to make her smile. But he hadn't, and then the moment was lost.

Instead, he waited until they pulled up to the hotel. In the darkness, he turned to her and, when her eyes met his, the only words he could mutter were "thank you." He kicked himself afterward when he was alone in his thoughts. What kind of man says "thank you" at the end of such a great night, without another word, without any reassurance of their future?

He suspected what was on her mind. The idea that he was here one minute and then leaving the next would be enough to make anyone angry. But their situation was different. They'd just reconnected. This wasn't a one-night stand. Or was it? He'd professed his love for her. And he meant every word of it. But maybe he was getting ahead of himself. She lived in Florida. He lived in North Carolina. His work was there. His dad was there. And his dad needed him now. He'd made a promise to himself years ago. After Tyler's death. After he deployed to Afghanistan and Iraq. After he lost himself to his demons. He promised to be there for the man who loved him, no matter what, who'd given up alcohol to bridge the gap in their relationship. To the father who loved him the best way he knew how.

By the time the suicide attackers hijacked the four planes on September 11th, Chance had already reenlisted in the Marine Corps and had been assigned recruiting duty. As a sergeant in a recruiting office, he was low man on the totem pole, working long, strenuous hours, but he didn't mind.

Then the Twin Towers collapsed. And then it was Tyler's funeral. And then he saw Claire. It was as if those moments were broken into a million little pieces, each one flashing red before his eyes as Chance slumped into the back seat of his ride to the airport.

It was 2001. Chance swung open the front door to the townhouse he rented in Woodbridge, Virginia, the day after he laid eyes on Claire for the second time in his life. Inside, he marched straight to the cabinet and pulled out a small glass, filling it with vodka and downing it in one gulp. Then he poured another and drained it just as fast, feeling the burn in his throat as it went down. Chance had to be back at work tomorrow, before sunrise, but he decided to pour one last glass before making his way to the couch.

The sound of a slow bugle echoed in his ears, and visions of Tyler's casket being lowered, Claire sobbing at its side, crushed him. He hated himself for being more upset about Claire than Tyler. The thought of the two of them together made his stomach churn. His chin quivered, and his shoulders shook as tears began to pool in his eyes. Lifting the vodka to his mouth, Chance sucked down the third glass and slammed it against the table before closing his eyes, letting his nightmares invade his sleep.

Waking up the next morning, dry mouthed and thirsty, Chance stumbled to the bathroom and climbed into a cold shower. Washing the fatigue away, his knees shook, and the room suddenly went dizzy. Or maybe it was him. He couldn't be sure. The only thing he could be sure of was Tyler was dead.

Ignoring the nausea, Chance rushed out of the shower and threw on his uniform, ready for a day of recruiting at the local high school. But when he arrived, already late, his cell phone vibrated with an incoming text.

Hurry up and get to the office.

What? No program today?

No need. Get here quick.

Confusion tugged at his collar, but Chance followed orders. Pulling into the parking lot at the recruiter's office only minutes later, Chance's eyes widened at the number of cars. Almost every spot had been taken, leaving him with the last one in the corner.

Chaos engulfed him the second he swung the door open. Greeted by more than a dozen boys and girls, Chance's gunnery sergeant was hidden from view.

"Over here!" he called out, his voice raspy and annoyed.

"What's going on?" Chance asked, touching his forehead, his dizziness suddenly coming back.

"You're late. I need you to start the paperwork for all these new poolees."

"Wait, what?" Surprise slipped from his tongue.

The gunnery sergeant eyeballed him. "You look like shit, but we'll address that later."

Chance turned to walk away, but his stomach became

queasy, and his forehead dripped with sweat. He made it two steps before he bent forward, acid rolling up his throat. The contents from the night prior spewed across the floor, just missing the boy standing next to him. The room fell silent, except, of course, for the noise coming from his gunnery sergeant's breathing.

Later that day, when the office was empty, after Chance had changed his uniform, he got his ass chewed out.

"What the fuck were you thinking? You smell like shit. You look like shit. You better get your fucking shit together." And those were his nice words.

Chance took the berating because he deserved it. He didn't like it, but he knew he'd fucked up. But he didn't care enough to change his behavior.

Later, as Chance sifted through the stacks of paperwork, he recognized a common theme among all the new poolees. They all wanted to go to war, to fight terrorism. And, over the next several months, Chance recruited more and more kids, all with the same ambition, the same desire. Rarely ever having to make a house call, people came to him, making his job all the easier.

After he was done each night, he stopped at the liquor store and bought a new bottle of vodka, drowning his sadness and anger and frustrations one sip at a time.

On the cusp of the new year, Chance found himself drooling on his couch when his phone woke him up. It was an incoming text from his dad.

Call me back. I'll be awake.

What the hell? His dad never texted him. Chance didn't think he even *knew* how to text.

Worried something had happened to Joe, Chance quickly dialed his dad's number.

"Chance?"

"Yeah. You wanted me to call?" Chance stiffened, suddenly

aware that the couch he'd been sitting on wasn't his. Breathing heavy, he looked around. Scattered newspapers, blankets, and pillows littered the floor. Empty beer cans and vodka bottles lined the coffee table, a few laying crushed on the floor.

"Chance. I heard the news. When do you leave?" Panic rang in his voice.

"Umm," Chance couldn't concentrate on his dad, on his words, when he had no idea where he was. His head throbbed, and he could still taste the remnants of booze on his tongue. His eyes shot to the door when he heard footsteps coming. His heart pulsed against his chest. He had to get out of there.

Racing to the door, Chance opened it and was greeted by an unfamiliar scene. He had zero idea where he was. Scanning the lot, his eyes caught sight of his car in the corner.

"Chance. Are you there? I'm worried about you, son. I want to be there when you leave." The sorrow could be heard in his dad's low voice, cracking on the word "worried."

Racing down the stairs, it dawned on Chance what his dad was referring to. "Yeah. Sorry. I was just..." *Crap, what was I just doing?* "I leave next week. I don't think we'll have time; we have a lot of training before heading to Afghanistan." Chance wasn't even sure how his dad had known about his deployment. He'd just recently requested a transfer, volunteering for a deployment he knew better suited him than recruiting.

"I still want to be there. I love you, son."

When push came to shove, his dad did make it in time to see Chance before he boarded the flight overseas. At the time, Chance didn't think much about it. He was too busy assessing his gear, ensuring he and his men had everything they needed. And, for the next six years, Chance deployed three more times. Each time, harder than the last. He watched his marines come together as a family, only to be destroyed by roadside bombs, ambushes, beheadings, and firefight attacks. And if it weren't those that were destroying his family of marines, it was the aftermath, the return to home, that claimed the lives of so many of his men. From car accidents to suicides, his men suffered.

After his last deployment, after he lost a few men in Iraq, Chance felt shattered. He was at the lowest of all his lows. He finally went home. For the first time in years, he drove back to Asheville. He wasn't even sure why. But he was there.

Pulling into the driveway, the sun peeked through the trees, casting shadows across the lawn. The idea of coming home suddenly worried him, causing his heart to beat faster. Chance raised an eyebrow as he trudged up the stairs of the creaky back porch, eyeing the assortment of lilies and peonies strewn across a dozen flower pots.

"Hey there! I wasn't expecting you for a few more hours," his dad said gleefully.

"I wanted to get on the road and leave earlier." Truthfully, Chance had been forced to leave earlier. All the marines were told to go see family when they returned stateside.

"Well, I have some things planned for us. Figured we could take a day trip to Chattanooga. Just the two of us."

Chance's eyes narrowed. "Chattanooga? Why the hell would we go there?"

"Oh, it'll be nice. Plus, we haven't been there since you were little."

"No, thanks," Chance said and went to his room. Throwing his duffel bag on his old twin bed, he noticed something out of the corner of his eye. His parents' room was across the hall, and at this angle, he could see the old cherry-wood dresser his mom had picked out years ago. On the newly polished wood, there lay a handful of medallions...silver, red, gold, and purple.

Curious, he took a deep breath before walking over. He touched the bronze one and noticed there were two of them.

"Sobriety chips. That's my one-year clean chip. Been sober for over two and a half years now." His dad leaned over him.

"Why haven't you told me?"

"Didn't think you'd believe me. Not like you and I've had the best relationship the last decade," his dad said with a genuine grin as he ran a hand through his white hair. "I've been attending those meetings your mom used to go to. Nice people. They've helped me quite a bit. Sometimes I hear stuff I wish I didn't. But it's helped. And I guess that's all that matters."

Chance wasn't sure what to say. He wasn't sure if he actually believed him or not, but he *had* noticed something different about him. The way his dad smiled. The way he talked. His appearance. He didn't look like he'd been run over by a bus anymore, and his hair was cut short, and he'd even shaved.

Placing the medallion back on the dresser, Chance stepped around his dad to get to the kitchen. He opened the refrigerator, hoping to find a beer, something to call bullshit on his dad. But there was nothing.

"So? How 'bout we head out? If we leave now, we can still get there before noon."

Country music filled the truck on the drive to Chattanooga. On occasion, his dad talked, trying to converse about the typical stuff, like the weather and whether Chance had a girlfriend. His demeanor had drastically changed since the last time he'd seen him, and Chance wondered when it happened, how it happened. People didn't just change overnight. He'd talked to Joe over the years, kept up with him whenever he had the time. Had Joe told him? Had Joe mentioned his dad's sobriety? Maybe. Maybe he had. He couldn't remember. His head began to hurt. He needed a drink.

"Can we pull over? Maybe go to a bar or something?" Chance didn't care what his dad thought. At twenty-eight, he was an adult, and if he wanted a drink, he would drink. He didn't care that his dad had given up drinking.

"We're almost there. How about we wait till afterward."

"After what?"

"You'll see."

Not much time passed before the truck pulled into a small parking lot with a sign that read "Lookout Mountain, Incline Railway."

Slumping in his seat, Chance grumbled under his breath. He was tired and hung over from the night before, and all he could think about was vodka and Coke. But when his dad told him to get moving, he followed orders.

Memories of his mom came rushing back as the railcar climbed the steep hill. Visions of her laughing and twirling around in the breeze. He smiled to himself as he remembered her lifting him up high so he could get a better view.

At the top of the mountain, he stretched his legs. His head was pounding.

But his dad continued to move forward. "Follow me."

They hiked over to the observation deck, where Chance was able to see sandstone cliffs and mountains for miles upon miles. It made him think of the picture from his childhood. Now, standing here as an adult, he wondered if they really could see seven states. He wanted to call bullshit on whoever made up such a lie.

"Have a seat," his dad said.

"Why?" Chance frowned.

"I've wanted to tell you this for a few years now. Damn, I should have told you this when you were a kid. As a boy, you had a right to know."

His dad proceeded to tell him what he already knew, about his real father and how he'd saved Chance's dad's life during the Vietnam War. But he included other details, details Chance hadn't known.

"Simon grew up here. He enlisted in the army when his parents and younger sister were killed in a house fire. Simon was at work when it happened. And I know it tore him up most nights," his dad continued, describing a hero, a man he was proud of.

He apologized for the years they lost due to his drinking and told Chance that he understood if he couldn't be forgiven. With tears in his eyes, he continued. "I'm worried about you. War changes people. You already had my baggage to deal with and now war on top of it. You're a walking time bomb, Chance. You've always said you didn't want to be anything like me. And here you are, already trying to be like your old man."

"I don't—"

"You wanted a drink before noon. Don't think I haven't noticed the signs. I'm an alcoholic, remember?"

"I'm not an alcoholic like you," Chance growled, his chest puffing out as he stood up. "I know my limits. My men need me. You don't understand what I've seen. I'm allowed to have a drink to forget about it all." He shook his head and clenched his fists, ready to defend himself.

"My men needed me, too, son. But I couldn't save them all. The ones who come back might be the lucky ones. But look at me. I almost drank myself to death. If it weren't for your mother, my nightmares would have killed me years ago." His dad's voice softened with each word, and he brought a hand to Chance's shoulder.

With that, Chance thought about his dad's panic attacks growing up. Him waking up in the middle of the night, his mom consoling him. His wild hair and the dark circles around his eyes. And then he thought about himself. He, too, had begun having nightmares, but that was expected. This was all new and fresh. They would stop over time, he told himself.

"I know I let you down. A lot. I wanted to be a good

father. I really did. I wanted to do it for Simon, for your mom, and, hell, I loved you more than myself, so I wanted to do it for you. I can't keep making excuses though." His dad brushed away his tears. "Your mom and I robbed you of ever getting to know who your real father was, and you deserved that."

Chance listened but kept his head down. He hadn't put much thought into getting to know who Simon was. He tried not to think of anything from his past. It was hard enough focusing on the present.

"Go see Joe when we get back home. Valerie too."

Chance finally turned to look at him.

His dad gave him a wry smile. "I know you've always felt more comfortable talking to Joe than to me. I don't blame you. He and Valerie are expecting you."

They didn't get home until close to midnight and, by then, they were both exhausted. Trying to sleep in his old twin-size bed was nearly impossible. He closed his eyes but tossed and turned late into the night. After an hour of no success, he reached into his backpack and pulled out a half-empty bottle of vodka. It was the one thing that helped him sleep at night.

After another hour, his eyelids finally became heavy, and his breathing slowed down. Sleep finally won. But, in his sleep, he saw the shadows of his enemies and the blood from his men. A loud metallic shriek and an explosion, followed by screaming. He smelled the gasoline from his tank and felt the heat from the fire. And then he saw his dad, shaking him violently, forcing him to wake up. It was another fucking nightmare.

The next morning, Chance went next door to see Joe. Valerie answered, her face soft as she gave him a tight squeeze.

"It's been a while since we've seen your face," she said, walking him through the house until they reached the back deck where Joe was sitting.

Pushing his hands against his chair, Joe stood up and gave Chance a pat on the back. "Good to see you. Have a seat." Motioning to another chair, both of them sat down while Valerie excused herself to make a cup of tea for Chance.

"Anything you want to talk about?" Joe asked once Valerie disappeared, his eyes narrowing as if he already knew the answer. Resting his hand on the handle of the mug, Joe waited silently, allowing Chance time to process his thoughts.

"I...I don't know what exactly I'm doing here. I...my dad seems to think I have a drinking problem. But you know me. You know I'd never end up like that...like him." Running his hand around the back of his neck, Chance pulled at it before going on. "I mean, I..." A long sigh released from his chest. Feeling defeated, he stopped. Who was he kidding? This was Joe. Joe was always able to see right through him.

Joe looked at his cup and then back up to meet his eyes. "Chance. You have a lot on your plate right now. I can't imagine what you're going through. But you have to know you have our support. Valerie works with people who have PTSD. She's been helping your dad. I think you should talk to her. Like, *really* talk to her. Before this shit gets worse."

Crossing his arms, Chance looked away, both uncomfortable and ashamed of how he got here. He'd known for a while he had a problem, but he had no desire to quit. Drinking was the only way to stop the nightmares.

"Your dad suffers from PTSD too. After September 11th happened, I think your dad kind of woke up. And when you went on your first deployment, that's when Valerie convinced him to go to AA meetings. He was pretty against it at first. He was also against therapy. And, shit, he's had more relapses than I can count. But look at him now. Did he tell you he's been sober for over two years? It'll be three here shortly."

When Valerie walked back out with his cup of hot tea, Chance thanked her and took a sip, savoring the hint of lemon that floated in his mouth. Closing his eyes, he twisted his neck and began talking. At first it was slow, but the more he said, the more poured out. Valerie pulled up a chair next to Chance, resting her hand on his arm when his body began to shudder.

"I can't close my eyes. I can't sleep. The nightmares, they consume me. And my men? Each friendship I form comes at the risk of loss. We all have our demons."

Valerie and Joe listened for hours that night, which was just one of many that followed. Over time, Valerie introduced Chance to dialectical behavior therapy, which included an array of skills to help manage his emotions. And, like a chain reaction, Chance and his father grew closer, recognizing lost connections and forgiveness. It was during that time Chance found his passion for psychology. With Valerie's lead, Chance built himself a roadmap, plotting out each class recommended to help his men in the field, and then what he needed to do to become a licensed psychologist himself.

But, at the core of it all, no matter what strategies Chance had for moving forward with his life, he could never forget about Claire, the one dream he wished for.

Chapter Twenty-Three
Present

Claire

Claire awoke to the sound of blue jays chirping outside her bedroom window early the next morning. She flipped the pillow over her head to drown out the sound, but that didn't work. The noise, while something she usually looked forward to in the early mornings, was deafening and overwhelming today.

Lifting the pillow, she stared at the ceiling for a few moments before finally dragging herself out of bed.

Shadow looked at her from the corner of the room, recognizing that it was still early.

"I know, but I can't sleep. Don't look at me like that."

Wagging his tail, he rolled over for Claire to give him a belly rub before sauntering out of his own bed.

After she fed him and let him outside, Claire made herself a cup of coffee. She couldn't stop thinking about the night before. It had started off so casual and carefree. And then the passion broke free as Chance grabbed and pulled her into that magnetic embrace. The rain cascading down their bodies as their lips met fervently. His fingertips tracing the small of her back, sending a wave of pleasure throughout her body.

It had been so unexpected, but she'd be lying to herself if she said she hadn't wanted it to happen. She'd wanted more, too, and when they reached her house, her body had been anticipating his touch so much that she got lost in his presence. Remembering it now felt like reading one of her romance novels. The desire. The burning passion. Their wet bodies. She could feel the words she so often typed come alive in raw detail.

But the abrupt stop threw her off balance, even though she knew it would be inevitable. Her heart sank as she recalled her behavior after Chance's phone call. She had only been thinking about herself and her wishes. Her desires. She wanted to comfort Chance; she really did. But in that instance, she was selfish and cold. She had dreamed of that moment for as long as she could remember, and while she knew it wasn't true, she felt rejected.

Sipping her coffee, Claire scolded herself. She left Chance believing she was upset with him, when the real person she was upset with was herself. He was probably at the hospital already with his dad, not giving her a second thought, which made her grow even more frustrated. But who was she kidding? It would never have worked out. They lived in two different worlds. He was only here for the weekend, and she wasn't one to sleep around or have a fling. She was much too old for that.

Claire decided to distract herself today. Since she'd just finished her manuscript yesterday, she pulled out her laptop and opened it on the kitchen island. Opening an email, she attached the document without reading it again. Then she pulled up Tessa's email address and clicked Send.

"There. Finished," she said to herself.

Just as soon as she opened up a new document to begin something new, her phone vibrated. It was Tessa, her editor.

Her eyes narrowed, curious if Tessa even had an opportunity to see her email.

Guessing that she didn't, Claire picked up on the fourth ring, saving Tessa from going to voice mail.

But before she was able to utter a word, Tessa's voice shrieked through the speaker. "Oh My God! Who is he?"

"What?" Claire asked, her eyebrows furrowing in confusion.

"Don't you toy with me, Claire! I want all the juicy gossip. You've been holding out on me!"

"What are you talking about?"

"You've got to be kidding me. Have you not checked your Instagram yet? Someone tagged you in a few very sexy, very steamy, very *wet* pictures!" Tessa's voice was sharp and high until the word sexy came out, deepening and slowing for dramatic effect.

As Tessa continued to yap away, Claire hurried to open her Instagram. She clicked on the heart at the top of the screen, and right there, right in front of her eyes, were three pictures of her and Chance, standing in the rain, embracing each other in a deep, passionate kiss. Someone had captioned them "Isn't this New York Time's Bestseller Claire Harding? Now we know where she comes up with her steamy romance ideas!"

"Claire? Are you listening to me? Why haven't you told me about this guy? I need details!"

"Tessa, I have to go!" Claire exclaimed.

"Wait! Whatever that was, and whoever it was, this is a good thing! It's going to help sell your —"

But before Tessa finished, Claire ended the call.

Chapter Twenty-Four

Present

Chance

I t was still early by the time Chance arrived at the hospital, the sun just starting to peek over the treetops. The warm summer air welcoming him back to Asheville.

When the elevator doors opened, Chance met a nurse, who directed him to the stroke unit where Joe was sitting, his crutches leaning against the wall. His gray hair had turned completely white but in a fashionable way that more than complemented his rugged face. Valerie called him her silver fox. At just over sixty, Joe was in the best shape of his life. Unfortunately, a bullet to the leg had been his undoing and, since it wouldn't heal properly, he was finally forced into an early retirement, or at least that's what Joe called it.

Chance bent down and gave him a quick hug, nodding at the magazine in his hand.

"Valerie's idea," Joe said, rolling his eyes. Valerie had been begging him to travel for as long as Chance could remember, but Joe had always prioritized work over anything else, saying there would be time for vacations later. The only thing he'd commit to was local travel, and Valerie wanted to go abroad.

When Joe and Valerie began dating, which had surprised Chance, they'd discussed flying to Italy to see the Leaning Tower of Pisa.

"When I retire, I'll take you across all of Europe," Joe promised before bending her into his arms for a kiss.

That night was ingrained into Chance's memory. Maybe it was because it had been the first time he'd seen Joe genuinely happy. He had never seen Joe with a woman other than his family or friends. He suspected Joe probably did meet other women, but with their age difference, Chance had never been privy to that kind of information. He'd never really thought about Joe with a woman. He was just Joe.

But there, in his house, on that night, he witnessed a happiness he never knew existed. Joe's playful jabs at Valerie's quirky lifestyle, still refusing to leave her apartment near the bar where Chance had first met her. Her ability to make him smile with just a sideways glance.

It was so different from what Chance had grown up with. He tried to think about his own parents, racking his brain to find these types of memories, but only fleeting moments came to mind of the spark that his parents once held for each other.

Joe had told Chance that he ran into Valerie a week after his initial introduction to her, the morning he'd picked Chance up from his drunken stupor. He was at the police station, finishing his paperwork on an arrest he'd made that morning. A call came in at the station claiming a "peeping Tom" was trespassing on a man's property.

"You better get over here and grab him before I take care of him myself," the man barked through the receiver.

Joe was the first one on the scene, and after chasing the "Tom" for a bit, he finally apprehended the man, cuffing him before bringing him to the station.

The man trembled, and his hands shook, looking rattled and slightly confused. He insisted he had to make a phone call, that he needed his medication. When Joe offered him a phone, he called Valerie, his therapist. At the time, Joe didn't know who Valerie was by name, but when she sashayed through the station, Joe immediately recognized her. Gorgeous from head to toe, her silhouette immediately triggered recognition. But it wasn't just her appearance that bore beauty. She was strong willed, never letting up on her pursuit of getting her patients treatment.

"My patient needs his medication. He isn't going to harm anyone. He just gets spooked when he forgets to take them." Her voice was sultry, but very matter-of-fact. Confident, as if this wasn't her first rodeo.

"If we can get these charges dropped, I'll call his psychiatrist, refill his prescription, and have him admitted to an outpatient program before you can blink."

Joe was hesitant, but something about Valerie's eagerness to help manage his behavior with rehabilitation rather than punishment tugged at his heart. He asked Valerie out that same night. And the rest was history.

"They're saying he should be okay," Joe told Chance. "Valerie is in there with the doctor now. You should go in too." Joe nodded toward the door.

Without another word, Chance stepped away, leaving Joe to browse articles on the best places to visit while in Europe.

Chance entered his dad's room, standing silently in the doorway until they noticed him, which didn't take long. Valerie was the first to acknowledge him and gave him a tight squeeze.

"You must be Mr. Johnson's son. I'm Dr. Kim. I was just telling your father and Mrs. Daniels that he's very lucky. He had a rather large clot blocking the blood supply to his brain. Since Mrs. Daniels was able to call 911 at the onset of his stroke, we decided to treat the clot with what we call recombinant tissue plasminogen activator. Typically, this only works within the first few hours of these types of strokes. He had a CT when he got here, and we just received the results back from this last one. He looks to be in decent shape." The doctor glanced down at his clipboard, ensuring his details were accurate.

"So, what does this mean? Can we take him home?" Chance asked, his voice heavy with concern as he looked at his dad, who looked anything but healthy.

"Definitely not right now. He needs to start rehabilitation. I'll send the nurse in with instructions on what will happen next. Just understand that recovery can, and will, be slow. I expect, with immediate care, Mr. Johnson will regain most of his functions." He scribbled a few things on his pad of paper and then clicked his pen under the metal tab of his clipboard before hurrying out of the room.

"Are you okay?" Chance finally asked, swinging a chair closer to his father's bed.

His dad struggled to nod his head. His lower lip on the left looked just a tad bit heavier than normal. And he couldn't fully lift his left arm when Chance went in for a hug. Chance glanced at Valerie, confused.

"He had some numbness, and then some paralysis, on the left side of his body. I stopped by to help him with his meds last night."

Chance thought about his dad's arthritis and how it had been painful for him to open his daily medication boxes in recent weeks. He was thankful for Valerie and her nightly visits to help his dad.

"When I knocked, I heard some commotion, but he never came to the door, so I let myself in. He was just standing there, between the kitchen and living room, staring at me." Valerie dropped her head, trying to hold back her tears.

"He tried talking. Like his mouth was moving a little, and he was making noises. But nothing comprehensible. When I tried to get him to sit down, I noticed he struggled to move his leg and arm. I figured, by the looks of it, it was a stroke. I called 911 right away. We got really lucky."

"Thank you for being such a great friend," Chance said, his voice low. He thought back to the day he met Valerie. Their relationship sure had changed. From waking up naked in her apartment, something he wished he could forget, to becoming his very best friend. He often wondered what life would be like without someone so selfless and compassionate in his life.

Pushing the chair out, Chance reached for Valerie and gave her a quick hug, worry still dragging her down.

"Go take Joe home. I'll keep you posted."

"Are you sure? Do you need anything before we go?" she asked, voice trembling.

"We'll be okay. I'll call you if we need anything." Chance gave a wry smile.

Once Valerie was gone, Chance sank back into his chair next to the hospital bed.

"Go ahead, you can sleep," Chance told his dad as he watched him fight to keep his eyes open. Placing his hand on top of his dad's, he let it rest for a few moments, turning his attention back to Claire.

Should he call her? Text her? Should he explain what was going on? Maybe later. He'd call later. He was needed here now. This was more important. Claire would understand.

But deep down, Chance wasn't even sure if he believed himself. Doubt clouded his judgment. What good would come from calling Claire anyway? He'd already left, looking like a fool, no doubt upsetting Claire. No, he couldn't. Claire was his kryptonite. He'd tortured himself once before, thinking of her, letting himself succumb to his demons. Not again. Claire was just a coincidence. A happy chance encounter. Nothing more.

He had to stay the path. He had to keep working toward mental clarity, toward his goals of helping others striving to achieve what Valerie helped him set out to conquer long ago. If it hadn't been for Valerie, he wasn't sure what his life would have turned out like.

Valerie had changed the trajectory of his life. As a therapist herself, she pushed for therapy when his drinking escalated with every deployment, his anger growing wild as he unleashed his verbal assaults on his closest friends. It was Valerie who taught him how to meditate, how to keep his cool. And it was Valerie who showed him how he could pay it forward, helping him create a map for his life outside the Marine Corps. And, in time, Chance embraced this plan. It was eat, sleep, and breathe mental health. He had to. It was everything he could do to stay of sound mind after what he'd seen on his deployments.

By the time he'd served twenty years in the Marine Corps, Chance had managed to earn both his Bachelor's and Master's Degree in Psychology, focusing on PTSD and Addiction Studies.

He'd spent the greater portion of the last decade helping fellow veterans work through their demons, just as Valerie helped him. He couldn't just stop. He couldn't leave. This is what he'd wanted all along. And he'd made peace with the fact that he was alone. Love just wasn't in the cards for him like it had been for some people. And he was okay with that.

And yet, Claire still infiltrated Chance's every thought. She'd never understand though. He still had nightmares. No amount of therapy took away his nightmares. And Claire didn't stand a chance against them.

Chapter Twenty-Five
Present

Claire

As soon as Claire hung up with Tessa, she dialed Molly's number. Terrified Molly would see the pictures, she felt an immediate urge to explain herself. Claire had been careful with who she introduced into Molly's life ever since she was a baby. She'd never had a boyfriend, never dated, and, heck, she had been so celibate that she hadn't even kissed another man in years. Unless she counted Molly's grandpa. But a kiss on the cheek was anything but promiscuous.

It wasn't that she'd planned it this way. To not date, to not have a man in her life. But after Tyler died, being a single mom became her priority. She was so focused on Molly that her life slipped by without her even realizing it. One day she was sending Molly off to kindergarten and, the next, it was college. Maybe that was why she lost herself to her writing. It was easy to daydream, to imagine what could be, what love might look like. Somehow, she had also grown into a cynic and didn't believe in true love, especially the kind worth fighting for.

Claire had her share of suitors, men who vied for her attention. It started in the Marine Corps. Men who wanted only one thing, with immaturity spilling out of their pores. But Tyler had helped her through that. And while Tyler was her best friend, and while they shared one drunken moment that resulted in Molly's existence, Tyler didn't have her heart. She loved him in a way one loved a friend, not a lover. There was no passion, no lust, no magnetic connection that drew her to him. And then, after Tyler, she questioned herself and her choices. Maybe Tyler was her one true love. Maybe she'd missed her chance at happiness.

As the years passed, Tyler's dad and brothers even began to worry about her. They all told her it was okay to date, to find love again. But all she saw were men who viewed her as a conquest, as a woman to be lured into bed. She saw through their phoniness. Their straightforward charm, continuous flattery, large egos, and boastfulness turned her off faster than the bat of an eyelash.

And now, here she was, a forty-four-year-old woman, who was afraid to show any public displays of affection with a man, where her twenty-four-year-old daughter could see it. It was hard enough when she told Molly that Chance was going to attend her show last night. Molly had questioned her insistently, but because Claire had never had to explain anything to Molly, she didn't know what to say to her except that he was a friend of both her and her father. She felt ridiculous after the call because her daughter read her novels. She read about love, lust, and sex. But she still found it incredibly difficult to mention anything of the sort about her own life.

After the second ring, Molly picked up in predictable fashion. "Hey, Moms! You're calling early. What's up? How was your date?"

But before Claire was able to answer, Molly continued. "Okay, okay, I'm just giving you a hard time. But he was hot! How could you not want to date him? Tell me again how you and dad knew him." she said, laughing through the speaker.

"Well, that's kind of what I wanted to talk about," Claire said as she stood up and paced the kitchen. Nerves ran through her body as she shared her earliest memory of Chance, sharing everything she remembered.

By the time she finished her story, there was a brief period of silence before she told Molly to open up her Instagram and search for the hashtag of Claire's name.

"*Mom!* That's you? OMG! This is great! I'm so happy for you. But wow…I'm speechless. I can't wait to *really* meet him," Molly said, rambling her words into almost incoherent sentences.

"Well, that's another thing. You won't get to meet him," Claire said sadly, admitting to herself the sad truth of her love life. It was just too good to be true. Too good to be true for her.

"I can't accept that! Look at the way he's kissing you, Mom!"

Claire *had* looked, a dozen times. She'd seen that kiss. She'd *felt* that kiss. In the moment, it was what gave her life. She wanted that kiss to be the difference between lust and love, and she wanted love to win.

But the more she thought about it, the more she got in her head, the more she realized it was just lust. She desired him, that was for sure. The saying "what will be, will be" was her mantra. And what was there? There was no Chance. He was gone.

And she was alone.

Molly did a great job at trying to cheer Claire up, trying to convince her that it was okay to date. She insisted that dating was fun and that she wasn't getting any younger. "If this Chance guy doesn't work out, that's his loss. I still think you should text him though. What's the worst that can happen?"

My heart breaks.

"Then you go out with another guy. You're a catch, Mom. I mean it," Molly continued.

Later that afternoon, Claire ran to the store to pick up

some groceries. She was checking items off her list in the fruit aisle when she suddenly bumped into someone.

"I'm so sorry," she said, peering up.

The man nodded and walked away without saying anything. He looked familiar, but before she could think about it, she heard her name being called from the other end of the produce section. She turned around, recognizing the voice. Her friend Brittany was racing toward her with cucumbers in one hand and a plastic bag in another. Joshua, her husband, was following behind, trying to keep up while pushing their cart full of food.

"Well, look who we have here! It's our girl, Claire," Brittany yipped as she waved a cucumber at her.

Brittany and Joshua were both in their fifties and were the first friends she made when she moved back to St. Petersburg. They lived down the street from her, and they brought over a baked lasagna the first night she moved in. As avid runners, they introduced her to the world of running. They participated in all the local runs and races, although Claire suspected Joshua preferred to run alone, rather than in large outings. But Brittany always had to know what was going on in the community, so she dragged poor Joshua everywhere she went.

"Hi, Brit. Hi, Joshua."

"Hi? Is that all you have for me? I've been trying to fix you up with Chad for years now. All the while you've been sneaking around with this beau of yours? What's his name?" Brittany asked in an accusatory tone.

Chad was their nephew. Claire had zero interest in him, but Brittany refused to take that as an answer. Chad was a few years younger than Claire and still lived at home with his parents. He also couldn't hold down a job. She'd met him one too many times over the years and, each time, was the same as the first. He followed her around, trying to impress her with what he considered were his good looks and strength. But

Chad wasn't her type. Unlike his aunt and uncle, he didn't run. And he wasn't interested in his health, for that matter, either. She recalled what he did care about...how many cans of beer he could drink before he belched. He thought it was hysterical, and it was all she could do not to walk away, since she considered both Brittany and Joshua her friends. She knew Brittany meant well, but she wouldn't stop pressing the issue. It made going to social events awkward in recent weeks.

"Oh, he isn't my boyfriend," Claire began.

"Not your boyfriend? So, you just go around making out with any guy?" Brittany looked at her in horror as she placed her hand on her heart. "I thought I knew you better than that. And to think, you've been allowing a man, who isn't your boyfriend, to hang around your house all this time?"

"It's kind of a long story, Brit. He's an—"

"Well, if he isn't your boyfriend, it looks like you're still on the market," Brittany said, cutting her off. "Chad was asking about you the other day. He said he'd love to take you to dinner one night. I can arrange it if you want," Brittany said, ignoring the fact that Claire had always turned down their offer.

Claire started to respond but caught herself. She didn't know what to say that she hadn't already said before. She wasn't on the market. And, even if she were, she wouldn't go out with Chad. But how could she tell Brittany this? She couldn't bear to hurt Brittany's feelings.

"Well, then, that settles it. I'll call Chad right now." Brittany walked over to Joshua and tossed the cucumbers into the cart. Then she pulled her cell phone from her big, baggy, black purse.

Before Claire could say anything, Brittany was already on the phone with Chad.

"Hey, sweetie! Guess who I just ran into? Okay, so you don't really have to guess. No. It was a rhetorical question. It means I was just making a statement. You don't have to really guess. Chad! I was just trying to grab your attention." Brittany started arguing over the phone, almost forgetting the purpose of her phone call.

Claire watched in horror, trying to figure out how to dig herself out of this grave.

"It's Claire. No, not Claire Morgan. Chad, I'm at the store with Claire Harding. She said dinner is a great idea. No, Chad, not with me. With you. Okay. Absolutely. That's a great idea. I'll tell her. Bye."

Claire's mouth dropped. What just happened? How did she not manage to say one word the entire time Brittany was on the phone?

Brittany smiled as she shoved her phone back into her purse. "Oh, Joshua, it's Claire's lucky day," she began in a sing-song voice. "Chad said he'd clear his schedule to take her to dinner tomorrow. Isn't that wonderful?"

Claire finally followed Brittany's gaze to Joshua and realized that his mouth was open just as wide as hers, if not wider.

"Brittany," Claire started to say.

"Oh, you don't have to thank me. It's the least I can do, Claire."

Just then, Joshua cleared his throat. "Why don't they have dinner at our house? No need for them to look for a restaurant on such short notice."

"Why, that's a great idea," Brittany began before looking disappointed. "Oh darn, our bathroom is being remodeled. That won't work. There's a mess all over the house, and I'll never get it clean on time." She looked up at Claire. "But I have a better idea. Let's do it at Claire's house. I'll make chicken marsala. That way, we can leave after dinner, and you and Chad can spend some time alone. Oh, Joshua, I'm so glad I thought of this. We need to run though. I need to grab some mushrooms for tomorrow's dinner."

And just like that, Brittany was rushing off in the other direction. Joshua looked at Claire and gave her a knowing look. She was thankful for Joshua. Thankful that he tried to downgrade the date. But the fact that she got conned into it in the first place left her speechless.

"Hurry up, Joshua!" Brittany yelled from the other side of the produce section. "We'll see you at seven tomorrow night."

Chapter Twenty-Six
Present

Chance

Chance drove straight to his dad's house after he left the hospital. The nurse told him his dad would most likely be there for a few days before they found him a rehabilitation center, so Chance should go home and get some rest. But, instead of going home, Chance wanted to grab some things for his dad. Some clothes, his slippers, his toothbrush, and, most importantly, the picture of him, his mom, and his dad. His dad still kept that picture of them in Chattanooga hanging on the refrigerator, after all these years. He refused to move it, always claiming that the kitchen was his mom's favorite room in the house and that he enjoyed seeing her whenever he walked by.

As Chance looked at the picture, now curling at the edges, he wondered what life would be like if his mom were still alive. How different *his* life might look. Would he have stayed in the Marine Corps for as long as he had? Would his dad have ever found sobriety, or would he still be an alcoholic? Would he have found out the truth about Simon?

Before he could dwell on it for long, his phone rang, interrupting his vicious cycle of self-doubt. His mind instantly went to Claire, hoping it was her on the other end. His heart paused as he looked at the caller ID, but no such luck. And why *would* it be her? He had let her down. He had been the one to walk away. First, he told her he loved her, and then he left. He knew she understood why he had to leave, but he also knew that his inability to talk about anything afterward must have left her hurt and betrayed. He wanted nothing more than to say he was sorry, but he also knew that words didn't always matter. Saying sorry wouldn't fix this.

I'll text her later.

The phone rang again. "Hi, Mark. How are you?" he asked, answering the call.

"Not so good. The nightmares are back. I'm having a tough time sleeping. Karen left me."

Mark was one of Chance's longtime patients. He came to the practice the first week Chance started working for Valerie. She suggested Chance take Mark on as his first patient, that he would most likely connect better to Mark than she would since Mark was also a veteran and had PTSD. Mark had served his country for four years in the Marine Corps, but it was during his third year that he witnessed the horrors of war. During an early morning attack, insurgents tossed a grenade into an Afghan home, killing an Afghan child and wounding countless others, both Afghans and Americans. Mark had had intelligence on what was about to happen, but he was too late. The blast hit when Mark was running, knocking him from his feet and tearing off his leg from the knee down.

Like so many others, Mark was frustrated with the mental health industry. Right after the attack, he was airlifted out of Afghanistan. He was well cared for and checked on constantly. But as time went on, and he moved back to Asheville, his treatment came to a rapid halt. Nightmares rolled in, making sleep impossible, and he found it incredibly difficult to be a supportive husband when his mind went back to Afghanistan, even all these years later.

"Do you want to meet me at the office? I can be there in an

hour," Chance said now, recognizing how difficult that phone call must have been for Mark.

"I'd appreciate that. Thanks."

Chance clicked End and quickly placed his dad's belongings into a plastic bag he found at the bottom of his bedroom closet.

On his way out of the room, a picture on his dad's nightstand caught his eye. He stepped closer and noticed it was the picture of his dad and his army buddies, including Simon. His hand tightened around the plastic bag, and he caught his breath. Now, more than ever, he saw the resemblance he bore to the man he'd never met.

Not knowing how to feel, he quickly turned around and left the room. He looked around the house one last time before closing the door behind him, thankful to be leaving.

Since it was a Sunday, no one was at the office, not even the associates who worked at the law firm adjacent to them. It was quiet, which suited Chance just fine. When he entered the building, he flipped the switches, turning on all the lights, and then keyed in the passcode, turning off the alarm system. He sent a quick text to Valerie.

Chance: *At the office for a bit. Mark called. I'll lock up when we finish.*

Just as he hit the send button, Mark walked in.

"Perfect timing," Chance said, motioning him to his office.

Mark sank into the couch. "I feel like I've been doing good. I really don't understand how all of this started again." Mark shifted his weight from one cushion to the next. "I mean, I think it's been at least a year since I had back-to-back nightmares."

"How long ago did they start again?" Chance asked, recognizing that Mark was only visiting once a month now, and the last time he saw him had been a few weeks ago.

"Only the past week. But they've been bad. And I've been on edge too. I've snapped a few times and scared the kids. Karen said she wouldn't come home until I spoke to you."

Karen was a good woman. Because Mark was also a marine, Chance didn't always look at him as just a patient. He was part of his extended family of brothers. That meant Karen was family too. Karen and Mark had been married prior to the grenade launch, before his amputation. So, Karen stuck it out with him through the thick of it. Together, they had three children, and Chance had met them all.

"Okay, well, you're here now. You know as well as I do, those nightmares can be a tricky thing. Just about anything can set them off. Let's just talk about what's been happening since the last time we talked."

For the next hour, Chance listened to Mark's vivid recollection of events that played out over the last few weeks, noticing that he got more agitated when he spoke about his teenage son.

"Learning to drive can be incredibly stressful on any parent," Chance responded, allowing Mark's feelings to be heard.

"Yeah, and he acted like I was the bad guy when I told him to get out of the car when he backed into the garbage cans. He broke a taillight." He sighed. "I see what you just did there."

"What do you mean?" Chance laughed.

"You know perfectly well; you slipped that stress word in there."

Chance smiled. "Honestly, I can't say it's the stress from having a new driver in the house or not. I mean, that has to be scary though. I can't imagine what it's like to have a kid behind a machine that weighs three thousand pounds."

Mark sat up a little straighter and exhaled loudly, placing his hands on his knees. "No, you're right. I should have seen it coming. And I know I need to apologize and work on this. I wish I could just stop them from happening though."

"Are you getting any sleep?"

"No, not really."

"Have you called your psychiatrist? You should ask for something to help take the edge off, at least to help you sleep. I can reach out to Dr. Jefferies if you want."

"I'd appreciate that."

Jotting some notes down, Chance reminded himself to leave a message on Dr. Jefferies' on-call line so Mark could pick something up tonight.

"Okay, so you know the drill. Call Karen. Breathe. One step at a time. I want to see you at the end of the week, if that works with your schedule. If there's a problem, I'll work something out on my end." They both stood up to leave.

"It'll get better, but call me if you need anything," Chance said, patting Mark on the back.

After Mark left, Chance turned back around to grab his car keys. Noticing a light on in Valerie's office, he peeked his head inside to find that she'd come in while he was in session with Mark.

"Oh, hey, Chance. I'm glad you didn't sneak away yet," Valerie said somberly.

"What are you doing here? I figured you'd be at home with Joe."

"I was. But when I saw your text about being here in the office, I figured I'd come by to check on you." Valerie nodded her head in the direction of the empty chair. "Sit."

Chance did as he was told and sat in the chair across from her.

"How was your trip? And I'm not just talking about the conference."

"It was fine," he lied.

Her eyebrows arched. "You know you can tell me anything, right?"

"Yeah. I know. But it was fine. I got a lot of support from the Q&A."

Valerie sighed. Then she turned her computer screen around to face him.

Chance's eyes widened as his body stilled, frozen in place.

Chapter Twenty-Seven

Present

Claire

Tossing her bags into the back of her Jeep, Claire felt an ache in her stomach that she couldn't get rid of. How had that just happened? How did she manage to get herself suckered into a dinner date with Chad? She didn't want to hurt anybody's feelings, but Chad was the farthest from her type. She wondered if he was anybody's type and immediately felt bad for thinking it, but she shuddered at the thought nonetheless.

She closed the back gate to the Jeep and climbed into the driver's seat before placing her sunglasses on her face. Before starting the car, she sat there a moment, the afternoon sun blazing down on her sun-kissed shoulders. Her mind criss-crossed back to Chance. If only she could find the courage to text him. Was it too soon? What would she say? *I miss you. I want to see you again. I loved you the moment I set eyes on you.* Or would she tell him about Chad and hope that he'd save her from the doomed date?

There was part of her that felt disappointed Chance hadn't thought to text *her.* But he was busy with his dad, right? He would be too busy to text her, probably for a few days, maybe longer. There were parts of her that held out hope. Hope that he would at least say something, even if just goodbye.

Claire was lost in her thoughts when her phone rang. Startled, she checked the caller ID. It was Tessa. Her heart sank a little. She couldn't help it. She knew it wouldn't be Chance, not so soon. But her body wouldn't let go of the hope it still held out.

"Hi, Tessa."

"Okay, Claire. I need you to fill me in on some details, because your story, well, it's definitely not what I expected. You've never done a 'girl gets boy' ending."

It was true. Claire's entire writing career had been set on the premise of girl finds boy and falls in love but can't manage to find lasting love. Whatever the reason that kept them apart, Claire always ended her novels with a cliff-hanger. She created a series to entice readers to come back for more. But none of her novels, even the last one in her series, had the happily-ever-after feeling to them. Her protagonists were strong, independent women, who weren't defined by love. Her readers were used to this and while, at the beginning, some were left angry, wanting a happy ending to ensue, they'd come to realize the underlying messages of her books. Growth and independence.

This novel, however, was a stand-alone. She ended it with her heroine finding love because of the growth and independence her character displayed. She hadn't anticipated it ending the way it did though. That part surprised even her as she wrote it.

"Claire? Are you listening?" Tessa asked.

"I'm sorry, I missed what you just said," Claire responded as she shook her head and started her car. *Snap out of it,* she thought as she tried to push visions of Chance from her thoughts, knowing full well that he was part of the reason she'd created her happily ever after.

"I need details. I mean, this is fantastic. But totally not like you. You've never written an ending like this. It's going to shock your readers to their core. And you'll probably open yourself up to a whole new group of readers. But I'd be silly not to ask you the obvious. Does any of this have to do with the man in the pictures?"

Tessa's question was expected. Claire knew she'd ask again and again until she got what she was looking for. Tessa was pretty ruthless and straight to the point. In all honesty, she was pretty surprised it had taken Tessa this long to call her back. But Claire didn't know how to answer her. She was still trying to sort through her feelings. Tears stung her eyes and rolled down her cheeks. If only she could push past this.

"I want to scrap the entire thing. Trash the novel," Claire said quietly, not believing her own words.

There was a long pause before Tessa spoke again.

"Toss it? You've got to be kidding me. Claire. This is one of your best pieces. There is no way I can scrap it. What's going on? You know you can talk to me, right? We're friends, too, I hope you know that."

Tessa's voice was sincere, and Claire knew she meant what she said. But Claire wasn't ready to talk about it. She wanted to. Hell, she even felt the need to. But something inside her wouldn't allow her to vocalize anything. It was the struggle of her life. It was what was preventing her from telling Chance that she loved him. It was what held her back from every relationship she'd ever had. When she lost her mom, a piece of her was lost too. And then Tyler. When he was killed so tragically and suddenly, surviving was all she could do to stay afloat for her daughter. She learned to grin and bear it. But the smile was often a lie.

Claire found that writing was the only way she could keep that smile going. Some people had friends they would call and chat with when the going got tough, when they needed a shoulder to cry on. But Claire, she was a young mom and hadn't made many friends, and the older she got, the harder it became. Sure, she was friendly with people. But she learned early on that, if she was upset, the only person she could rely on was herself.

"I mean it, Claire. I've known you for how long? Five years now?" When Claire didn't respond, Tessa continued. "Okay, how about this? Tomorrow, my house. We'll talk about the novel and this mystery man. I'll grab some wine, and we'll make it a ladies' night. Just you and me."

Claire heard the enthusiasm in her friend's voice and wished she could take her up on her offer. Having a night out to vent sounded nice.

"I can't. I kind of have other plans tomorrow, and I don't know how to back out of them," she said, biting her lower lip.

"You're too nice. Just tell whoever it is that you forgot you had plans with me. Look out for yourself first. What are these plans, anyway? And why are you being so passive about all of this? You sound terrible today."

Claire placed her head against the steering wheel, still holding the phone to her ear. "It's Brittany. She and Joshua are bringing Chad over for a so-called...I can't even believe I'm saying this out loud. A date." She winced as the words fell out of her mouth. She heard Tessa gasp. And then there was silence.

Tessa knew Brittany well. They used to belong to the same runner's group. Before Claire came along, Brittany had hounded *Tessa* to go on a date with her nephew. She had spoken so highly of him that Tessa agreed to the blind date. She expected a man who was tall, dark, and handsome. A successful, hardworking gentleman. Instead, she met Chad. A short squarish man-child, who could barely remember her name. At their first meeting, he'd unbuttoned his pants at the table, without hesitation, sitting that way for the entirety of dinner. Tessa told Claire it was so terrible that she'd paid the bill herself and walked out on him while he was still eating.

"He smelled like gasoline when he walked in," she'd told Claire, "and his T-shirt had what looked to be chocolate stains down the center. I mean, it was my first impression of him. Who goes out wearing a dirty T-shirt to meet a girl?"

"Tessa? You still there?"

"One word. How?" Tessa was not typically one of few words. But she couldn't blame her friend right now. How indeed had this happened? Claire chalked it up to being spineless. She had no idea how to stand up for herself when it came to situations like this.

"You know how Brittany can be," Claire began, but Tessa interrupted her before she could finish.

"I don't mean Brittany. I mean, *how* did you go from *last night* to *Chad*?" Tessa applied extra emphasis on "last night" and "Chad," and Claire knew why.

Claire requested a rain check. She told Tessa they could get together on Tuesday, if she made it past dinner tomorrow night, promising to fill her in on all the details of the mystery man.

"Good luck, Claire, you're going to need it."

Chapter Twenty-Eight
Present

Chance

Chance's eyes grew wide, and his mouth dropped open when he saw the picture on the monitor.

"You saw Claire. And you aren't fine. You're processing a lot right now," Valerie said, her voice steady.

"How?" It was the only word that escaped Chance's mouth. He was confused in so many ways. Where had that picture come from? How did Valerie have it? How did Valerie even know that Claire existed still?

"I almost didn't recognize you. Someone hashtagged Claire on Instagram last night. I just saw it a little while ago. That's why I'm here."

Chance's jaw tightened. His chest was restricted. Growing angry, Chance tried to stop his hands from becoming fists, but it was futile.

"Chance. I'm so sorry. I saw the time it was posted, and it looks like I probably interrupted you and Claire."

"Interrupted us?" Chance's eyes narrowed, placing his hands on Valerie's desk. "What do you even mean? My dad had a stroke. You didn't interrupt anything." His voice was quick and heavy and filled with impatience. "But I'd like to know one thing. How did you happen to know about Claire?

The last time I talked to you about her was over twenty years ago."

There was silence again. Valerie was good at thinking before she spoke. She was used to processing her feelings before sharing them. It's what made her an incredible psychologist. But the silence was suffocating right now. Chance didn't want her to process her thoughts. He wanted the unprocessed truth, not the sugarcoated version of it.

"Spill it, Valerie. What is this all about? How did you come across her Instagram page in the first place?"

Letting out an extended sigh, Valerie began to talk. "Some of this isn't my story to share. So, I'm not comfortable telling you everything. You'll have to talk to Joe about some of it. But the reason I have her on my Instagram is because I saw her novel in your office a few years ago. I mean, you don't read romance, so imagine my surprise when I saw a romance novel on your desk with Claire's name on it."

"It wasn't mine. But, either way, how did you know it was the same Claire?"

"That's something you'll have to ask Joe. But I was curious. I figured she was history. You hadn't spoken her name in years. Not once. And then you and Becca broke up. It left me feeling kind of curious. I mean, don't you find it odd that you and Becca could never really commit?"

"That novel wasn't mine," Chance said defensively. "And Becca had nothing to do with it."

"Can we start over? I am not accusing you of anything. I'm just checking in to see how you are. I can see you're hurt. This picture shows another side of you, though. One I've never seen. Just look at you." She pointed to him on the screen. "Look how happy you are. I've seen you smile, but I've never seen you passionate. After a night like this, you should be glowing. But you're not, and I feel at fault."

Chance thought about her words, but didn't say anything.

He *had been* happy last night, but only for a brief moment. He couldn't allow himself to be happy; it wasn't in his cards. But none of that mattered anyway. He had work to do, classes to finish, and research to conduct. And now he had his dad to take care of. His plate was overflowing, and he had absolutely no time for someone else to rely on him.

"Claire is none of your business. Nothing happened last night, and my happiness doesn't come from women."

"That's not what I'm saying. I feel like I'm making this worse. I just don't think you're looking at the big picture right now. I want to help, but if you don't let me—" Her voice came to a stop when Chance slammed his fist onto her desk.

"I don't want your help. You've done enough," he yelled. His blood pressure was higher than a hot air balloon, and he almost got dizzy from the frenzy. He felt sweat drip from his forehead, and his arms started to tremble. His heart felt like it was pulsating out of his body. He was sure Valerie saw it too. He had to get out of there; that much he knew. He needed fresh air. He bolted out of the room before either of them could say another word.

Once outside, and after a few deep breaths, Chance's heart rate began to slow back down. It took a little longer for his hands to stop shaking, but regret instantly flooded him. He felt bad for his reaction, but anger still bubbled in his chest.

Valerie knows about Claire? And let's not forget Joe has been speaking to her over the years without a word to me about it?

A few hours later, Chance was back at his condo in downtown Asheville. He paced the living room, trying to numb his feelings with a glass of Chardonnay.

While Chance had recognized that he had a drinking problem years ago, he never attended AA meetings like his dad and never gave up alcohol completely. He accepted the fact that vodka was his enemy and only indulged in a glass of wine, or an occasional beer, at special events. Tonight may not have been a special event, but he had to cover up his anger some-how. The taste was smooth as it hit his lips. After he poured himself another glass, he sat down and opened his laptop. He stared at it for a few minutes, thinking about his dad. He knew he had to run back up to the hospital before it got too late. Maybe after a quick nap, he told himself. But how could he nap with so many thoughts swirling about?

He thought again about his dad, but this time, visions of the picture of him with Simon appeared in his head. He looked at his computer and opened up Ancestry.com and typed in his password. He saw the pending message that had been there for the past few years, unopened and unread. He had never been able to pull himself together enough to open it and doubted he'd be able to today either. The unknown scared him. Would it say he had a match? Would he find any of Simon's family? Maybe a relative he didn't know existed? Were any of them still alive? And would it even matter anyway? For years, he questioned why he even tried in the first place. But here he was again, debating on opening the unread message.

Chance poured himself a third glass of wine without any hesitation. His phone rang. It was Joe. He ignored it. When his phone rang a second time, he sent it straight to voice mail. He had no intention of listening to another person worry over him or talk about Claire.

Slowly, his eyes began to feel heavy, and Chance struggled to keep them open. Visions of his mom and dad danced in his head. He could see them hugging as he watched from his bedroom door, his younger version standing in the dark. Only the outline of his mom's back could be seen, but she looked so happy from where he stood, he was sure of it. His dad leaned his head on her head and held her in a tight embrace. He smiled as he looked up to see Chance watching. Then he pulled an arm out from around his mom's waist to give him a slow wave. Then he closed his eyes again, smelling his mom's hair as if he were taking her in for the first time.

Chance woke to the sound of pounding on his door. It was dark inside, and he was still sitting at his desk. The pounding grew louder.

"Hang on a minute," Chance grumbled, pulling himself out of his seat. His head was throbbing, and he remembered finishing off the second glass of wine on an empty stomach, thankful he hadn't started on the third. He hadn't eaten anything all day.

As he stood up, he felt a little dizzy and grabbed the desk. His eyes flickered back to his laptop to see he'd somehow managed to open the message on Ancestry.com, but before he could read it, the pounding started up again.

"I said hang on!" Chance yelled.

He walked over to the door and unlocked the deadbolt. Then he turned the knob, and Joe fell into him as the door swung open. His crutches flew in opposite directions. "Damn it, Chance. Do you ever check your phone?"

Chance helped Joe back to his feet and grabbed the crutch that had fallen backward, out of the room, while Joe reached for the one closest to him.

"I must have fallen asleep," he said, rubbing his eyes. "What time is it anyway?" He patted his pockets to feel for his phone. When he didn't find it, he turned to look at his desk. It was there. But so was the bottle of wine that stood, half finished, completely visible.

"It's only seven o'clock," Joe said, following his gaze. A wave of disappointment fell over his face, Chance could tell, but he didn't say anything, which he was thankful for.

"The hospital tried calling you. When they couldn't reach you, they called me. Your dad had another stroke. He hasn't regained consciousness."

Chance turned toward the desk and grabbed his car keys and wallet.

"I don't think so," Joe shook his head, acknowledging the elephant in the room. "You can ride with us. Valerie is downstairs waiting in the car."

Chapter Twenty-Nine
Present

Chance

"I can't tell you if your dad will ever regain consciousness. The swelling is pretty substantial and, with any coma patient, we just can't predict what will happen," Dr. Kim said once they arrived at the hospital. "It's still incredibly early, but, at this time, your dad has scored a three on the Glasgow Coma Scale, which means he's not responsive to any stimuli. That doesn't mean he won't eventually wake up. But, for right now, we just have to wait."

Inside the intensive care unit, Dr. Kim told Chance, Valerie, and Joe that only two visitors were allowed in the room at a time and, since visiting hours were almost over, they would have to make it short.

Chance knew Valerie would want to go, but she hung back with Joe to give him some space, probably because of their argument earlier that day.

Pushing open the glass door that led to his father's room, Chance slowly stepped inside, alone. There was a tube in his dad's skull and another that came out of his mouth, which was connected to a ventilator, helping him breathe. Hospital blankets covered his body from the neck down, and the skin on his face was pale and gaunt, making him look every bit his age.

Chance was told that coma patients couldn't see or

respond, but there was a small possibility they could hear. But what would he say to his dad?

Looking at his father now, lying in this bed, with so many machines hooked up to him, Chance wanted to burst out crying. He remembered when his mom was in the hospital and how he never had a chance to say goodbye. He remembered how his dad laid over her, holding her, sobbing until he couldn't sob any longer.

Wiping away the tears that fell down his face, Chance went back into the hallway and called Valerie over, his voice strained as he said her name. When she stood up from the chair, he motioned for her to follow him. At the door, he grabbed her hand and brought her inside. Neither of them spoke until Valerie let out a cry.

Turning to her, Chance gave her a hug. "I'm sorry," he whispered, "for earlier."

Her body shook, and she began to sob. "I'm sorry too. You have so much on your plate right now. And I want to help. I just don't know how."

They stood like that for a few minutes. The comfort of another person soothed him. He wished it was Claire he was hugging or who was hugging him back.

As if Valerie sensed his thoughts, she pulled away and looked up at him. "You deserve to be happy, Chance. You really do. But you know me. I can't sugarcoat anything, not even to save my life." She wiped at her face; her mascara streaked at the corners of her eyes. "We need to talk. You know that. But not now. Now, you need to be with your dad."

"Stay with me?" he asked when he realized she intended on leaving him alone.

"I'll come back. You need time alone with your dad," she said softly as the tears began to fall down her face again. And then she slipped out of the room, leaving him alone with his thoughts.

Chance pulled up a chair and sat as close as he could to be near his dad. He listened to the loud rhythmic hiss of the ventilator that kept oxygen flowing into his father's lungs. He watched the heart monitor and blood pressure machine working steadily side by side with one another. His tears began to dry on his cheeks as he sat there by himself. Reaching under the sheet, he pulled out his dad's hand and held it loosely, afraid of hurting the frail man.

What should he say? What *could* he say? Over the last few years, he and his dad had grown closer than they had ever been. When he retired from the Marine Corps, his dad flew out for his ceremony. It was the first flight he had been on since his tour in Vietnam. When Chance graduated with his bachelor's degree and was sick with laryngitis, it was his dad who insisted he still attend the ceremony.

"You don't need a damn voice to walk across a stage. You've earned this recognition and I'm proud of you. Your mom is probably crying from the heavens above right now. You can't disappoint her. And you never know what the future holds. Don't be a sissy. You're a marine. Toughen up." With that logic, how could Chance say no?

And it was his dad who Chance finally confided in about his failed relationships. "There's something missing. It's like, even when you were at your worst, Mom still loved you and supported you. You two were happy. I don't think I'll ever find that kind of love."

"That's just plain foolish," his dad told him. "I fell in love with your mom the minute I laid eyes on her. I felt so bad because there she was, grieving over her new husband, who she had to bury. And she had to do it alone. She had to be the one to choose where to bury him since he had no family to help her. I didn't tell her how I felt. Hell, I couldn't even show her. But, over time, I think your mom knew she wasn't getting rid of me. And, eventually, she somehow managed to fall in love with me too. But, you see, the way we both fell in love with each other was different. When we both knew it was love, we weren't willing to let it go. I am the luckiest man on Earth to have found someone like your mom." His dad's eyes sparkled as he recalled the events that led him to marry Chance's mom. "And you'll find happiness too. You'll know it when it happens. You just wait and see."

When asked if he felt like he could fall in love with Becca, Chance had looked away. "How can I fall in love with someone when I think I missed my chance at love?"

His dad took a sip of the sweet tea he was drinking before he asked him to elaborate.

"It's just, well, I think I fell in love already. But she didn't love me back," Chance said, lowering his voice, almost ashamed of himself for admitting he was in love with a woman who clearly didn't love him back. A woman who married another man. A woman who had to grieve the loss of her husband, who had died in such a traumatic way. The thought stung him like a tattoo.

While these thoughts floated around in his head, he still longed to have her back. To be near her. To kiss her one more time.

Knowing his dad wasn't one to pry with more questions but was deeply interested in building their relationship, Chance continued. He told him about Claire. How he met her the night his mom died. How he saw her again at Tyler's funeral, only to find out she'd become widowed. And then he told his dad that he'd found Claire's novel in his office the year before, as if the world was mocking him for his failed attempt at love with her.

"Well, there are only three things you can do then."

"What would those be?" Chance smirked, lifting his eyebrows.

"One," his dad said, sticking a finger into the air, "dump Becca and go find Claire."

"Two?" Chance asked, pursing his lips and tilting his head.

"Two, keep dating Becca. You'll fall in love with her, even though you clearly love someone else."

"Gee, thanks. What about three?" Chance asked, giving him a dirty look.

"Oh, there isn't a three." He laughed.

But it was also his dad he'd confided in when he ran into Claire at the small café. He would be lying if he hadn't wanted to find Claire the moment he was told he'd be traveling to St. Petersburg, but it happened so fast he didn't even know where to begin. The moment he saw Claire, he told his dad through text messages that he felt like fate was giving him another chance.

His dad responded with smiley emojis and three words. "Go get her!"

That was the last time he texted his dad. He had no idea that Chance had had the best night of his life. And he had no idea that he'd ruined it the same night. It was just like fate to play games on him.

Chance started to cry. The tears fell like boulders. "I wish I could talk to you. I wish you could hear me. I'm sorry it took me so long to come back home. I'm sorry we weren't closer growing up. I know I've never told you this, but you've been the best dad a man could ask for. You've taught me more about myself than I ever imagined. Thank you for your sobriety. Thank you for being strong for me when I needed it." Chance rambled on, not wanting to filter his thoughts or miss anything. He held on to his dad as if he might slip away like a boat floating away from its dock, and yet gentle enough, recognizing how fragile he had become over the last few days.

"And Claire. I wish you could meet Claire." Chance slowed down as his words shifted in topic. "There's something about her I can't shake. She's gorgeous, even more so after all these years. And she is kind and compassionate. There's a calm to her that I know you'd appreciate," he said as he recalled the way she pulled at his hand on the beach. Or the way she casually walked with him along the river walk. "I know you'd absolutely love her. But I'm pretty sure I blew it. I froze up, and I still haven't called her."

He bent his head and continued. "I'm sure you'd be disappointed in me right now too. Not only have I not reached out to her, but I had a few drinks tonight." Chance pulled at the collar of his shirt, suddenly feeling warm. He moved the hand that lay on his dad's bony and bruised hand and realized it wasn't him who was warm.

He placed his hand, palm up, on his dad's forehead and furrowed his brow when he realized his dad was burning up. His tears came to a sudden stop as he pressed the button for the nurse.

Chapter Thirty
Present

Chance

Two young nurses hurried his dad's stretcher out of the room to run some tests and to get another X-ray and CT scan after verifying his temperature had spiked. Chance felt like he couldn't catch a break as he watched the brunette make eye contact with the redhead. It was a knowing look, like they had seen this before but couldn't share details until Chance talked to the doctor.

Valerie rushed in with Joe close behind. His crutches hadn't slowed him down one bit. "What happened?" she asked, out of breath, a look of alarm on her face.

"I don't know. He was burning up. They took him up to CT." Chance sank back into the chair. "I'm worried. What happens if he doesn't wake up?" Chance didn't let himself cry this time. He was too tired and out of fuel.

"Are you hungry? I can go check the cafeteria for some food. Maybe some coffee?" Valerie asked.

"I'll take a coffee if they have any down there. Grab Chance one too." Joe said, leaning in to kiss Valerie on the cheek. Valerie pressed her lips together and then pulled a chair over for Joe to sit in.

For the first few minutes, they remained quiet, both feeling the weight of the room. And then Joe cleared his throat. "Valerie told me you saw Claire this weekend." While his sentence was a statement, it came out more like a question. Chance knew Joe was trying to start a conversation. And it was a conversation he wanted to have. He had a lot of questions for his friend, but Chance wasn't sure this was the right time for it.

"I know you two had an argument. I'm not here to give you a hard time. You have a lot going on, a lot of stress. I just wanted—"

"Why didn't you tell me you contacted Claire when I went to Okinawa?" Chance interrupted Joe, suddenly angry. "And why didn't you tell me you visited her when she was at Camp Pendleton? Or the fact that she changed her name twice and moved back to St. Petersburg a few years ago?" His face felt flushed. He felt exasperated and resentful toward Joe. "You kept in contact with her all these years, and you never said anything to me."

"Whoa, whoa, whoa. I have not kept in contact with her all these years. Let's get that out of the way first," Joe snapped back. "I knew she was in St. Petersburg, you're right. And I only found that out through Valerie."

Chance watched as Joe exhaled.

"I was put on as lead detective once you left the States. The Jacksonville Police Department felt it was necessary to have an outside perspective handling the case since they had to arrest their own cop. I couldn't tell you anything, you know that. And I'll be honest. I had no idea you'd want to know anything as it was. When you came home, you never spoke about it again. You never mentioned her name."

Chance dropped his head into his hands, resting his elbows on his knees. He knew Joe was right. He hadn't talked about Claire. But he thought about her all the time. He even tried looking for her before he found out she was living in New York City, before he knew her name was Romano.

Before the attack. The years following Tyler's death had been some of his darkest days. He was too hurt, too angry, too drunk, to say Claire's name aloud. And even when he began to get his shit together, he assumed he'd missed his greatest opportunity at love. She had been the so-called "girl that got away."

"I guess what I don't understand is, why did Valerie say it was your story to tell? She made it seem like she knew more but couldn't tell me."

Joe nodded, as if he knew exactly what Chance meant, even though Chance had no clue.

"I'm telling you this as a friend. Even though I'm retired, you do realize it's an ongoing investigation, right?"

Chance shook his head. He had no idea what Joe was referring to. An ongoing investigation? After all these years? He hadn't even thought about it. Hadn't considered the idea that they were still doing anything for a case that old, figured there was some statute of limitation or something.

Joe looked uncomfortable. He glanced out the door and then back at Chance. "What I'm about to tell you has to stay between us. Do you understand?"

"It's been more than two decades. What else can be happening?"

"A year after Claire's brother gave us their names, David Swift and Larry Richardson were convicted of first-degree murder, thanks to the plea deal Alex took. By the time he dropped their names, we had them hauled off in cuffs and behind bars. Like Alex, David was also a cop. He committed suicide the night he was convicted. He never gave us any information. Anything we found out was from Alex and Larry. Neither of them knew the fourth guy's name. He was the ringleader, the mastermind. It took us a long time to figure that out. But the guys had no idea back then. They thought they were all equal in their shenanigans. They were told by this fourth man that they were being hired to steal a few loose diamonds, along with some jewelry from a local jeweler in downtown Jacksonville. In turn, they'd receive a handsome payout. The women were just decoys. Larry put an ad in the paper for an escort at some of the nearby colleges, promising them a hefty wage just to dress up. Both Larry and Alex stand by their word that they had no intention of harming any of the women. They claimed that this fourth man got hostile, that the women got greedy and were stealing the diamonds.

"Anyway, the case went cold for a few years. We looked into every angle we could think of, but we never found this fourth man. Eventually, we started thinking there *was* no fourth man. It was just an evil manhunt they sent us on to divert attention away from them. Jacksonville wanted me to close the case, but I couldn't do it. I agreed to take a step back. To get off their toes. But having worked it for so long, I knew I was missing something. Last year, Larry was released. He'd served his full twenty years. The day he was released, I had him followed. I wanted to know where he was going, who he was going to see, who he was going to talk to. The missing diamonds and jewelry were another case, and I figured, if Larry was hiding anything, he would lead us right to it. Instead, someone else had the same idea. They beat us to it each time. Larry went to his sister's house in Oak Harbor. The next day, their house was ransacked. The day after that, Larry's sister found him with a syringe in his arm. He overdosed on fentanyl. His sister was a mess. She couldn't comprehend why he would do that to himself."

Chance listened as Joe talked, but he couldn't imagine how any of this pertained to Claire. He grew impatient waiting for the connection and finally spoke up.

"Can you cut to the chase? How does any of this involve Claire?"

Clearing his throat, Joe continued. "A month after Larry

died, Alex was severely beaten in prison. A few inmates held him down, while another one stabbed him with a makeshift knife, lacerating his liver as a result. The same inmate also tried to cut out his eye. It didn't work, but Alex had to get twenty-five stitches to fix his face. They also broke his nose and his arm. When Alex was questioned, he told the guards his sister was in danger."

Chance's eyes grew wide. His heart pulsed. "Danger?"

"Yeah. I got a call from the superintendent at the jail one night, telling me that Alex needed to talk to someone working his case. Now, imagine my surprise after all these years of staying silent. Now Alex wanted to talk. Obviously, I was shocked. I hadn't expected anything from his case to head my way. When I got the call, Valerie was with me, so naturally, I told her. It was then that Valerie told me about Claire. She told me how she found her novel in your office. That Claire was living in St. Pete. That you might not be over her."

"Why would Claire be in danger?" Chance asked, hyper-focused on the girl he loved.

"Alex told me that, since he was in so much debt, he took one of the diamonds for himself. When he knew things were going downhill, he hid one of the largest diamonds in Claire's belongings. When Claire left that night, he panicked. He searched her room for hours but couldn't find it. He figured, after all these years, either the police found it, or Moe found it."

"Moe?" Chance asked.

"The fourth guy. Alex said that's what they called him but doubted that was his real name. Alex also doubted Moe made any appearances at the jail. Said he was too smart to have his face on camera. Said he probably had someone else come in and convince the crooked inmates to rough him up. And that's when Alex cracked. He let it slip about Claire."

Chance stood up, not sure what to do. How to react to this information.

"How long ago was that? Have you been in contact with Claire since? Does she know?"

"It's been a few months. Right after, I called the St. Petersburg police and notified them. Then, well, that's when this happened," he said pointing to his leg.

Joe was the reason Valerie didn't go to St. Pete that weekend. She was the one who was supposed to be at the conference. But Joe's leg wasn't healing correctly, and he had to undergo a second surgery. So, Valerie stayed back to help him with recovery. A few months back, Joe was shot while on a morning run. There had been tons of people out that morning, and no one had any idea where the bullet had come from. Witnesses said they heard the pop one minute, and the next, there was blood all over the sidewalk. One man tore off his belt and tied it around Joe's thigh to help cut off the artery, which stopped the flow of blood. But the bullet still fractured his femur, causing Joe to be wheelchair bound for the last few months. The second surgery was already planned, but because of complications, Joe had to go into emergency surgery sooner than expected.

Joe was tough. But a bullet to the femur was enough to send him into retirement. He argued against it. Told his superiors he would bounce back stronger. He didn't want to retire. But no one was having any of that. They said it was his time and that he should take his time recovering and appreciate time home with his wife.

"So, Claire could still be in danger?" Chance asked frantically as he studied Joe's expression.

"Honestly, I don't know. It's been a few months, and I haven't heard anything yet. I do believe this Moe person is smart, and he might wait it out until the time is right. I also don't think he'll draw attention to himself by hurting her. My concern is her being in the wrong place at the wrong time."

Just then, the door creaked, and the doctor walked in with one of the nurses from earlier. Both Chance and Joe looked up at the same time.

Chance knew immediately from their body language what they were going to tell him.

Chapter Thirty-One
Present

Chance

"I'm sorry," Dr. Kim said in a low voice, looking straight at Chance. "Your father didn't make it out of CT."

Chance didn't respond. Instead, he stared, unable to take his eyes off the doctor's white lab coat. Looking at an object that was stationary was a coping mechanism for stress. By focusing on that one object, he could keep his anger at bay. Stop it from boiling over so that no one would become his target. He had practiced this for years, ever since he began his own treatment for PTSD. It allowed his emotions to stabilize, giving him time to process and think before he reacted.

"His X-rays showed that he had pneumonia, which is common in coma patients. But we also wanted to rule everything else out. So much can happen in such a short amount of time. Unfortunately, your father wasn't receiving enough oxygen in his bloodstream. Due to his DNR, we didn't resuscitate."

Just then, Valerie stepped in, holding two coffees. Everyone turned to look. At the silence, Valerie looked at Joe, who was already shaking his head. Tears began to fall on her face. Unable to catch them, she rushed to Joe, placing the Styrofoam cups on the table and burying her face into her husband.

"Can I see my dad?" Chance asked, ignoring everything else in the room.

When they wheeled his dad's bed back into the room, the nurses told Chance to take as much time as he needed. Joe and Valerie started to leave, to give Chance some time alone, but Chance asked them to stay. "I can't do this alone. Not again." He grabbed the chair Joe had been sitting in earlier and motioned him to come back.

Valerie, her face flushed and swollen from crying, helped him hobble back to the chair. When he sat down, Chance dragged another chair over. Valerie took a tissue from her purse and sank down next to him as she wiped at her nose.

Chance stood. Not a word was spoken. There was no more sound. No more beeping. With the door closed, they couldn't even hear the shuffle of feet in the hallway.

He was gone. His dad was gone.

Chapter Thirty-Two
Present

Claire

Claire stared at her phone for at least an hour as she lay in her bed, trying to fall asleep. Shadow curled up beside her, snoring, half his body covered up by an oversized blanket. On a normal night, Claire would readjust the dog or make him get down. But tonight, she didn't notice the noise. Instead, she petted Shadow's sleek black fur as she scrolled through the Instagram comments attached to the pictures of her and Chance, trying to tire herself from the long day. But that wasn't working. Instead, she found herself more alert than when she lay down, and it was all because of the comments the pictures were receiving.

There seemed to be a general consensus that Claire and this mystery man were the real deal. Her fans were overjoyed at the idea that Claire was living out her own love story. One comment read, *Don't let that one get away,* while another one said, *Now, he's a keeper.* Even her daughter commented on one of the pictures with a bunch of hearts, which made her smile.

Claire shifted under the covers and wondered what Chance was doing at that very moment. Was he trying to sleep too? Was he with his dad? Was it possible that he was thinking about her? Claire couldn't stop the questions from circling inside her head, and she hated herself for it. She was beginning to feel pathetic since Chance hadn't so much as sent a text. But she knew there was reason for it. She didn't know much about strokes, but from the little knowledge she did have, she knew they affected people to varying degrees. She prayed Chance's dad was one of the lucky ones.

She remembered his sullen expression when he received that heartbreaking phone call last night and felt a pit at the bottom of her stomach. It was the same expression he wore on the bus all those years ago when he shared the news of his mom's declining health. Why was it that they kept meeting under these awful circumstances? It felt as if the world was conspiring against them. Last night was the first night she had felt alive in years. And today? Today she felt as if she got suckered punched right in the gut, having been conned into a date with the least desirable man alive.

Still scrolling through the comments, one suddenly caught Claire's attention. *He needs you.* She raised an eyebrow, curious. The time stamp was just a handful of minutes ago, according to her watch. She clicked on the person who sent it, but it was a private account with very limited information. When she looked back at the comment, she noticed more comments were flooding in underneath. *Yeah, he really needs you, in bed,* one person replied, while the next few followed suit with *in the car, on the beach,* and her favorite, *naked.*

That one made her laugh out loud, which woke up Shadow. "Okay, Okay. I'm shutting it off now," she said to her sleepy pooch. And she did.

Before she closed her eyes, she held out her phone in the darkness to check her text messages one more time. Nothing. Maybe she should text him? Maybe he was still too busy to reach out to her. If anything, she wanted to check in with him to see how his dad was doing. That's what people did, right? She hated the way she felt when she questioned her actions because she hated the idea of rejection. *What happens if he doesn't respond? Just do it,* she told herself. *Just get it over with.* So, she finally did. She sent a straightforward text.

Claire: *I've been thinking of you and your dad today. I hope you're both doing okay. Call or text me when you get a chance.*

And then she fell asleep.

The next morning, when Claire woke up, she temporarily forgot about her text message to Chance. She knew she should get out of bed and head over to the café to start work, but she had zero motivation. She didn't want to think about writing today. But, when Shadow whined at the foot of her bed, indicating it was well beyond potty time, she finally pulled herself out from under the covers. "Okay, let's go," she said, more to herself than her dog.

Knowing she was already running behind, she made herself a cup of coffee for the road. Then, like a balloon bursting in midair, the recollection of words transcribed into her phone came flooding back to her. She rushed back into her bedroom and seized her phone. *Great. It's dead.* She was searching for her charger when the doorbell rang.

Still in her oversized black-and-red-striped pajama bottoms and black tank top, she looked out the window to see Brittany standing alone on her front porch. "Brittany. Why are you here so early? Is everything okay?" she asked after opening the front door, the sun almost blinding her.

"Oh, Claire, I'm a terrible friend," Brittany said, maneuvering herself into Claire's house without being invited in. Her hair was in hot pink curlers, something Claire hadn't seen since her mom was alive. And she wore a matching flannel top-and-bottom pajama set, something much too hot to wear in Florida during any time of year.

"What do you mean?" Claire was confused. It wasn't like Brittany to come over so early in the morning. Unannounced, yes. But never before noon. Brittany was old school and always made sure she was dressed, with hair and makeup done, before she left her house, even if it was to run out to fill up her car with gas.

Brittany sank into Claire's sofa, sighing with dramatic effect. "Do you have any coffee?"

"Sure, let me go grab you a cup. I just made it." Claire walked back to the kitchen, quickly plugging her phone into the charger before she poured a fresh cup of coffee for Brittany.

Placing the mug on the table in front of her, Claire asked again, "What's going on?"

Brittany clutched the mug tightly in one hand before realizing how hot it was and quickly set it back down. "Okay, Joshua told me I was being a little too pushy yesterday at the grocery store. He said you weren't interested in dating, let alone dating Chad. He insists I need to stop pushing Chad on you. But, well, Chad is such a sweetheart. He's not just my nephew, he's my godson, you know that. I want him to be happy too. And I think you both would make an adorable couple."

Upon hearing Brit's words, Claire knew what was happening. Brittany was laying a guilt trip on her. She knew how to push and what to say before she would cave.

"Poor Chad hasn't been very successful with the ladies, and he isn't getting any younger. He keeps meeting the wrong types of girls. And you, well, you have it together. You'd be so great for him. And if it didn't work out for you two, at least he could see what the right type of girl is. Truth be told, sometimes I wonder if he is all there in the head, but he deserves love. Did you know he lost his job? They wanted someone with more experience. He just told me last night."

Claire cringed when she heard Brit acknowledge her nephew's flawed behavior. But what could she say? She felt bad. Brittany meant well. What was the worst that could happen? Maybe dinner wasn't a terrible idea. They could all eat quickly and then be on their way.

She hesitated as Brittany sat, waiting in anticipation for a response. "You aren't a terrible friend, Brit. I can't promise anything. We can still have dinner tonight, but—"

"Oh, I knew Joshua was just being silly. See, I told him you'd still love to have dinner tonight. I was worried all night over nothing. Joshua insisted I cancel the whole thing. Boy, do I feel foolish now."

Grabbing the coffee mug, Brit stood up and walked toward the door. "I knew you'd come around about Chad, but I was beginning to worry that the man you were seeing was someone serious. It wasn't like you to have male company that often. From the looks of it, though, I think he might be stalking you. You should keep your doors locked." She opened the door and nodded toward the mug. "All right, I'll see you tonight. I'll bring the cup back with me when I come back for dinner. Oh, and wear something nice, would you?" she asked, giving Claire the eye, telling her she wasn't pleased with what she had on now, even though it was the morning.

Claire squinted and pursed her lips, confused. How did she manage to get herself back into a situation she could have climbed out of? Only Brittany would make something so simple sound so inappropriate. Who called it "male company" nowadays? And Chance came by *one* night, not "often" as Brit claimed. And stalking? Chance was over six hundred miles away. It was highly unlikely he was stalking her, especially since he hadn't even given her as much as a reply text.

Text! Claire ran to the kitchen after Brittany had headed back to her own house. Maybe Chance had texted her. She touched the screen, illuminating the background. No new messages. That meant nothing from Chance. She felt defeated. Tonight would be a long, disastrous night.

After Claire let Shadow back inside, she went upstairs and

took a quick shower. When she finished, she combed her wet hair with her fingers and pulled it back into a tight ponytail. Quickly grabbing her bag, purse, and car keys, Claire ran out the door, slamming it behind her, but gasped when her feet hit the porch.

The black truck was across the street again. And the man in the driver's seat looked like he was staring at her, though she couldn't make out any of his features. She clasped the handle to the door, waiting to head back inside, but just as she began to twist it, the truck peeled away from the curb. Her heartbeat ran wild. Who was that? Was he watching her? Or was it just a coincidence?

Chapter Thirty-Three
Present

Claire

The afternoon was sizzling, even by Florida standards. Sitting at her usual table at the café, Claire noticed a few squirrels quarreling in the bushes. One leaped out and knocked over an abandoned plastic cup that still had remnants of water in it from ice cubes that had long since melted away. Another squirrel popped its head out and ran over as they both tried to drink the small puddle underneath their tiny little feet. Claire laughed to herself, amused at the small creatures. It sure was hot. Sweat was dripping down her neck and back, soaking the light tank top she wore.

Standing up to stretch, Claire decided to head inside to buy another water. While she needed caffeine, she also knew staying hydrated was more important on a day like this. It reminded her of her Marine Corps days. They called it a Black Flag, indicating that it was too hot to conduct any kind of physical fitness outdoors, citing safety and hydration were more important. The potential for marines to fall out of a run, pass out, and hurt themselves was too high to wage the risk.

Claire smiled to herself, remembering her days in the Marine Corps. Remembering her friends she still stayed connected with, as well as those she didn't. She remembered

Tyler and his smile. It was funny how one thing could make you remember so much.

Walking into the café, the cool air hit her skin and gave her goosebumps.

"Why don't you work inside today?" Sasha asked, wiping the counters with her washcloth.

"It might be hot, but there's something about the salt in the air that helps me focus."

"You sure it ain't the coffee?" Sasha laughed.

The bell on the door jingled, and both Sasha and Claire looked up. Claire's heart skipped a beat, hoping to see Chance's face. She knew it was ridiculous to think Chance would come back, especially since he hadn't returned her text. But now, standing in the café where she and Chance both stood together just two days before, Claire couldn't help but hold out hope.

When a tall, older gentleman walked in wearing a baseball cap, Claire turned back to Sasha, feeling slightly disappointed. "Can I get another water bottle?"

"Sure, hun," she said, handing her an ice-cold water.

When Claire turned to leave, she was startled to see the older man had inched closer to her. She gasped out of surprise, as her face was almost in his chest.

"I'm sorry," she said out of habit, trying to be polite for something she was sure wasn't even her fault. She found it uncomfortable when people didn't give others their personal space and couldn't recognize that everyone had a right to their own little bubble.

He took a step back, but when she looked up, she caught his eye behind his sunglasses. There was something familiar about him. She'd seen him before. Something about his eyes. His face. His physical presence. For a solid second, she stood there without moving, not quite being able to put her finger on it.

"No problem," he said in a monotone voice, both deep and raspy.

When he looked away, she shrugged it off. The older she got, the more people looked familiar. She could hear her daughter now. "You think you know everyone!" She smiled and walked back outside. "Thanks for the water, Sasha."

Later that afternoon, after Claire enhanced her knowledge on the world of veterinarians, a topic central to her newest endeavor, she decided it was time to pack it up and head home. She knew she couldn't push off the inevitable. Tonight would happen whether she liked it or not. She placed her laptop inside the bag first and then shoved the power cord on top. After her notebook and pens were stored away, she stood up to look for her phone. When she couldn't locate it, she began to panic. Her phone was her lifeline. Everything was on it.

She bent down and looked under her chair. Then she retraced her steps from earlier, looking inside the café. She even asked Sasha if she'd seen it. When Sasha shook her head, she asked if she could call her phone for her. Maybe she would hear it somewhere. But no such luck.

"It went straight to voice mail," Sasha said with a sympathetic tone. "Did you leave it in your car? Check under your seat," she suggested, feeling hopeful.

But Claire knew that wasn't possible. She had it out earlier. She and Tessa had been texting about tonight. The last message she remembered was the crying emoji she sent in response to Tessa asking if she needed an emergency getaway. She sent the yellow emoji with tears flooding out of its eyes as a way to express how sad she was that she couldn't escape her own house. *Damn,* she thought.

Of course, on the one night she needed her phone the most, she couldn't find it.

Chapter Thirty-Four

Present

Chance

Chance woke up the next morning at his dad's house. It had been so late when they left the hospital that he didn't want Valerie and Joe to drive across town just to drop him off at his apartment. On any other day, he would have called an Uber to spare anyone the trouble. But last night, he found solace in the idea of going to his dad's house.

It hadn't dawned on him until he dragged himself out of bed that he'd left his phone on the desk at his apartment. *Crap.* He needed his phone to cancel his appointments for the day. Or did he? Remembering that his dad had a computer in the guest bedroom, Chance walked down the hall and pushed open the door. Behind it lay boxes of old photo albums and files. Chance reached down for the closest album and lifted the cover. There were baby pictures of him tucked inside a filmy cover with worn yellow edging. His mom held him in one picture. Her long brown hair wrapped around her face, dangling in front of him as a toddler. Something he hadn't remembered. As a nurse, she typically had it pulled back and away from her face. She was beautiful. He could see the resemblance between them now that he was older. They shared the same smile, the same large oval eyes.

He lifted the page carefully. More pictures came into view. His dad held his hand as a small boy, waving at the camera. His dad with a ball in his hand and Chance with a bat, standing in a baseball dugout. His dad carrying him on his shoulders while he ate an ice cream cone at a carnival. A few tears formed at the corners of his eyes. Remembering the good moments had been so difficult for Chance as he grew up. His memory latched on to anything negative he could find, and he hated himself for it. As a psychologist, he knew it wasn't his fault. But the man who just lost his father couldn't consolidate the truth.

Chance placed the worn photo album on the desk, promising to go back to it later. Turning on the computer, he wasn't the least bit surprised to see he didn't need a password. His dad was predictable. As he began to open a web browser, he noticed there was already one minimized at the bottom of the screen. He clicked on it. Ancestry.com popped open and along with it a message:

Dear Jeremy,

I am sorry to hear that you've been having a tough time locating any blood-related relatives for your son. Unfortunately, at this time, we have no matches. This isn't to say someone might not match him in the future. Our data is based on people who have provided their DNA and are currently in our database. We wish you and your son the best of luck on your search.

It was signed by the chief communications director.

Chance couldn't believe his eyes. His dad had reached out to Ancestry.com. He hadn't told his dad that he, too, had reached out, that he'd provided his swab of skin cells years ago. He had believed that telling his dad, now, after all these years, would have felt like he was betraying him. He had worked so hard at building their relationship that he felt guilty about the DNA test. It was part of the reason he couldn't bring himself to read the message that sat unopened for so long on his own computer. And now, knowing he had zero blood relatives, he felt more alone than he did before. But his dad must have felt guilt, too, or he would never have reached out to Ancestry.com, and that made Chance's heart feel heavy.

He cried, tears spilling from his face. His chest heaved as he wiped his eyes with the back of his hand. He missed his old man. He missed his mom. How would he get through the next few days? The next few weeks? He had no family now. None. Joe and Valerie were the closest he had to family.

As the tears continued to fall from his face and land on his arm and the desk, Chance moved the paper under his elbow. It was a yellow sticky note. It read *One day at a time.* It was written by his dad, probably meant for his own sobriety. A way to remind himself to stay sober one day at a time. And then Chance looked back up and noticed another sticky note attached to the edge of the computer screen: *Don't look back. Only forward.* And then another on the printer: *I'm proud of you.*

Chance looked at them again, blowing out slow steady breaths. It was almost as if his dad had chosen these words to talk to him right now. As if he knew these words would help bring Chance comfort. And they did. But there was absolutely no way his dad had written them with the intention of Chance seeing them. No way he wrote them for Chance. Or had he?

No, he told himself. His dad wrote them for himself. It was a way for him to stay positive. He had started writing little Post-it notes to himself once he became sober and continued to do it over the years. Chance vaguely recalled the idea coming from another AA member. As a therapist, he knew how important it was to write these affirmations on paper.

There was something about using your hand to physically write them that caused one to develop a stronger conceptual understanding of the words. But Chance had never really read the words through his own lens. They had always been words his dad had chosen.

Now, those little sticky notes, and the words they presented, resounded in Chance's soul, and he felt like his dad was with him. Right there. In that moment.

If I had one more day with my dad, what would I say to him? What would he say to me? Chance sat in silence for a few moments, thinking about the last few days. The last time he'd seen his dad was before he left for the conference. They'd talked about Claire. Talked about his mom. Discussed how his dad fell in love with his mom. How Chance was more like him than he wanted to admit.

"Go get her," he had told Chance, smiling, encouraging him to rekindle the spark he and Claire once had. And, suddenly, Chance knew he'd say it again, a million times, if he was still here. He'd tell Chance he was a fool for leaving Claire. He'd tell him to go get her.

Pushing the chair out from the desk, Chance stood. He knew what he had to do. What he had to do all along.

Chapter Thirty-Five
Present

Claire

The doorbell rang exactly at seven o'clock. Not a minute sooner. Not a minute later. Brittany walked in first, carrying a glass dish with foil on top, filled to the brim with chicken, and dressed in an oversized pink sundress with hair curled tight. Joshua followed, carrying a pot of noodles, wearing khakis and a white polo shirt.

"Hi, Claire, sweetie!" Brittany sang out as she sauntered in, bringing her dish to the kitchen counter. "Do you have a potholder I can stick underneath this? It's still hot."

"Yeah, over here." Claire reached for the silicone potholders she kept in the drawer next to the stove. She pulled an extra one out for Joshua's pot of noodles and placed it on the table.

"Do be a dear," Brit said, facing Joshua. "Can you run down and grab the French bread I left on the table? We can't eat without bread."

"I'll be back in a few minutes," he grumbled, not looking pleased.

Behind him was Chad. Claire hadn't noticed at first. He was being quiet, which wasn't like him. Typically, Chad made an appearance and was just as loud as Brittany.

"Hi, Claire. You have a lovely house. I can't believe I haven't seen it before."

Claire eyed Chad. She felt a twinge of guilt creeping up inside her chest. She could see the fear in his eyes. The look of "I'm in over my head" darted across his face. He, like Joshua, had on khaki shorts and a polo, but he hadn't bothered to tuck his in, at least not until he made eye contact with Claire. On instinct, Chad began shoving his shirt down his pants, making Claire feel all sorts of awkward as his hands reached down farther than they needed to go.

"Yes, Claire, your house is very clean," Brittany said, joining the conversation but looking displeased with her aesthetics. "Why don't you two have a seat on the couch, and I'll set the table. Do you have any wine or beer?" she asked, looking impatient.

"Yeah, I have some wine on the table already." Claire began walking toward the kitchen to help, but Brittany told her to go sit back down. That she had it all under control. "Tonight is about you and Chad. Sit next to him," she added, pointing her nose in the direction of the loveseat Chad had already claimed, his body on both cushions.

Claire winced, her insides screaming as she squeezed in next to Chad and the armrest. She could see the sweat already beginning to form around his temples and the back of his neck.

Once Brittany was out of sight, Chad began biting his fingernails. Turning to face Claire, he apologized. "Sorry, bad habit." The words were tiny as he gritted his teeth with his finger between his front incisors.

She responded with a fake smile and a nod of the head. She winced again as he spit the nail pieces from his mouth, not wanting to imagine where the nail clippings would land.

She could get through this, she thought. *Just keep that pretend smile on your face, and it will all be over before you know it.* She had to give herself a pep talk. It was the only way she'd get through the night. That and a few glasses of Cabernet Sauvignon.

There was a quick rap on the door. Claire knew it was Joshua and figured he could let himself back in, but she couldn't resist the urge to get up and open the door to help him. It gave her an excuse to stand up and gather herself.

"Hey, where's your TV?" Chad asked as Joshua walked back in with the loaf of bread.

"I'm sorry. I don't have one down here. I don't really watch much TV," she replied. "You can have a seat anywhere, I'll go bring this to the kitchen," she said, turning her attention to Joshua.

"For real? Like, what do you do all day?" A look of stunned disbelief crossed Chad's face.

"I work. I read. I go for walks with Shadow."

And then, as if Shadow heard his name being called, he scratched at the back door to be let inside. Claire had almost forgotten about him. Shadow would stay out all night if it were up to him. He loved it out there.

"I'll be right back; I should go give this to Brittany and let my dog inside."

"You have a dog?" Chad's face morphed from stunned to disgust. "I'm not a super huge fan of dogs, Uncle Josh," he said, scrunching his nose.

Claire heard Chad complaining as she left the room. He sounded like Molly when she was five years old. She remembered Molly complaining about peanut butter and jelly sandwiches the same way Chad was complaining about the dog right now. "But, Mom, I don't like this stuff," she'd whined. The difference, though, was that Chad was a grown adult and Molly had been a kid.

Just get through this. You can do it. Almost halfway there.

Claire laid the bread on the kitchen table as Brittany poured the wine into four glass goblets.

"Looks like we're ready to eat," Brittany called out to the boys.

Claire was about to slide the back door open for Shadow when Brittany placed her hand on top of hers. "Just don't mention Chad's job tonight. That's a touchy subject. Oh, and don't ask how today was. He rear-ended an elderly couple, and he feels terrible that he fled the scene before the cops arrived. He doesn't have insurance. They dropped him the last time he got into an accident."

It took a few moments for Claire to register the words, realizing that Brittany was being serious. She nodded, and Brittany let go of her hand, allowing her to open the door for Shadow. Before the door was fully open, the doorbell rang. Shadow squeezed through the small opening and made a mad dash for the living room.

"Are you expecting anybody tonight?" Brittany asked, a frown forming at her lips.

Meanwhile, Shadow had torn his way to Chad, his attack stance prominent, growling, eyes glowing.

"No," Claire said, making her way down the hall to the front door, curious who was there. "Shadow, heel," she called out before turning the handle to open the door.

Shadow sat down at Chad's feet but continued to growl, glaring up at him.

"Somebody get this dog away from me!" Chad whined, but Claire could barely hear him.

She opened the door. "Tessa, what are you doing here?" she asked as her friend stepped inside.

"You didn't really think I'd let you do this alone, now did you?" she whispered softly in her ear, handing her a bottle of Pinot Noir. Her jet-black hair swept across her bare back as she strutted her way into the living room, making a beeline for the couch.

Claire followed, not quite sure if she should be thankful for Tessa's presence or not. On the one hand, Tessa would be a great distraction. She would take away the awkwardness, and she might actually be able to have some good conversation. On the other hand, she knew Brittany would be furious, which could turn the night upside down.

"Shadow, what's wrong, boy?" Tessa asked, reaching down to let him sniff her hand. Her black, strapless romper lowered ever so slightly, revealing some of Tessa's cleavage.

Chad looked away, appearing embarrassed at the revelation of her skin.

Tessa! Claire thought, amused. Tessa was teasing Chad. But she knew Tessa better than that. She wasn't doing it to embarrass Chad. She was doing it for Brittany's sake. Brittany despised women who bared too much skin. She called them slutty.

Shadow stopped growling almost instantly and lay down on his back, allowing Tessa to rub his belly.

"That's a good boy," Tessa said in her best dog voice.

Claire laughed. Leave it to Tessa to intervene. But her laughter stopped short when she noticed Brittany glaring at Tessa from the kitchen. *Crap. Crap, crap, crap,* she thought. *This is bad. Real bad.*

"Is there enough to make another plate? Tessa drove all this way. I'd hate to send her home," Claire asked Brittany politely, trying to deescalate the situation.

"There's plenty," Joshua responded, coming into the kitchen, placing his hands on Brittany's shoulders. "Right?" The look they shared made Claire uncomfortable.

Brittany frowned. "Yes, I suppose there is enough. We should go eat before it gets cold."

The five of them sat around Claire's kitchen table. None

of them seemed to be enjoying themselves, at least none of them aside from Tessa. Claire saw she was getting a kick out of her surprise visit.

"So, are you two still running?" Tessa asked Brittany and Joshua, glancing up at them between bites of her chicken. Tessa was great at small talk.

"Yes, we meet the group every Sunday and Wednesday morning," Brittany said, lifting her chin as if that was one of her proudest accomplishments. She took a sip from her glass and set it back down on the table. And then she twirled her noodles around her fork, lifting enough to stuff her mouth as Tessa directed her next question toward Chad.

"And you, Chad? What's new with you? How's your job?"

"Well, how's your job, Tessa? Aren't you the nosy one today," Brittany said more as a statement than a question, almost spitting noodles back onto her plate.

Tessa hadn't known not to ask about Chad's job. "Did I say something wrong?" She looked from Claire to Brittany and then from Joshua to Chad, her eyes puzzled.

"Chad, dear, sit up straight," Brittany yipped, switching gears. "You should really put your napkin in your lap in case you spill something." She grabbed a napkin and began to put it in Chad's lap. In doing this, she knocked over her glass, spilling red wine on the table, which dripped onto the floor and onto Chad's lap.

"Oh, this is just great. I can't believe—" Brittany began before being cut off by Joshua.

"Oh, just stop already! He is a grown-ass man. Let the poor guy take care of himself." Joshua shot up from his seat, throwing his own napkin onto the table. "This is getting ridiculous. He doesn't want to be here. Haven't you noticed? Haven't you asked what he wants? And what about Claire? Have you actually apologized to her? Did she want this dinner?"

The room fell silent. Claire had never seen Joshua stand up to Brittany before. He'd never yelled, let alone raised his voice.

"Well, I…"

"This has to stop. I can't take it anymore. If you don't stop, I want a divorce."

All of their eyes grew wide. Divorce? Brittany's mouth dropped. But before anyone could say another word, the doorbell rang. Again.

"Mom?" Molly's voice rang out from down the hall.

Claire stood, thankful for a distraction. "In the kitchen," she yelled. She tore a handful of paper towels off the roll and quickly began wiping whatever she could from the table and working her way to the floor, careful to avoid eye contact with anyone.

"Oh, I didn't realize you had company," Molly said, surprised, as she stepped into the kitchen.

Tessa stood and straightened her romper before giving Molly a hug. "Hi, sweetie. I feel like I haven't seen you in ages. Your mom tells me you're dancing at the Straz Center."

"Yeah, we just finished up with *Cinderella*. We had auditions tonight for the *Sound of Music*. That's actually why I'm here. I've been trying to call you all afternoon, but your phone keeps going to voice mail," she said to Claire, clearly concerned.

"Oh, I lost it earlier at the café while I was working. I have no idea where it is." She stood up, crossed to the garbage can, and tossed the paper towels inside before walking over to Molly for a hug. "How'd it go?"

"Awful. I'm pretty sure I bombed it. It was seriously the worst audition I've ever done. I mean, I went left when I was supposed to go right. And I did that every single time. They must have called me out there four times, and I just couldn't get it together," she said, leaning her head into her mom's shoulder.

"I'm sure you did better than you think. But, in case you didn't, you know you can always audition anywhere else. There is no reason you can't spread your wings." Claire was proud of her daughter. Molly was independent and strong-willed, always working hard at her dreams to make them come true. And she knew Molly had come to realize that every setback was actually a learning experience, a chance for growth.

"I'm sorry, Claire, I think it's time for us to go." Joshua stood and pushed his chair in. Then he looked at Chad, his eyes narrowing in on him as if speaking with his eyes.

"I'm sorry, too, Claire. I should have told Aunt Brittany that I didn't want to come tonight. It's just, well, sometimes it can be hard to say no to her." His head hung low, as if ashamed of himself for not being able to speak up. But Claire understood. It was the same reason she'd agreed to the dinner too. Brittany was a force to be reckoned with, and it took guts to stand your ground around her.

"What do you mean you didn't want to come to dinner?" Brittany demanded, looking bewildered at what was happening. "You told me that you always wondered what it would be like to marry Claire. I was just trying to help navigate that so it might even be a possibility."

It was Chad's turn to look surprised. "Marry Claire? I said I always wondered what *Mary* did at *Claire's*! You know, the girl who works at the mall? I've wanted to ask her out for the past year." He stood up and shoved his seat into the table so hard the glasses shook. "I'm going to ask her out."

Claire smiled as she watched Chad puff out his chest, feeling more confident in himself. Together, he and Joshua wiped their dishes into the trash and gathered their belongings.

Molly scooted to the side to let Joshua and Chad walk by as they headed for the front door.

"It was nice seeing you, Molly." Joshua nodded his head. And then he was gone.

"I'll come back tomorrow for my dishes. I honestly don't know what came over those two," Brittany said, not too far behind the boys. But once she was on the porch, her expression turned to confusion. She turned back to look at Claire, who was ready to close the door behind her. "Are you still seeing that boy? The one from the picture?" she asked suspiciously.

"No. I was never really seeing him. It's a long story," Claire responded, feeling defeated. She was trying to forget about Chance, but it was no use. In every instance, she felt like she was being reminded of him. And, without her phone to confirm or deny if he was thinking about her, too, she felt glum.

"Well, like I said, I think he's stalking you then. That truck out there. He keeps coming by every day. You should be honest with him and tell him you aren't interested. Or get a restraining order on him. Something." And, with that, she walked down the stairs and chased after Joshua.

Claire looked across the street. That truck *again!* Her body went rigid, and she sucked in a deep breath before slowly releasing it. Nobody seemed to be in the truck, but she was too nervous to walk over there. She looked to the right and then to the left. Nobody was outside. Nobody was around at all. It had to be a mistake. That truck must belong to somebody around here. But as she closed the door behind her, there was a part of her that felt uncomfortable. A part of her that felt like she was being watched.

Chapter Thirty-Six
Present

Chance

She isn't answering. Why isn't she answering? Chance dialed Claire's number for the fourth time. He paced his room, thinking about Claire's text message from last night. He hadn't realized there was a message from her until now. Not until he saw his phone sitting on his desk where he had left it. He wanted to talk to her. To hear her voice. To apologize for his silence in the car the night she dropped him off at his hotel. For everything. But her phone was going straight to voice mail.

He knew what he had to do. He couldn't wait any longer. He knew he should call Valerie and Joe, but he didn't have time. He checked the flights leaving Asheville Regional Airport and found one that was flying straight into Clearwater/St. Petersburg in just over an hour. If he hurried, he'd make it in time.

His fingers worked their magic, and he had a boarding pass in less than two minutes. Then he booked an Uber to drive him to the airport. His clothes were packed tightly into a small black duffel.

Trying to call Claire one last time, Chance dialed her number, but when it went to voice mail again, he shut off his lights and walked out his door.

Chapter Thirty-Seven
Present

Claire

Molly and Tessa helped Claire clean up as they talked about what happened that night, laughing as they recalled Brittany's expression when Joshua finally confronted her. None of them thought they would really divorce, but the idea was interesting. Claire liked them both. She really did, even if Brittany was a bit over the top. And she hoped they could work out their problems. She knew it would be hard for Brittany, but she had no doubt she'd put forth the effort to save her marriage, especially because Joshua was such a good man. She was beginning to envy what they had. The thought of a man supporting her every last move sent a shiver through her body. In her mind, it wasn't just any man. This man happened to have Chance's face. His dark brown hair. His muscular arms. And his rock-hard abs. She blushed as Tessa brought her back down to reality.

"Hey, did you notice the comments on your mom's picture last night?" she asked Molly, snuggling onto the couch with her glass of wine.

"Which ones? There're so many. I still can't believe that was you," Molly joined in, sitting across from Tessa in the oversized plush chair.

"Why? Because your mom is incapable of kissing a man? Having a great night? Living a little bit on the edge?" Claire laughed as she took a seat next to Tessa where there was more room. "You do know, I can live on the edge. I can be fun."

Tessa was scrolling through her phone, clicking away, when she suddenly gasped.

"What? What is it?" Claire asked, alarm in her voice.

"You'll never believe who messaged me." Tessa shared a look with Molly. They knew something she didn't.

"Who? What are you two up to?" she asked, feeling the warmth of the locket along her neck.

"So, did you see the comment that sparked like a hundred other comments, 'He needs you?'" When Claire nodded in acknowledgment, Tessa continued. "Well, I did some digging and found out that user was from Asheville, like your *friend,* Chance." She emphasized the word "friend" and looked at Claire as she said it. "I added her as a friend and saw pictures of your hottie. My first thought was that he was dating this woman, but then I saw her with some other man. I reached out to her and asked what she meant by her comment. I told her I was your friend and, well, she messaged me back."

Just as quickly as Tessa's smile appeared, it disappeared when she reread the message. Claire could tell it wasn't good news. In any other moment, she would have chastised her friend for reaching out to a stranger about a man she longed for. But her curiosity was stronger than her anger, and so she asked, "What does it say?"

Molly came over and joined them on the couch, sitting on the armrest closest to Claire as Tessa began to read.

Valerie: *Hi, Tessa, thank you for reaching out. Chance is a close friend of mine, and I consider him my family. My husband and I live next door to his dad. I was the one to call Chance the night this picture was taken. His dad had just had a stroke. I hadn't realized Chance reconnected with Claire. Anyhow, Chance's dad took a turn for the worse, and Chance is taking it really hard. He feels everything deeply, and while he is always the one to put a smile on everyone else's face before his own, he could really use some support right about now. I know he loves Claire. He's never not loved her; I can see that now. If you can somehow pass this message on to Claire, I would appreciate it.*

After Tessa finished reading, the three of them went silent. Claire shifted in her seat, knowing they were waiting for her to say something. To respond. But what would she say? Love was such a strong word. And this wasn't a movie. It wasn't one of her novels. People just didn't fall in love this way. Did they? She wanted to believe real life could have happily ever afters, but she didn't. She was a cynic. Dreadful things were around every corner. Her parents had died. Her stepbrother was in jail. Molly's dad died. Hell, he died trying to save people. The world was against her.

"Well?" Molly said, finally breaking the silence. "Are you going to explain? You made it sound like it wasn't going to work out between you two, but this sounds like there was a legitimate reason he had to leave."

"He lives in North Carolina. I'd be fooling myself to believe it would work out," she said, beginning to feel emotional at the thought of Chance's dad at the hospital. She thought about the unanswered text message, and now she didn't know what to believe. Did Chance just overlook it? He must have been too busy. But he didn't say anything in the car when she drove him back to his hotel. She could have supported him then. She could have reached out for his hand. Told him she was there for him. But she didn't. She was just as much at fault. And now she felt like crap because he needed her.

Tessa put her phone down and turned to Claire. "Who said it has to work out? You're allowed to have fun. You're allowed to date. If it works, it works. If it doesn't, it doesn't."

"Yeah, don't you always say, 'What will be, will be?' This isn't over. Fate hasn't sealed the deal. Nothing says you two won't work out. Mom, a total stranger is telling you this man is in love with you. That must mean something. And you deserve to be happy." Molly rested a hand on her mom's shoulder.

A tear rolled down Claire's cheek, and a lump formed in her throat. She hadn't expected her daughter to be so supportive.

"What do I do?" she asked, surprising herself with her own words.

"First of all, you call him and then—" Tessa began, but Claire interrupted.

"I texted him last night. He hasn't responded. But maybe he has. I don't know. I lost my phone, and his phone number is saved in it. I don't know how to get hold of him."

"Mom, you can track your phone on the computer, you know that, right? Find out where you last had it." Molly got up and walked to her office to retrieve Claire's laptop, handing it to her when she returned.

"I already know I lost it at the café. I had it while I was there, and then it went missing. It won't show up where it's at now because it's dead." But as soon as Claire finished talking, her mouth dropped open.

"What is it?" Both Tessa and Molly asked at the same time.

Claire turned the laptop around, making the screen visible to them. "It last pinged out front, two hours ago."

"Did you maybe drop it when you got home today?" Tessa asked, standing up and walking toward the front door.

Claire and Molly followed Tessa. She opened the door, and they all looked outside. While Tessa and Molly searched the ground, Claire's eyes immediately locked in on the black truck across the street. The same truck that was parked there earlier. The same truck she'd seen all week.

A wave of nerves rolled through her body, but adrenaline forced her feet to move.

"Where are you going? Mom?" Molly yelled as Claire continued to walk down the sidewalk and into the street, ignoring her. Cupping her hands to the window, Claire peered inside the dark vehicle. Her eyes shot around the front seat, hoping to find something, anything. She was about to turn around and give up and then...there it was. Her phone. Her unmistakable camouflage Marine Corps phone case. Sitting right there on the passenger seat.

What the hell? Whose truck is this? Why is my phone in there?

"Hey! It's in here!" Claire shouted, waving them over.

"Whose truck is that?" Molly asked, just as curious as Claire.

"I don't know. I thought maybe Kelsey invited someone to stay at her house while she was on vacation, but no one's there." Claire pointed to the house in front of her. And then she remembered what Brittany said. Something about someone stalking her. She'd seen the truck too.

Suddenly, Claire felt chills running down her spine. She scanned the quiet road. The dim street lights cast eerie shadows that bounced across the trees. Claire wanted nothing more than to get everyone in the house. Her throat tightened as her heart picked up speed.

"We need to get inside," she demanded, pressing her hand to each of their backs. "Quick."

"What's going on? Claire?" Tessa asked, confused.

"Mom, you're scaring me," Molly added, but followed Claire's orders.

They ran quickly and were up the stairs within seconds. Tessa reached for the handle and opened the door first. Molly was right behind.

Claire was about to lay her hand on the porch railing when she felt a sharp pain in her shoulder. And then the world faded around her.

Chapter Thirty-Eight
Present

Chance

After landing, Chance tried calling Claire one more time. The plane hadn't even finished taxing to the terminal, but he had grown impatient while in the air. He hoped her phone was back on. That she would answer this time. He'd apologize. He'd tell her he was on his way to see her.

He went to his call list and clicked her name. Bringing the phone to his ear, he waited a few seconds for the call to connect. His heart began to beat faster. His stomach tightened. And his hand became sweaty.

But the call never went through. *Voice mail. Damn.* He knew he was nervous, but he hadn't expected these feelings to wash over him. But that's what love was. It was your brain releasing prominent levels of dopamine, which caused your body to react differently than it would normally.

He hung up, feeling disappointed. Why was it still going to voice mail? Still nervous, he decided to send her a text in hopes she'd charge her phone before he tried calling her again.

Chance: *Hi, Claire. I got your message. I'm sorry I'm just now responding. I was at the hospital and left my phone at home. Call me when you get this.*

He clicked Send and waited for it to register "delivered," but that never happened. It wouldn't, since it was off.

Chance's stomach continued to twist, and he tightened his lips. This was his fault. He shouldn't have waited so long. He was going to make it better. He had to make it better.

Clearwater's airport was small, and Chance easily made his way to the front, where both arrivals and departures were right next to one another. He stepped out into the humid air just as his Uber driver pulled up in a red sedan.

"You headed home or just visiting?" the young man in the driver's seat asked as he adjusted his phone in the cradle attached to his dashboard.

"Visiting," Chance replied, thinking about where life would take him if he and Claire worked things out. Asheville was his home, and it was where he wanted to work. His patients were there. But he would move anywhere for Claire. He could finish his doctorate degree anywhere and find new patients. He just wanted to be near Claire. He'd wasted years without her in his life, and he wasn't willing to lose more.

The ride was short, but as they pulled into the subdivision where Claire's house was located, they came to a screeching halt.

"Damn, sorry about that," the driver said.

Red and blue lights lit up the street, and the driver had almost plowed right into the car in front of him. "Wonder what's going on down there." he continued as he looked at his driver's app.

Chance watched as the man zoomed in on the app, noticing he was less than two blocks from Claire's house. He could see traffic was stopped all the way down the street. There must be an accident. Chance checked his phone for the hundredth time since he'd been sitting in the car. *Damn*. He'd missed a call from Valerie. He should have told her he was leaving. That he was going to see Claire. That he had already landed. He didn't have time to talk now, so he sent her a quick message to fill her in and promised he'd call as soon as he had the chance. He was too close now.

No sooner had he clicked Send than his phone rang. It was Valerie again. Reluctantly, he answered and began talking, but Valerie cut him off.

"Chance, listen to me! Claire's been abducted!"

"What? What do you mean?" Just as the words escaped his mouth, he looked back up. The lights. Were those lights because of Claire?

"Claire's friend Tessa messaged me. It's a long story. But someone took her." She spoke fast, but rationally. She was good at staying calm under pressure, which came in handy, which he was thankful for.

"How long ago? Do you know who?" Chance asked, clutching his duffel bag, ready to jump out of the car. But as soon as he asked, he knew the answer.

"Joe thinks it's that guy. Moe. But we can't be certain."

"I'm almost there. I'll call you back. You said her friend's name is Tessa?"

"Yes. Be careful, Chance." And with that, they hung up.

"Stop here," Chance instructed the driver with urgency. "I'll walk the rest of the way."

Chapter Thirty-Nine
Present

Claire

Claire woke to the sound of sirens. Her eyes were blurry, and her head hurt. She strained to see where she was as the memory of looking for her phone came rushing back to her. She wanted to reach for something, anything, but her arms were wrapped behind her, secured by zip ties that rubbed at her bare wrists. Panic ripped through her. All she could see were red and blue lights illuminating the walls through the window across the room.

A scream raced out from her throat, only to be muffled by the tape placed over her mouth. Her chest heaved, and her heartbeat raced, scared, and frightened and confused.

Eyes darting around, Claire's body began to tremble. Where was she? No one was in the room with her; she was alone. A twin-size bed with princess blankets, lined with stuffed animals, stood along one wall. A doll house sat in the corner next to a giant Barbie Jeep. White blackout curtains draped the windows, parted in the middle, allowing the lights to flood the room.

The last thing she remembered was looking for her phone. And then. *Oh my god! Someone has me!* A sharp pain tore at her insides at the realization. *Those sirens. Please be for me.*

Think. Think. Find a way out. Use what you know. You can escape. You can't be too far from your house.

But, as if he heard Claire's thoughts, a man appeared. He stood tall. His physique was both solid and sturdy, but she could tell he was thin underneath his layered clothes. His eyes, hard and cold beneath his glasses. He was older, with graying hair. In his younger days, it would have been jet black. She could tell by looking at his eyebrows. He had a familiarity about him. She was sure she'd seen him before.

He looked at her and then walked to the window, opening the curtain carefully to gain a better view. After assessing things, he turned toward her, the light creating a shadow around him, making it difficult to see his features. Just the outline of his body.

"The sooner you talk, the sooner we can get this over with." He pointed at the tape. "If I take that off, you'll scream. So, we need to establish a few rules first." His voice was deep and raspy.

His voice. There was that familiarity again. She looked at him with more clarity as her vision adjusted to the darkness. And that's when she recognized him. It was his eyes. His glasses. He was the man at Beach Brew. The man she bumped into. But why was he here? What did he want with her? What could she have possibly done to upset this man?

He stepped away from the window, pulling the curtains closed tightly, creating total darkness in the room. "You don't remember me, do you?"

She closed her eyes, but still felt him getting closer. His breath against her face.

"First, I'm going to peel this tape off. It might hurt. Second. You won't say anything unless you are asked a question or told to speak. If you scream, I press this button. It's connected to a bomb that's located in your house."

Claire's eyes grew wide. *A bomb? Why on Earth would this*

stranger have a bomb in my house? She thought about Molly and Tessa. Even Shadow. They were all at her house. And those sirens, they might mean the police were there too. She couldn't be the cause of so many deaths. She had to figure out how to give this man what he wanted. But she also had to figure out how to get out of this alive. There was no way he'd let her go now that she'd seen his face.

"Let's establish a baseline, shall we?" he asked, bending down at eye level. "What's your name?" He began peeling the tape, which started at the back of her head. She winced as the tape pulled loose strands of hair. When he got to her face, he repeated his prior statement. "If you scream, I press this button."

She nodded. As the tape came away from her lips, she mouthed her name, but her throat was so dry it was barely audible. She cleared her throat and tried again. "Claire. My name is Claire. But you already know that. Why am I here?" Her voice was quiet but strong. She wouldn't let him sense her fear.

"I ask the questions," he said, standing back up but not taking his eyes off her. "You have something that belongs to me." He reached down with his free hand and touched his leg, scowling in pain. Her eyes followed, noticing a bloodied bandage.

She was about to open her mouth, to ask what she could possibly have that belonged to him, but he put his hand up, blood smeared across his fingers, and placed it in front of her face, stopping her before she made that mistake. Her eyes shifted directions. She looked at the button on the device he held in his other hand. It was red, which meant it was activated.

"I'm going to ask you again. You don't remember me, do you?"

Claire waited for his hand to lower before speaking. "I

remember I ran into you at the café. I don't have a clue what I have that's yours. If you tell me, I'll gladly give it back to you."

Throwing his head back, he laughed.

Another gasp fell from Claire's lips.

"I also ran into you at the store. The other day. Didn't I? That was you."

The laughter continued for a few seconds before his face went serious. "Why, you know me from somewhere else, Claire. We've met before. A long, long time ago."

And then it hit her. His eyes. That stare. He was the man she'd seen inside Alex's house that night. The one in the hallway. The fourth guy the police never found.

Shit. Shit, shit, shit! He'd been following me. Alarm took over her body. She felt nauseous as images of the dead woman came back to her, half naked, lying in Alex's bedroom, and the smell...the awful smell. Then she thought about the money she stole from Alex's dresser, with the bloody hair. Tears began to form in her eyes when she realized the seriousness of the situation she was in.

"If you want that money, I can give it back to you. It really wasn't much. I didn't know it belonged to you." But even as she said it, she doubted he'd be doing all this for that little bit of cash from over twenty years ago. Her body went rigid with fear. He'd killed before, and he'd do it again.

"There has to be some kind of mistake," she breathed out before looking back into his dark, icy eyes.

"Oh god," she whispered to herself. And then she closed her eyes.

Chapter Forty

Present

Chance

Once outside in the fresh air, Chance looked around to survey the neighborhood. He knew he would look suspicious just walking around in the dark. The police would take one look at him, and he'd be on the ground in seconds, cuffs behind his back. He took out his phone and called Valerie back. She picked up on the first ring.

"Hey, do you have Tessa's phone number or a way of getting in contact with her?"

In less than a minute, Valerie had Tessa on the phone, putting them on a three-way call.

"Tessa, I'm down the street. Maybe two blocks. There are a lot of cops out here. I want to help, but I'm afraid they won't let me through," Chance said quickly, letting her know he was on foot.

"I'm coming for you. Meet me at the stop sign where the cops have the street barricaded off. Stay on the phone with me though. I don't want to lose you." Chance heard the unsteadiness in her voice. The worry and stress of losing her friend was being transferred to him. He knew he had to do something. He had to help.

"I need you to walk me to the corner and let my friend

come in," he heard Tessa say to somebody, probably an officer. "He's Claire's boyfriend. He can help."

The word boyfriend would complicate things. He knew that. But it didn't matter. What mattered was finding Claire.

He continued walking, inching his way closer to the stop sign, where a man in uniform was waving him away. "You can't be here. This is an active investigation site."

"He's with us. Let him through," a woman in a black dress yelled as she ran toward him, escorted by another officer.

Out of breath, Tessa hugged him like they'd known each other for years. "Molly said she's already met you. She's down there talking to another cop. This is all too much. I just don't understand any of it. One minute Claire was looking for her phone, and the next minute she was freaking out, telling us to hurry up and get in the house. And then...then someone was driving away with her in his truck." Mascara ran down her face as they made their way back to Claire's house.

"Did you get a look at the guy? What did he look like? Did she put up a fight?" Chance asked, his heart pounding out of his chest.

"That's what I don't understand. It's like...she was right behind us. We were running, but she was right there. And then...when I turned around, the guy had her in his arms. She didn't fight. She didn't move. It's like he drugged her or something. I don't know." Tears poured even faster, and she sobbed into his chest.

Molly came up behind them and hugged Tessa, tears in her eyes too. "The detective over there wants to ask you a few more questions. You can describe the guy better. I told him it was dark, but he insists any information is helpful. I already told him about Shadow."

"What about Shadow?" Chance's eyebrow lifted.

"When we got inside, it was like Shadow instinctively knew what to do. He darted out the door and ran after the man, after Mom was already in the back seat. The guy kicked him, but Shadow tore into his leg before he managed to get inside himself. He drew blood, that much I saw. He took off that way," she said, pointing in the direction Chance had come from. "Shadow ran off in the same direction. We haven't seen him since."

"I think I can help. I might know who did this. I mean, I could be wrong. And I don't know where to find your mom or the guy. But I might have a lead." Chance let out a sharp, painful breath.

A few moments later, the three of them were sitting in Claire's living room with a detective, listening to Chance tell them about Moe and what happened over two decades ago. Molly, he noticed, was in shock. He remembered Claire saying that she didn't know any of the details from her past, only that her grandparents had died in a boating accident. Tessa was equally in shock but seemed to take it better.

"I'm sorry. I know you haven't heard this before," he told Molly.

"I never knew. How could Mom not tell me any of this?" Molly shook her head, sobbing as Tessa grabbed her around the shoulders and pulled her in, a look of sorrow spreading across her face.

"I've been in contact with a retired detective. Joe Daniels from Asheville, I think he said his name was." The husky detective sat straighter, flipping his notepad through previous pages. His dusty brown hair was high and tight, and it reminded Chance of the military. "He contacted me a few months back, maybe over the winter sometime. We kept an eye on the house for a while, as a courtesy. But we never saw anything out of the ordinary. We couldn't keep our officers on patrol over here when a crime hadn't been committed."

He stood up, about to shake their hands, when Chance heard a woman's voice yelling for Molly and Tessa. "I can help!

Tell them I'm here. I can help!" Whomever was holding her back must not have been doing a good job because, just then, before anyone could react, a round lady with bright pink curlers and a flowered nightgown pushed her way through to them.

"Molly! I know the license plate for that car. I heard what happened. I can help!" she yelled again, trying to push the cop off her. "Don't you touch me there. I'm married!" she growled, glaring at the man who was trying to keep her from inching any closer.

"Sorry, boss. She thinks she might have the license plate number for the black truck that took her," a shorter, scrawnier man, probably half the woman's size, said, casually shrugging.

"*Think* I might know? I *do* know. I told Claire that somebody was stalking her. You better believe I wrote down his license plate number. I even pulled a background check on him when she told me she wasn't dating anybody."

Everybody's mouth dropped. Could this woman be serious? A background check? On a random stranger? How likely would it be that it was the same man though? It was probably a stolen vehicle. No way would he be driving his own car.

"Officer Scott will take down the number. We'll look into it. Thank you for your help, ma'am. My name is Detective Spencer. If you have any other information, you can ask for me." He turned back around and looked at the three of them.

"His name is Morris Hurley. I have a picture at my house," she shouted as Officer Scott was redirecting her back to the front door.

Chance and Detective Spencer looked at each other, their eyes wide.

"Did you say Morris Hurley?"

Chapter Forty-One
Present

Claire

"You have a very expensive diamond that belongs to me. A red diamond. And I want it back," the man sneered, his face twisting in angst. He carefully paced the room. His hand on the black box that contained the trigger.

Claire watched him, unsure how erratic he might become if she told him she didn't know anything about a diamond. Her heart was almost leaping out of her chest. She could feel it pulsing. She knew if she denied it, he'd hit her, hurt her, even torture her. If she played along however, she might be able to buy herself some time. She needed a plan.

He glared at her. She saw the impatience spread across his face as his nostrils flared.

"What if I told you I sold it?" Claire choked out with a raspy breath.

"I'd say you're lying to me. A diamond like that would set off alarms. Only specific people can buy a diamond like that without raising questions." His eyes grew serious, and he licked his lips.

He inched closer to Claire, crouching down to eye level, glaring at her, burning a hole into her soul. From where he squatted, she could see a scar that ran down the side of his head where an ear used to be. She held in a gasp, afraid he'd see her fear. She didn't want to lose control.

"Well, what happens if I found the right people?" She tested him, trying to restrain from shaking.

His eyes narrowed and his lips tightened, his nose against her nose. "Then I'd say today was the unluckiest day of your fucking life. A diamond like that costs millions. At least three on the black market. Don't be fucking stupid."

Out of the corner of her eye, she noticed his arm dropped. The device he had in his hand looked cheap, possibly not even real. But she couldn't be certain. She had to get a better look. If she planned to escape, she needed to know if he was bluffing about the bomb. She couldn't go off intuition. She needed facts. The fear almost suffocated her, but she had to keep going. She had to stick to her plan.

"Well, maybe I got three million for it." Her voice cracked as she tried to sound serious, trying to play it cool.

Looking past him, Claire was suddenly aware that the red and blue lights were no longer cascading across the room. And the sirens had stopped echoing against the walls, causing the room to go eerily quiet. It was just her and her own luck now.

The man stood back up and flinched, wincing in pain from the wound on his leg. His head turned to the side, as if he were thinking about her words, how truthful she might be or what lies were spilling from her lips. She had to distract him. She needed to catch him off guard.

"I can give you a few hundred thousand up front, but the rest is spread out across a few locations. I'd need your word that you won't hurt me or my family. Then it's all yours. All of it." She pleaded with him. She needed him to believe her. She needed the assurance that he would keep her alive, at least until he found out she was lying. But, by then, she was hoping she'd have escaped.

Claire thought about her mom. "Always have a plan," she

had said. *It's too hard to plan under this kind of stress.* There were too many variables. Too many things that could go wrong. But Claire knew she could piece a plan together. The Marine Corps taught her to improvise. First, make him believe there is money. Second, find out if the trigger is real. The rest would fall into place.

"I don't believe you," he growled, limping back to the window. A thin streak of light crossed his body. His hand still held the box. He looked down like he was looking at someone. Something.

And then she heard it. Barking. There was barking outside. He closed the curtain, but it got caught on the edge of the bed, leaving a small sliver of light. The man placed the box on the dresser and looked at her.

"How the hell did your dog follow us here? If he doesn't stop barking, I'll kill him." He pulled out a knife from his back pocket, showing her he meant business.

And then he was gone, closing the door behind him, not giving her a second to say a word.

Claire frantically tried to untie herself, to loosen the zip ties on her wrists. She didn't want to make too much noise, afraid he would come back and catch her. But she had to hurry. She had to save her dog. She knew he wasn't bluffing about killing Shadow like she had been about the diamond.

The zip tie tore into her skin as she tried pressing her arms out and away from her body, the way she'd been taught, but it was difficult with the chair in her way. She continued pulling away, in quick movements. Repeatedly. Her wrists felt raw with every swing. And then, she felt one snap. One wrist was free. She swung again, this time harder. And then that one snapped too. But they were still behind her. She needed to find the end of the rope and untie it.

She heard Shadow barking, still outside from what it sounded like. She was so close. After she got this untied, her legs would be easy. Then she'd move the device for the bomb and find a weapon to protect herself.

Suddenly, as she managed to come loose, the barking stopped. There was silence again, except for the beating of her own heart. She stilled. And, in that moment, her thoughts went to Chance. A single tear fell from her eye as the realization came that she might not make it out alive. She'd never see Chance again.

Chapter Forty-Two
Present

Chance

"Detective? I think we might have something," Officer Scott called out from the front porch.

"Could be unrelated, but I wanted you to know about it. Dispatch said there was a dog barking a few blocks from here. A woman called in complaining of a black dog barking at a house. She said she was outside on her porch with her husband when a dog ran up and started barking at her neighbor's house. Told us a man is staying there while the family is out of town. They rented it out about two weeks ago."

"That's Shadow!" Molly cried. "Shadow found Mom!" She jumped up from the couch, with Tessa right beside her. "We have to go."

"Did you get an address?" Detective Spencer asked, turning his attention to the officer. "I want you to get back on the phone with the woman and find out if she's seen the man or his car. Get a description. We need to do this right. It might be completely unrelated, and we don't want to make any mistakes."

Chance watched as the detective pulled out his walkie talkie.

"This is Detective Spencer. I'm requesting backup to

follow me to a suspect's location. Could be armed and danger-ous. We're going in silent."

The short ride following Detective Spencer felt like the longest drive of his life. It was only six blocks away, but it felt like Chance had driven miles as he gripped the steering wheel tightly between his fingers. He could hear his heart thumping against his chest as he turned down the last street and pulled up behind an unmarked cop car.

The detective wouldn't allow him to ride along, but that didn't mean he couldn't follow him. Molly tossed him her keys and told him to be careful, to give her an update the second he heard something.

Watching the cops enter the house from the side brought back flashes from Iraq and Afghanistan. He wanted to be there, to run in the house and help. But he was unarmed, and he hadn't trained with these cops. They were a team, and they would do whatever they could to get her out alive. He had to trust them.

And so he waited. He sat firmly in his seat, pulling at his nails, every second he waited harder than the first. The antici-pation was excruciating. What was taking so long? There were no lights, no sounds, nothing.

He closed his eyes for a half second, praying she would be safe, promising himself he would tell her again that he loved her. This time he wouldn't leave. This time he would hold her and never let go. He had to tear down his wall. Love was more important than anything else in this world.

When his eyes opened back up, he saw lights flooding the house.

He watched, nervously, waiting for something to happen. Something to tell him Claire was okay. But as each second ticked by, his muscles grew tighter with fear.

Chapter Forty-Three
Present

Claire

Claire's panic worsened as each second ticked by, praying and hoping Shadow was okay. Shadow had been with her since she moved back to St. Pete. She adopted him from a rescue in downtown Tampa. At eight years old, he had been one of the oldest dogs there and labeled unadoptable by the volunteers. But she fell instantly in love with his pouty little face. He looked so sad, with his puppy dog eyes, but unlike other people, she knew he had some spunk left in him. And he did.

When she took him home, he proved to be a great companion. He loved playing catch, going for runs, and cuddling up with her while she read. And Shadow proved the age-old saying that you couldn't teach an old dog new tricks to be inaccurate. Shadow was more than eager to learn new commands. And now, here Shadow was, showing his loyalty by trying to protect her from this man. But the silence was deafening, and she couldn't take it any longer.

There was no time. Claire had to hurry. That man would be back for her any second. She tossed the rope across the room once she managed to maneuver herself out of it and reached for the small black box from the table. She grasped it in her hand, careful not to touch the button. It was light in her hand, but she didn't have time to look it over. She had to move it, hide it from him.

Standing straight and motionless, Claire heard footsteps as each stair creaked beneath his feet in the hallway. He was coming back for her. Her eyes darted from wall to wall, looking for a weapon. She looked toward the window. She could jump. But she didn't know what was down there, the curtains closing off the outside world from her view.

Her breathing quickened, and her throat tightened as uncertainty yanked on her collar. Her eyes settled on the four-poster bed, hopeful she'd be able to unscrew one of the posts.

Placing the box carefully on the floor, Claire pushed it as far back as it would go underneath the bed. It couldn't be noticeable. Then, with urgency, she began twisting and turning until she had one post unscrewed. She could use it as a bat, she thought to herself.

Without wasting another second, she quietly ducked behind the door and got ready to swing.

The footsteps stopped, and the door handle rattled. Claire prepared herself as her heart jumped from her chest. She held her breath, and then the door swung open.

"You're lucky that dog stopped barking. It must not have been yours after all," he said before looking up.

This was her chance. His eyes would have to readjust to the dark. *Swing. Just swing the post. And then you can run.*

But she swung a second too late. He noticed she wasn't in her chair and instinctively looked in her direction.

"What the—" he started to say, but caught the post as it swung toward his head. With one hand, he yanked it from her hold.

"What the fuck?" he screamed at her. "Get back over there now!"

Claire caught a look of surprise and panic in his eyes when

he looked toward the table. He'd forgotten he put the trigger down. This was her chance.

Jump on him. Reach for his arm and use what you learned. Use your training.

It may have been a few decades, but she was still confident she could hold her own.

His eyes widened when he realized she wasn't going to listen. He reached down and pulled out his knife from the sheath behind his back.

Claire would have been lying if she said she wasn't afraid. But she lunged at him anyway, trying but failing to kick the knife out of his hand with her knee. She wouldn't hold back. She wouldn't give up without a fight. He stumbled backward but reached for her leg with his other arm, knocking her down onto her back. She wrinkled her nose in pain as she caught her breath.

He laughed at her while waving the knife in her face. "I want my fucking diamond."

He isn't going to kill me. He wants me alive. The thought invigorated her. She had the upper hand. She could do this all night if she had to. Pain was just weakness leaving the body. She could handle any pain he brought to her because she was ready to do the same to him.

She narrowed her eyes, keeping their gazes locked on one another. And then, surprising even herself, she swept her leg behind his knees, knocking the knife to the floor. She lurched toward it, but he was faster. Her hand caught the blade as he yanked the handle away. A gash appeared, stretching from one side of her hand to the other. Blood oozed out, and the pain felt like hot oil being poured into her palm. But she couldn't let that hold her back. Couldn't let him see her pain.

Get back up and dust yourself the fuck off, she told herself. She had to use the element of surprise in her favor since she was smaller, and she had to move quickly, without hesitation.

"This is ridiculous. Just sit down before you keep getting hurt," he bellowed, this time waving the knife toward the chair.

Claire pushed her hands against the ground, lifting herself to her feet. Taking a few steady breaths, she calmed her nerves. This was it. It was now or never. Her lips twisted as she zeroed in on his eyes. Watching. Waiting.

And when his eyes shifted for a second, she lunged again, blasting him in the side of the neck with her fist. His face turned toward her, and she kneed him in the genitals with all her might. He went down, his knees hitting the floor first.

Standing over him, Claire swung her elbow back, cracking the side of his jaw, feeling the sweat from his face. He yelped, unable to get back to his feet. A burst of adrenaline ran through her body, and she began swinging at his neck and face, then at his rib cage and torso, knocking the wind out of him.

She finally pressed her knee into his open thigh wound, her weight digging into his flesh. She swung her arms so hard and so fast she didn't hear the door open behind her.

The room began to fill with officers and paramedics. She was out of breath, barely able to breathe. She hadn't remembered when she'd stopped, but someone stood over her, cleaning her hand and wrapping it with something soft and dry. Someone else shone lights in her eyes, while another person called her name. She wasn't sure where it was coming from. The room was light, but she couldn't make out any of their faces. She watched as the man was handcuffed and pulled to his feet. His face was bloodstained and swollen.

"Claire? Claire Harding?"

The man finally came into focus. "My name is Detective Spencer. I have someone waiting to see you."

Chapter Forty-Four
Present

Chance

Chance made a beeline up the staircase the moment he received clearance from the officer at the front door. Not knowing what to expect, his pulse quickened with every step. His mouth was dry, and his head began to throb. He needed to get to Claire. He had to see her.

He reached the bedroom on the second floor as a few men in uniform were exiting. Detective Spencer was crouched down, facing Claire, as a lone paramedic tended to her hand. He stood in the doorway, unsure what to do until the detective made eye contact with him and waved him over.

As she sat with her back to him, Chance felt an intense urge to pick her up in his arms. To hold her. To protect her from everything. But when he walked around to face her, he didn't need to do anything. She jumped to her feet and hugged him first. The bandage, not finished being wrapped around her hand, fell to the floor.

Chance immediately pulled her into an embrace, squeezing her tightly, their hearts beating in unison. After a few seconds, Chance lifted one hand and placed it on her head, stroking her hair, breathing her in. Pulling her away, just a little, Chance peered into Claire's round eyes. Tears pooled while she tried to form a smile. He brushed what he could away, his thumb caressing the skin right above her cheeks.

"It's you!" she whispered, staring at him.

"It's me." His thumb traced the side of her cheek, and she leaned into it, closing her eyes.

"I'm sorry, ma'am, but I'm going to need you to sit down so I can finish wrapping this. Then we'll have to take you to the hospital. I'm sure you'll have to get an X-ray to verify if any tendons were cut," the young paramedic said sympathetically.

Chance sat down beside her and watched the man wrap her hand. The cut was deep. Studying her face, Chance wanted to know every detail, what happened, how it happened, but knew Claire would tell him when she was ready. Instead, he sat close to her, supporting whatever it was that she needed, unable to pry his eyes off her.

"All right, this should do for now," the man said as he got back to his feet. "Are you okay to walk or do you want me to grab the stretcher?"

Claire's body trembled. "I..." she started to say, but the words were lost in her sobs. The paramedic gave Chance a look, and Chance nodded reassuringly.

When the paramedic left to grab a stretcher, Chance bent down and kissed Claire's forehead, not once letting go of her good hand. "Is there anything I can do? Molly and Tessa know you're safe now. They're going to meet us at the hospital."

"My dog. Shadow. He..." she gulped, not finishing her sentence.

"You mean this guy?" Detective Spencer announced, reappearing in the doorway with their new favorite four-legged friend. He unhooked his leash, and Shadow ran to Claire, jumping and licking her, almost knocking her over.

"Shadow? I thought. I don't understand...when you stopped barking, I thought you were..." Claire cried, nuzzling her head into his black fur.

"This dog is a hero. He saved your life. And the neighbors over there. We wouldn't have found you as soon as we did if they hadn't called it in. But, looking at Morris, I don't think you needed us at all. You kicked his ass." The detective laughed.

"Before they take you to the hospital, I have a few questions. Do you think you're up for answering them now, while it's fresh in your head? I can always check on you later, that's no problem. But I figured I can give you some information in return."

When she nodded, he took a seat on the bed, across from her. "First, have you ever seen that man? Before today?"

"Yes, a few times. Up till today, I hadn't recognized him. It was over twenty years ago since I've seen him, and then I ran into him at the store the other day, and the café. But I didn't know who he was at the time. It had been so long.

"You didn't see him with anyone else, did you?"

"No, not that I'm aware of."

"Do you know what he wanted with you?"

Her eyes went wide. She suddenly remembered the bomb. Her expression alarmed the detective, and he immediately stood up. "What is it?"

"I forgot. He said he had a bomb at my house. He had a trigger, but I managed to get a hold of it when I got my wrists free. It's under the bed."

Officer Spencer turned on his walkie talkie. "I need the bomb squad over at the Harding residence. Everyone needs to evacuate the premises immediately. And send somebody over here to check the detonator. We don't know if it's live." The static came back, acknowledging the immediate threat.

"What else? Can you tell me anything else?"

"He said he wanted a red diamond. He claimed that I had it, that Alex told him he hid it in my belongings the day I ran away. But I don't know anything about a red diamond. The only thing I knew about was what Alex was hiding at his house, but the police found that years ago."

Chance held her good hand as she spoke, circling his thumb across the top. He couldn't imagine what she was going through. The trauma. The fear. He squeezed gently, bringing her hand to his lips and kissing it.

He helped her to her feet as the paramedic came back with the stretcher. She tried fighting it at first, saying she was fine. "I feel silly having to be strapped in. I'm fine," she said as the men began tightening the straps over her legs.

"We'll be going down the stairs, so this is for your safety," Chance assured her. "I'll be here the entire time."

He kept her hand in his until the very last second, when they picked her up and descended the stairs. But, once in the ambulance, sitting by her side, he clasped her hand in his again, promising never to leave again.

Chapter Forty-Five
Present

Claire

The air cooled as the temperature dropped, and the raindrops danced on top of tiny puddles in the backyard. Claire sat on her back patio, under the awning that hung from her roof, with Shadow at her feet. She looked down at her hand. It had been three weeks since the attack, and her hand was still wrapped up. The doctor told her it should heal on its own, but it could take weeks, if not months, for her to regain full mobility. She tried to flex it but wrinkled her nose in pain. She was just thankful she hadn't needed surgery.

"Take it easy. It's going to take some time," Chance said tenderly, coming up behind her. He rested one hand on her shoulder as he set a cup of tea in front of her. Looking up, she smiled at him, the tranquility of his eyes relaxing her.

Shadow's ears perked up, as if hearing Chance's voice meant it was snack time. "Not yet; it's still early," Claire said, as if reading his mind, but then reached into her pocket and pulled out a small dog biscuit and let him take it from her hand. She thought back to when she didn't think she'd get another chance to give Shadow a treat. She was sure Morris had killed him.

Morris, they found out, was Morris Hurley of Hurley's

Jewelers in Jacksonville. Detective Spencer told them while they were all at the hospital, that, with the help of Brittany's one-woman neighborhood watch, they didn't have to do much digging at all. For some reason, Morris got sloppy at his old age and drove his own car down to St. Pete to canvas the area. He rented the Airbnb using another identity, but the car was registered in his own name.

"Hurley's Jewelers had a few burglaries back in 1993 and 1994. His insurance covered all the missing jewelry, including some loose diamonds. But they required him to get cameras in and around his store to keep his insurance active. Come to find out, Morris was the one stealing from his own store. Insurance fraud. Your brother was in charge of retaining help. That help retained those women as a decoy. But, just like any other scam, everyone was double-crossing each other. With high stakes, like diamonds, paranoia can be a problem. The lack of trust often leads to mistakes and accidents. What I'm surprised about is your brother never revealed who Moe was," Detective Spencer had said at Claire's bedside in the hospital, where she'd stayed overnight for observation.

"I spoke to him a few times after I moved back to New York. I honestly don't think he knew who Moe really was."

"Do you think you'll ever talk to your brother about any of this? Ask him where he placed that diamond?" Chance had asked.

"Nope," she said smiling, touching her locket around her neck. "I have my family right here." And then she squeezed Molly tight as she sat snuggled up against her on the hospital bed. She was relieved when the bomb squad announced the bomb was a false alarm. Nothing had been found in her home, and the trigger was what she suspected, fake.

Now, as she sat on her back patio, she felt the locket once more. She thought about her mom, wishing she could be there with her. These next few days were going to be the happiest of her life, and she wished so badly her mom could be there to see her.

"Are you ready to come inside?" Chance asked, holding his hand out. She rested her good hand in his palm and let him help her out of her seat. She was still bruised badly. She couldn't remember anything specific causing her to hurt so much. Moe hadn't put up much of a fight. But here she was, needing help getting out of a chair three weeks later, stiff and sore.

Chance closed the door behind them once Shadow scrambled to his feet and followed behind. And then, before she realized it, Chance was scooping her up in his broad arms, carrying her across the house to her bedroom.

He placed her down at the edge of the bed before going back to shut off all the lights. When he walked back into the room, he stood in front of her in the dimly lit room, his eyes locked on hers. Reaching for her shirt, he lifted it over her head, careful not to snag it on her hand. The intimacy of him undressing her rippled through her body. He removed his own shirt, exposing his broad, muscular chest. Looking at his bare skin brought warmth to her, something she would never get tired of looking at.

Ever so slowly, Chance bent down and kissed the side of her neck, starting behind her ear and working his way down to her collarbone, his hands gliding over her soft skin. He inched closer, lifting her higher onto the bed until she was lying down with him above her.

Touching her lips with his fingers, Chance guided her face toward his and swept his lips across hers.

"I love you," she finally breathed out between kisses. Something she couldn't stop saying since the moment she let those words slip from her tongue at the hospital. Something she wanted to say every day for the rest of her life.

"I love you, too, Claire. I love you too."

Epilogue
Present

Chance

"And there you were. Changing my life in more ways than I could have ever imagined. The day I first met you, on that bus, I fell in love with a girl I barely knew. And while I wish I could go back and tell myself how crazy I was for letting you get away, I'm also glad I don't have a time machine. We wouldn't be the people we are today, and I love the people we have grown into. But then, as if destiny knew we belonged together, there you were again, that day I saw you getting coffee. And, in an instant, I fell in love with you all over again."

Chance stood confidently, looking into Claire's eyes, holding her hands between his own. His heart raced, adrenaline running through his veins. He licked his lips before continuing.

"I love your strength, your ability to kick ass completely on your own. And I love that you allow me to take care of you, even when you clearly don't need it. I love that you have such a beautiful outlook on life. That you can turn the sourest of lemons into the most delicious lemonade. And I love the look you have on your face when you're reading a good book and when you're enjoying the rain.

"Claire. I promise to make you smile every day for the rest

of our lives. To make you laugh when you're taking yourself too seriously. To be a shoulder you can lean on. And to support you in everything you do. From this day forward, my heart is forever yours."

Chance finished saying his vows, never taking his eyes off Claire, who now had tears running down her cheeks.

"Repeat after me," Joe said, turning his direction to Chance. "With this ring, I thee wed." Chance repeated him, placing a brilliant oval diamond ring gently on Claire's finger. He was careful not to move her hand too much. It was the first day out of her bandage, and it was only because of the wedding.

Claire went next, repeating after Joe and placing a black tungsten wedding band on Chance's finger.

When Joe announced them as spouses, Chance gazed into Claire's eyes as she stared back, a smile tugging at her lips. Taking her hand in his, he drew them to her face, brushing his fingers across her flushed cheek. Then, when her eyelids lowered and her lips parted, he pulled her in and pressed his lips to hers. He'd kiss her like this until the day he died.

Later that night, as Chance and Claire arrived at their bed and breakfast, they smiled, recalling how lucky they were to have all their friends and family come in for their wedding on such short notice. Chance asked Claire to marry him only a few days after she was released from the hospital. He would have asked sooner, but he had to pick out the perfect ring and ask Molly for her permission. He didn't want to waste another day of his life without living it with Claire.

Claire had accepted without hesitation. Together, with the help of Molly, Tessa, and Valerie, they were able to pull off a beautiful beachside ceremony in just over three weeks. Tyler's dad and his new wife, along with his brothers and their families, all flew down for the event. They even convinced Joe to become an ordained minister for their special occasion.

And together, they decided to move to Asheville for as long as Claire could stand it. "Stop being silly. I already love Val and Joe. And I can write anywhere. I want you to do your thing. Help people. They need you," Claire had said, kissing his nose. "As long as Molly can visit whenever she wants, and as long as I can keep my house so we can get away whenever *we* want, I'll be happy anywhere you are."

"When are Val and Joe leaving for Italy?" Claire asked him as she sat on the bed to take off her shoes.

"They leave tomorrow afternoon. I can't believe they're doing it. Three weeks in Europe." Chance chuckled.

"Can you help me out of this dress?" Claire asked, standing back up. Her eyes danced with excitement. Chance ran his fingers down her back as he unzipped her. She stepped out of the white gown, wearing just her lace undergarments, all while staring into his eyes. He was about to reach for her when she held a finger to his chest.

"Help me with this too?" she asked. It was the locket from her childhood, the one her mom gave her before she died. The same locket she dropped on the floor of the bus the day they met. It was old and broken, but she kept it close to her heart, all these years later, because it reminded her of her mom.

"You know, I've never seen the pictures inside," Chance said, unclasping the new chain it hung on.

"I know, but it's been stuck for years. I'm afraid if I try hard enough, the whole thing will break, and I won't have anything."

"No, I get it. I understand. But if you let me try, and I do break it, I can always solder the hinges back together."

Claire looked hopeful. "Really? It's been so long since I've seen them myself. There's a picture of my mom on one side and one of the both of us on the other. Don't laugh though. I was little when that picture was taken." She placed the locket, chain, and all, in Chance's soft hand.

Chance used his fingernail as a wedge to lift the top of the locket open, but it wouldn't budge. He groaned after a few failed attempts. On the fourth try, he pressed harder until he felt a sudden pop. Losing his grip, the locket fell to the floor with a clink and a thud.

"What was that?" Claire asked in surprise, dropping to the floor, looking at what had fallen out of the locket. She picked something up and held it between her fingers. Her mouth dropped open as the realization hit her.

"What is..." Chance began to say before he stopped himself.

It was the red diamond. It had been inside her locket all these years.

"What do we do with it?" she asked, already looking alarmed.

"I want to call Detective Spencer. You heard what he said about paranoid, double-crossing accidents. I don't want that diamond anywhere near us."

She hugged him and gave him a kiss. "And that's why I love you." She handed him her cell phone.

"I hope that call is fast though...because I have plans for us," she said coyly.

Acknowledgments

Behind every book, there is a village of those who help turn visions into reality. So, a very special thanks ...

To my editor, Shannon Cave, who took my manuscript and created a novel. I'm blown away by your ability to refine sentences, catch inconsistencies, and provide feedback that keeps me fueled to push through to the end.

To Susie Howard, my first reader and writing partner. The one who motivated me during the entire process. The one who said my first draft was great when we both knew that was a lie. Thank you for always being by my side, laughing along the way. I love you for not only that, but for the friendship you've awarded me these last three decades of our lives.

To my Beta Readers, Maximiliane Smith and Kate Waverly, who provided the tough love I needed once I thought I'd created a masterpiece. Your eyes and feedback helped make this novel into what lies in our hands today.

To my Cover Designer, Amanda Walker PA, and Design Services, for knowing exactly what I wanted and providing me with so much more.

To my Proofer, VB Edits, for coming into my life at the tail end and cleaning my last draft. I'm beyond grateful for our established connection. I won't be able to live without you now. Your eyes are pure gold.

To my Formatter, WickedGypsyDesigns. I cannot thank you enough for not only your creativity and formatting skills, but the insight you've provided me with as a new author.

To my sister, Angela Kroemer, for *always* being my biggest

supporter. Without you, I would never be where I am today. You're my rock, and I'll be forever grateful for your love and friendship. Anyone who has you in their life is one lucky duck!

To my husband, Pat. Thank you for allowing me to follow the dream I had when I first met you. For allowing me to hole myself up inside my office (our closet) night after night without knowing anything but a word count. That's true love!

To my children. Thank you for inspiring me. For reminding me that dreams don't have expiration dates and that anything is possible with some hard work.

To my mom. For always telling me to write a book. For asking me about my book, even when there was no book. Thank you for always keeping it in the back of my head.

And finally, to my sisters and brothers of the Marine Corps. Without you, this book would never have been possible. Semper Fi.

Sneak Peek

❧

UNDER THE MAPLE

Sasha

"**G**et out!" Sasha screamed, her voice sharp as she threw a ceramic mug at Greg's head, missing by mere centimeters, only for it to explode against the wall and shatter into a million pieces.

"What the fuck, Sasha?" Greg yelled through gritted teeth as he jerked away.

"Get out! Get the fuck out!" Sasha screamed again, grabbing another mug off the countertop and raising it in the air. Her heart thundered while long exasperated breaths escaped her lips as she waited. Waited to see what he'd do next.

"Okay. Damn! I'm leaving," he grunted, raising his hands in truce before reaching for the door handle, his dark eyes not trusting her. Not trusting that she wouldn't throw another one straight at his face if he didn't listen.

Turning the handle, Greg pushed the door open. "You'll be sorry about this. Don't think I didn't warn you." His eyes darted from her and then to Blake. Sasha's breath caught in her throat as she narrowed her eyes at him, praying he'd just leave.

A second later, he disappeared, and then she exhaled, her arm falling to her side. Her chest heaved unsteadily as she placed the mug back on the counter, though her fingers still gripped the handle. If he came back, she wouldn't hesitate. And she wouldn't miss.

"Sasha," Blake said her name, his voice soft and full of concern.

"I want you to leave too," she said quickly, looking down at her trembling hands.

"Sasha, can we talk about this? I want to…"

"Help? You want to help? Haven't you done enough? Please. Just get out." Sasha lowered her voice as it wavered, avoiding his gaze. She couldn't look into his dark green eyes. If she did, she'd lose it. She hated him for ripping apart her life. For shattering everything she'd ever known. He destroyed it the moment he walked into the coffee shop last week. He was pure sin. And yet, she craved him. More than anything. She wanted his muscular arms to wrap themselves around her. To lean into her. To touch her lips the way he did yesterday.

Standing on the other side of the café, Blake walked toward the front counter, slowly, as if each step might break the wood beneath his feet. Stopping only when he was mere inches from Sasha. His large frame stood still, watching, waiting, but she wasn't about to cave in like he thought or hoped she would. She could hear his breath as he inhaled, and it took everything in her not to look up.

"Sasha." His words were nothing more than a whisper. A plea.

"Blake, I need you to leave," Sasha bit back, holding in the tears that promised to escape. She wouldn't let him see her cry. She wouldn't let him see her fall apart.

Sasha heard his feet move again, his shadow following as

he turned toward the same door Greg just exited. When the rattle of the door handle echoed in her ears, Sasha sucked in a deep breath, her heart racing.

"I'm sorry, Sasha." His voice broke.

And then...he was gone.

Throwing her hands to her face, Sasha crumbled to the floor, letting the tears flood from her eyes. The cries came out muted, unable to catch her breath. "Why? Why me? Why is this happening?" She sobbed uncontrollably, hating her red hair. Hating that Blake had moved here. That he'd found her. Hating that she never knew she'd ever been lost. Hating that she'd let Greg back into her life. She was a stupid girl. Stupid, stupid, stupid.

About the Author

Manda Mazanec is a United States Marine Corps veteran and educator, committed to shaping a better and brighter future. While being an avid reader, writer, and runner, Manda is also an advocate for breaking the stigma associated with mental health illness, bringing to light how trauma can affect our everyday lives. Manda lives in Illinois with her husband, three daughters, and her two dogs and two cats.

Manda Mazanec Instagram : @mandamazanec

www.ingramcontent.com/pod-product-compliance
Lightning Source LLC
Chambersburg PA
CBHW021112110726